Acclaim for Elinor Lipman's

The Way Men Act

"A BREEZY, BRAZEN BOOK. . . . CHEERFULLY UNPRETENTIOUS. . . . A LEADING AUTHORITY ON THE WAY WOMEN—OR SOME WOMEN—THINK, TALK, GROPE, COPE, AND FIGHT BACK."
—*Entertainment Weekly*

"A lovely early bud of spring. . . . Sparkles more than most recent novels—and funny books with bite are getting rarer all the time."
—*Philadelphia Inquirer*

"This stylish, witty, entertaining concoction is a lesson in the social graces, '90s style. . . . Lipman's take on modern life and the problems of the post-'80s yuppie are so on target that it's frightening."
—*West Coast Review of Books*

"PUTTING A WICKED 1990s SPIN ON THE GAME OF COURTSHIP, LIPMAN COMES UP WITH A WINNER—a wry, witty, fond look at decent people attempting to make connections with each other. . . . RECOMMENDED."
—*Library Journal*

"ELINOR LIPMAN'S SMART DIALOGUE AND LOOPY SUPPORTING CHARACTERS WILL, MORE THAN ONCE, MAKE YOU LAUGH OUT LOUD."
—*People*

A Book-of-the-Month Club Alternate Selection

Also by Elinor Lipman

Then She Found Me*
Into Love and Out Again*
Isabel's Bed*
The Inn at Lake Devine

*Available from WASHINGTON SQUARE PRESS

The Way Men Act

A NOVEL BY

Elinor Lipman

WASHINGTON SQUARE PRESS
PUBLISHED BY POCKET BOOKS

New York   London   Toronto   Sydney   Tokyo   Singapore

This book is a work of fiction. Names, characters, places and incidents are either products of the author's imagination or are used fictitiously. Any resemblance to actual events or locales or persons, living or dead, is entirely coincidental.

WSP

A Washington Square Press Publication of
POCKET BOOKS, a division of Simon & Schuster Inc.
1230 Avenue of the Americas, New York, NY 10020

Lipman, Elinor.
    The way men act / Elinor Lipman.
        p.   cm.
    ISBN: 0-671-74841-6
    I. Title.
PS3562.I577W3   1992
813'.54—dc20

91-31878
CIP

First Washington Square Press trade paperback printing February 1993

10   9   8   7   6   5

WASHINGTON SQUARE PRESS and colophon are
registered trademarks of Simon & Schuster Inc.

Cover design by John Gall
Cover art by Debra White

Printed in the U.S.A.

For my mother

The Way
Men Act

1

Harrow

The shops stand three across: mine in the middle, Dennis Vaughan's to my left and Libby Getchel's to my right, fronting on Main Street in Harrow, Massachusetts. We like the quaint sound of that, "Main Street," because all of us lived somewhere more irritating for a time and returned home with the conviction that a gentrified college town (cappuccino machines, poetry readings, bike paths), with shade trees and paper ballots, with stylish food and parking meters that still took dimes and nickels, would give us Quality of Life.

I arrange flowers for a living, a barren business for a single woman, just one of the reasons I'm in transition. After high school I went to the West Coast to be in the sun and to earn money for some mañana idea of college I had, picked carnations in Leucadia, and ended up on the allegedly artistic side of things, arranging them. I came back to work for my cousin Roger and his wife, Robin, the sincerest couple in America. They flattered me and talked about my "art," as if what I do has lasting value. I admit to being good, certainly the best around here; but "here" is Harrow, home of MacMillan College, home to real artists, to tenured scholars of national standing, to people who write books, who *review* books.

Our friends in the big cities began to hear of Harrow from style section features on our Left Bank life-style. The out-of-state checks in our cash drawers are signed by culture-loving tourists, Tanglewood types, who believe they are discovering arts and crafts on this awninged, charming Main Street a season ahead of their friends. It makes me proud and a bit show-offish about living here. I am a native, a townie; I dart among the tourists, displaying my dry cleaning or my bag of groceries as if to say, "I *live* here, this place you choose as a weekend retreat, this Brigadoon, this movie set of a college town come to life. I live here, work here, dry-clean here, am known here. This is my home."

My name, legally, is Linda Louise LeBlanc, if you can imagine anything more forgettable. I became Melinda, chose it myself the summer between eighth grade and high school, suspecting that the next four years would require something sexier. They did. It was the same summer I successfully pierced my own ears with a sewing needle and an ice cube, and convinced my mother that the platinum streaks in my dark hair were caused by the sun. I dated, I graduated, I moved away to California; I came back, half believing that if I had once been the belle of Harrow, or at least the belle of Harrow High School, then I absolutely could go home again.

It was not a terrible idea: the town had changed. It was chic now, practically a vacation destination; and with the new Harrow came new Harrowites. I'd be a fresh face to them, someone's great idea of a lifetime partner, not just the ever-popular Melinda

LeBlanc, good dancer and fun date, qualities that haven't worked so well for me in a very long time.

I moved in with my mother, a nice woman who passes out coupons and food samples on toothpicks at local supermarkets. We call my living arrangement temporary, because I'm not the type who lives at home at thirty. I agreed to be flexible, and tolerant of her ways: Yes it *was* her right to tape every incoming Christmas card to the banister, and to see that every horizontal surface in the living room had its own set of coasters. In turn she would not pass judgment on my friends, my eating habits, or my evening activities.

It helped that I took the rental unit, a linoleumed room with a claw-foot bathtub on the third floor, which she had painted and wallpapered one winter with extra income in mind, happy to evict the MacMillan lecturer/tenant when I said I'd return. The gray linoleum is patterned to look like carpeting, and the slanting eaves give it a garret feel. I painted the underside of the tub deep rose and begged one quilt and three rag rugs from my grandmother's lifelong output. I share the kitchen downstairs, which means microwaving my mother's leftovers and taking the plate up to my room. I like her company—it isn't that; I don't want to get used to having someone always there to talk to. Occasionally she telephones me at work over some extravagant menu item that requires purchases in exact numbers: lobster, cornish game hens, veal chops, take-out Chinese. Count you in or not? It means my traveling stepfather, who sells pacemakers up and down the east coast for a Minnesota company, has dropped in for one of his conjugal visits, and my mother thinks my being there would prolong the dinner hour.

We worked this out, my third-floor privacy, before I returned to Harrow. She had no idea how homesick I had been and how few concessions she had to make. I'll work for Roger and Robin at

3

Forget-Me-Not, I said; I'll take classes at the community college. I'll think about a degree.

What I didn't say aloud was the real pull: that the only place I ever felt successful—even for lame, teenage reasons—was here.

Next door to Forget-Me-Not is Brookhoppers, a fly-fishing boutique and mecca for fly fishermen. Customers flock here from all over to buy Dennis Vaughan's hand-tied designer trout flies and to attend his weekend workshops at the Harrow Inn. It's the kind of shop nonfishermen pass and say, "This guy must deal drugs in the back room." Or, "This has to be a front for the Mob." But his disciples understand; they wait patiently for his attentions, declining help from anyone else with a, "No thanks, I'll wait for Dennis." He introduces himself, unnecessarily and modestly, as he moves from professor to stockbroker to radiologist to playwright, answering their questions as if each were fresh and penetrating.

Dennis is black, and attractive in a compact, wire-rimmed way that other men admire. He and his two salesmen wear earthbrown T-shirts with *Brookhoppers* silk-screened in speckled salmon across their hearts. The photograph on the back of his catalogue shows him in waders and a New Zealand sheepherder's hat, casting in a rocky turn of the Starkfield River. By popular demand, it is available as a poster for $14.99. Men have their secretaries write to say they hang it on the back of their office doors to soothe them while they close deals, traffic honking fifty floors below.

Two doors up from Dennis, on my right, is Rags for Sale, Libby Getchel's dress shop. The name is ironic, of course, because her dresses are one of a kind and expensive for Harrow. I had known her in high school where she was in the class behind Dennis and me, and hard to miss: Libby was broad-shouldered, taller than most of us, thin in a big-boned way that made her slow walk look Southern and sexy. She wore her straight blond hair chin-length with bangs as if a weekly trim nonchalantly undertaken with sewing shears were not carefully considered for effect. As a daughter of MacMillan employees, she could have gone to the college tuition-free but hadn't studied hard enough in high school. Instead she bought Vogue patterns and made her own dresses from translucent cotton blends, even in winter when her class-mates wore wool and corduroy.

She returned to Harrow a year after I did, still wearing out-of-season party dresses; still wearing her blond hair at lengths that had nothing to do with fashion. She confided to me around that time, a time when we were still confiding in each other, that Dennis was a factor in her choosing Harrow for her store—I knew, didn't I, that they had meant a great deal to each other in high school?

I said no, I hadn't known—

"In a high school not particularly tolerant of an artistic kid who didn't conform, surrounded by professors' kids on one hand, and popular, cheerleading types on the other? Dennis was very nice to me."

I nodded, willing to downgrade my old popularity to be a better audience and friend. "How long did you two go out?" I asked.

Libby said never, unfortunately.

I asked why not.

"My own fault," she said. "A misunderstanding. A mistake I hope to correct."

I said, "Look, if I'd known at seventeen who'd be left to date at this age, I'd have kept a few lines open, too. But we're not Detroit—we can't very well announce a recall of all the defective parts of our life."

Libby didn't answer, and didn't have to. Her gray-green eyes

explained that I was an ex-cheerleader, she was a proven noncon-
formist, and clearly there were no parallels.

All she had done back then was sew, starting with the easiest
Butterick pattern: a shift from 98-cent-per-yard cotton, solid
turquoise. The sewing instructor at the Girls Club taught her
about the straight of the grain and threading the old black Singer;
of the importance of pressing and pinking each seam. The first
project was supposed to be an apron with a bib—lots of straight
lines and no zippers. Libby said she had no use for an apron; she'd
prefer to start with this dress. How hard could a zipper be if a
pattern marked "E-Z" had you install one on Step Two?

"I need this for school," Libby confided. "We can't afford to
spend money on material for aprons when I don't have enough
dresses." Mrs. Christede, a volunteer, gave in. She'd been told that
many of the girls were from underprivileged homes. She thought
of donating material for Libby's apron—a yard of gingham was
nothing—but sensed something in Libby that she mistook for
pride.

"I'll make an exception this time," Mrs. Christede said.

Libby added the optional pocket and stitched extra large
rickrack at the neck and hemline. It was an exercise only, a means
to an end. She gave it to her mother, who wore it with a white
patent-leather pocketbook and white cardigan. Libby graduated
from Butterick and Simplicity to "Very Easy, Very Vogue"; then to
designer patterns with linings and bound buttonholes.

Many girls without her gift took up sewing. They bought
ambitious patterns and delicate material and cut out their dresses
on kitchen tables with their mothers' help. After one bad mistake,
they abandoned the project. They put everything back in the green
bag from Goldenberg's Department Store—the pattern pieces
pinned to the fabric, the notions, the white envelope printed with
the beautiful design. Their mothers reminded them weekly of the

$7.98 per yard fabric wasted on someone who had only made an apron out of sheeting five years before. Some offered their leftovers to Libby; some had never even pinned the pattern to their fabric. Most she examined and declined.

Dennis Vaughan sat next to Libby in trig her junior year in high school, and shyly teased her about her flowing party dresses. She noticed that being on the wrestling team did nice things for his neck muscles and his biceps. He was broad and about her height—short for a boy. Libby liked the idea that she was such good friends with a black classmate. He was nice and shyly funny at the same time—charming was the word that fit adults like him. Libby saw all of this, appreciated all of this in Dennis Vaughan, but didn't see herself as the beneficiary. She was a white girl and Dennis was her friend. They talked outside her next class until the bell rang (Dennis had study hall with the wrestling coach and could be late). One day they talked with Libby leaning against the lockered wall. Dennis, his books against his left hip bone, pressed his palm against the wall above Libby's shoulder, smiling as if fully aware of the effect. He was making the first move.

"We'd better go," he said when the bell rang, not taking his hand off the wall.

There seemed to be an audience suddenly, girls walking by extra slowly in pairs; packs of wrestlers; every homeroom teacher Libby had ever had. They were a boy and a girl people noticed anyway. In this pose, one muscular brown arm outstretched above a broad Caucasian shoulder, they might just as well have had an electronic billboard flashing a run-around message, "Dennis Vaughan is asking Libby Getchel out."

She thought about him for the next fifty minutes in American History and decided that she could not kiss a Negro boy. She was free of prejudice herself; she hadn't seen any unpleasantness toward the half-dozen black families who lived in Harrow, or

7

toward the half-dozen smart black girls in each class at MacMillan. But Libby couldn't date Dennis Vaughan. She liked him certainly; there wasn't anything she didn't like about Dennis. She might even have a crush on Dennis, which was beside the point.

And now Dennis had misunderstood.

At some point, weeks or months later—who could remember after all these years—she had had to say something explicit about his attentions: that she was a friendly person; that maybe he'd taken her friendliness for more than she had intended. He answered, his face reset in a new, hard way, saying Libby didn't have to worry. He certainly hoped she would recover from the embarrassment of their association.

And here we are, she said, twelve years later, Dennis and I entrepreneurs in Harrow; wiser, more honest, and, amazingly enough, both free.

I answered carefully. I needed a friend on Main Street and wasn't going to eliminate a candidate on the basis of one unrealistic goal and one insult to my high school character. Too many people were coupled in this town; too few were available for the kind of old-fashioned girlfriend/confidante role, for singles' night at Buddy's, for collaborating on unsent personal ads, for me not to welcome Libby.

So I said I understood completely: when there's no one else in our lives we tend to reignite the old flames, no matter how minor. I did that, too, I said. Everybody did. We scanned our romantic pasts for candidates the same way we pushed the Seek button on our car radios, hoping to find a song we wanted to hear.

She shook her head. Maybe I did that because of my large inventory of old flames, but it wasn't like that for her. She had come to realize what Dennis Vaughan meant to her, and she was fairly certain he loved her back despite the peculiar way he was ignoring her return. Meanwhile, there was much to do.

8

THE WAY MEN ACT

Carpenters, electricians, painters and carpet installers took their turns at 333 Main. Libby ordered a sign carved in teak by the same artist who had made a mahogany trout leap over the door of Brookhoppers. Soon, above Rags for Sale, painted dresses danced in relief from a curly clothesline as if they were ecstatic and alive.

I was embarrassed for her for that trouble. It seemed an awfully literal thing to do—to marry her store to Dennis's by commissioning a sister sign.

Luckily Forget-Me-Not, my perch, was in the middle with its painted brick façade and scalloped green awning. I thought its triteness saved the block, though; broke up the implied partnership; reminded Libby that if she had some rosy fantasy of merging into one big hand-wrought storefront, she'd have to work through me.

2

More About Dennis

Dennis does commentary for our local public radio station, three minutes a week about men and rivers, on trout psychology, about reading the water and thinking like a fish. His voice is getting croonier, his material dreamier as his following gets larger. More and more listeners write to him saying they see in the lives of trout metaphors for capital punishment and race relations. Dennis says no, his pieces are allegory-proof. What we hear is what we get. Of course, the broadcasts bring more customers to Brookhoppers: the station identifies him at the end of each segment with an understated, "Dennis Vaughan ties flies for a living not far from the shores of the Starkfield."

Dennis didn't always tie flies for a living. For the longest time he was a cameraman for "Newsbreak New England," on the road five days a week covering flower shows, ribbon cuttings, ground-breakings—the soft news with local flavor which preceded the real news at 6 p.m. "Live from the Kielbasa Festival," is how Dennis sums up his entire tenure with Boston TV. He fished whenever these road trips took him out of cities. He carried with him a map of New England trout streams. One day the "Newsbreak New England" anchor made Dennis the subject of a short interview: he tied a gray nymph on camera. He was wry and natural, speaking in front of the other cameramen and the anchor with the baritone chuckle. The piece remained in the can, half-serious, an eternal filler, ready for a spot that was chronically filled by actresses in plays on pre-Broadway tryouts and retired Red Sox infielders who were honorary chairmen of disease phone-athons. But it didn't matter. It gave Dennis ideas. He wanted to be an expert at something and he wanted to do it in a place where people knew him, remembered his wrestling trophies, remembered his receiving the Paul J. Johnston Jr. Memorial Award at Harrow High School for best combined performance in scholarship and athletics. Harrow, his hometown, newly fashionable since the old Woolworth's had become a downtown mall of craft galleries and cafés, was clearly the answer. People would drop by, at first just to wish him well, but then might tell their friends who fished about this guy, this Dennis Vaughan—the black guy, the wrestler from the high school, remember?—who, believe it or not, opened a little shop right on Main Street for fly fishing and nothing else. No guns, no permits, no ammo, no cross-country skis, no night crawlers.

Dennis's parents were delighted to have him back. They said they'd help; they'd work for free whenever he needed them. His mom said she'd bake cookies for the customers—remember that tray of grapes and cheese in that fancy men's store in Boston? Dennis said no: he pictured overqualified young men with college degrees wearing silk-screened T-shirts engaging customers in both practical and esoteric fly-fishing conversation, helpful, even charming; knowledgeable but never patronizing.

He rented the space, a thousand square feet on Main. He commissioned the mahogany-and-gold wooden sign with the leaping trout that would become his trademark. He hired two earnest and attractive young men—"associates" he called them— who he'd met at the fly-fishing-only waters below the Quabbin Reservoir. Nick had been raised in Montana, and Lyman in Vermont, and had found each other among all the bait fishermen matriculating at Bowdoin. Nick led all three on a trip home to Montana where they fished and camped and agreed at the end of the ten days that they were lucky men indeed to be making their greatest pleasure in life their occupation. Dennis said that technically, as CEO and principal investor, he would have to be their boss; but surely they would be partners in spirit.

Great! said Nick and Lyman. Sounds great. If we had any money at all, if our student loans were paid, we'd help you out. We want to do this, man. We can't fucking believe you asked us to start this thing. We're in. We are *in*. And all those girls from MacMillan right up the street! said Lyman, the louder one. How bad can Harrow be?

They opened three April firsts ago and sent announcements to every man and woman in the county who had secured a fishing license the previous year, inviting them to the grand opening. Twenty percent off everything in the store, free fly-tying lessons by Dennis, smoked trout pâté, salmon-colored balloons, blackened-trout cooking demonstrations outside. Hundreds came, filling the narrow store from when it opened until the balloons and food were gone. Men told Dennis they had heard of stores like this but far away, places a guy could visit on a Saturday morning and just talk to other guys who felt the same. "That's why we're here,"

Dennis repeated, shaking still another grateful hand, making eye contact.

"I tie my own flies," some said apologetically, "so I may not be your *best* customer. But I'd sure like to talk to you sometime when it's not so crowded."

"Absolutely," said Dennis. "We're open six days a week. And Nick and Lyman, my associates, they never get enough fishing talk. Did you know we have supplies here for people who tie their own? The finest, we think. Special for the local hatches."

"I must be dreaming," Dennis heard one man murmur to another.

Despite his high profile and his famous rapport with everyone he's ever passed in the street, Dennis is a quiet man. What I know about his last ten years I gleaned in my capacity as family florist—his sister's wedding last June, specifically. The bride, after a dozen increasingly chummy consultations, invited me to the reception where, under the influence of ice-cold champagne, I danced with her brother and made him talk.

There is an ex-wife, Iris Lambrix, whom he met in the store that first year. It was not kismet: Iris had been told by a colleague at MacMillan that an attractive black man had opened a successful shop at 329 Main, a townie actually, but someone who'd been away, worked in TV in Boston. Iris strode her long strides into Brookhoppers and did not fabricate a fly-fishing mission. She said, "My name is Iris Lambrix. I teach at MacMillan. There are few enough of us in this town. Would you like to have a drink after work some evening or dinner at my place? I don't cook but I have one tangerine chicken dish that works." She said this, Dennis recalled, without irony or charm, and he should have realized that Iris was not his life's partner. He said yes.

"So you're not involved with anyone in an exclusive relationship?" she asked in her same clinical tone.

"That's right," said Dennis. If only she hadn't been attractive and long-limbed and smart and black and an assistant professor at MacMillan. Then he would have seen more clearly that there was not much to recommend Iris Lambrix. The guys in the shop teased him, said she was Ms. Right. They were white; they thought she must be a perfect match with Dennis. He had scheduled himself to work that night, but Nick and Lyman said, "Go. We'll handle things here. You need a woman."

Iris lived in college housing, in a three-room apartment on the first floor of Stedman House. That made her Stedman House's resident adviser, a job for which she was poorly suited. Students outside of class annoyed her. Iris had commuted to Barnard from Queens, then to graduate school at NYU. She had decided that students who could afford to live at college were spoiled. It didn't matter that Stedman House was known for its diversity, that she had homesick girls upstairs from East Africa and Singapore, and Vietnamese refugees on scholarship from poor towns in southern California.

She posted hours on her door and underlined them. She wouldn't answer except for the emergencies where angry roommates yelled, "She's hemorrhaging down there," or "The police will only release her to an adult."

Dennis announced himself at the front desk at Stedman Hall at 7 p.m. He was carrying a bottle of wine and looked particularly handsome in a new-wave aloha shirt of soft gray and pale yellow. "I have an appointment with Iris Lambrix." The student receptionist had a ponytail that sprouted from her head in perky, asymmetric fashion. She smiled knowingly, a smile that said, "We all hate Iris Lambrix. You obviously have no idea." She pointed to a door off the main reception area. "That's her apartment," said the student.

14

He knocked, noticing the rather forbidding language of her posted hours. It reminded him of his resident couple's nameplate his freshman year at UMass, designed for parents, really, but very sweet: "Annie Caruso and Jay Steinberg (yes, we're married)."

Iris's said, "I am usually not here during the day. My office hours (Pinckney L202, x 646) are Tuesdays and Thursdays, 3 to 4:30. I go to sleep at 10 p.m. weekdays and you wouldn't want to deal with me if I've been awakened." Iris opened the door with a sour expression on her face he knew was meant for a dorm intruder. She smiled when she saw it was her date.

"I may be a few minutes early," he said.

"No one's ever early," said Iris. "You must be an exceptional person." It was a nice beginning. There was cheese and crackers first, sliced ahead and arranged in rows. Her tangerine chicken was technically correct, even though she took no joy in the serving or the eating of it. Iris told him about life as the smartest girl in the class. Asked him where he went to school, looked worried when he said UMass. He felt it necessary to explain not immodestly that he had not been the *best* student at Harrow High School but had done well enough to win the award for combined excellence in scholarship and sports—really a big deal here in town.

Iris frowned. "What kind of guidance counselor did you have?"

"A nice guy, Mr. Alberghini. He also was an assistant hockey coach."

"A black student in—what? the top five percent of his class? An athlete? He should have had Yale and Princeton fighting over you. What did you get in your SATs?"

"Five-hundred-something in verbal and six-something in math," he said obediently.

"Twelve-hundred in your SATs?" she said indignantly, "and you went to a state school?"

"I applied to Yale," Dennis said. "I also applied to Harvard, Dartmouth, Brown and Amherst."

"And?"

"I didn't get in. The wrestling coach at UMass had me to his house for dinner. He came to a few matches here and brought some guys from the team to cheer me on. I got a letter from Doctor J. telling me how glad he was he had gone to UMass. I didn't need much more convincing."

Iris had shaken her head sorrowfully.

"It's a fine university," said Dennis. "I had some great professors."

She asked what he had majored in and he told her, communications. Iris didn't like that either. She said she'd be right back with dessert, strawberries and melted chocolate; the same person who had given her the tangerine chicken recipe had said this was a good dessert for someone with no interest in cooking.

The strawberries were bruised and slightly shriveled. Dennis, wondering if they'd been washed, considered saying he was allergic. He drank her weak coffee and faked involvement with dessert by dipping and decorating his berries. She wasn't interested in the culinary part of hostessing, so it didn't matter. She interviewed him further: what was there to what he did that made him do it? Was it art and thereby creative? Was it so unique a skill that one would build a business around it? A successful business?

Dennis said tying flies was rather tedious. He was known for a few special designs and that was it. He sold other flies for a full inventory, but people seemed to come for his.

"Tedious," Iris repeated. "How odd."

"It's not so much the product. It's the store, the atmosphere. We created a small community, a place where people who love fly fishing or want to learn about it can come and talk to other aficionados—in fact I tried to do something with that when I named the store—Afishin'ados—but it was too much of a reach."

"Did you go to business school?" Iris asked.

Dennis laughed.

"You seem to have done your market research."

"It was a hunch."

Iris shook her head as if his assessment was annoyingly humble. "You've got excellent business instincts, that's obvious. There's always people in your store no matter when I go by. You must be bringing people in who are attracted to the premise as much as the product."

"I'd say that's true."

"Someone should write you up as a case study."

"Someone wrote me up in *New England Monthly* and in the Boston *Globe*."

"I mean an academic."

"Do you do that sort of thing?" he asked Iris.

"I'm writing a book on African-American Fortune Five Hundred middle managers so it's not my territory, but I could certainly imagine a slot for you on my syllabus."

"Doing what?" he asked.

"I do a thing on entrepreneurs and the owner-operated business. You'd be perfect."

"What kind of things would I have to say?"

"Just answer their questions. I'll have them drop by the shop first to get an idea of what you—"

"A field trip! I love it."

Iris said no, not a field trip. He was walking distance from campus and they'd drop in when he wasn't too busy; what time was that?

Dennis smiled, thinking how happy Nick and Lyman would be to have a large contingent of women coming in to watch them work. He said the slow times were when he met with salesmen and tied some flies. Would the kids be interested in that in class? He could bring what he needed and demonstrate a couple of basics.

Iris said with strained politeness, "Maybe one or two." She

17

thought it over and said, "The boys would like it. They're always complaining about MacMillan still thinking of itself as an all-women's school."

"How many guys in this class?"

"Five? Something like that. There are only a hundred and thirty or so in the whole school. I'm not one of the happy simpletons who gets high marks in congeniality so I don't get oversubscribed."

Dennis shrugged. "I'll do it. It's probably good practice for something or other."

"The women will fall in love with you of course. You're the type they like."

"*They?*" he repeated. "Women?"

"MacMillan women. They'll find you cute and while they're listening to you they'll think about Mummy and Daddy back in Beverly Farms and how an African-American boyfriend would be just the right stunt to get their attention, which would be quite doable from their end, too, because you are educated and own your own business and are a commentator on public radio. And your features have an East African cast which to the rich white girls might appear Caucasian. An entirely plausible third-world boyfriend who meets all the criteria."

Dennis smiled slowly and said he wasn't interested in little white sophomores. Why was she describing such a long and detailed scenario?

"Why else would you live in a town like Harrow? Do you want your children to go to Harrow public schools and be the only black faces in their classrooms?"

"That's a long way off. I'm twenty-seven years old and I have no plans other than to expand to catalogue sales by this time next year. I'm sure as hell not thinking about where I'd send my children to school."

"I'm quite attracted to you," Iris said. "I'm two years older than you are, which is immaterial to me. The difference in our heights doesn't bother me at all."

Dennis smiled, sensing that Iris was sweet-talking him as best as she could. He didn't stay the night, but did accept her offer to make love before he left. Iris was not distracted when two girls stood outside her door, discussing the sanctity of the posted hours, wondering if the results of a home pregnancy test could be false-positive, whether it was just cause for disturbing Professor Lambrix after 10, and whether they'd get any help at all from a bitch like her.

He'd been attracted to the wrong parts of Iris, he told me at his sister's wedding. But sometimes you deny stuff, especially when the woman you're with has everything figured out for the both of you. And he'd never do that again—get flattered into a relationship, or let the voice inside him saying "Something's not right here" be drowned out by the one saying "Nobody's perfect."

They were married for one year, after which Iris moved in with a woman named Wilsa, a humorless lesbian, whose line of silk-screened greeting cards suggested female genitalia. Dennis never talked about them as a married couple, but did volunteer that when he brought Iris home to meet his parents they took him aside and said, "She won't take care of you."

He said, "Take care of me? What am I, an invalid? She has her Ph.D. from N.Y.U."

They said, "We shouldn't have said anything. Forget it. She seems like a fine woman, son."

"Then why say it? If it's hardly worth mentioning, why ruin things?"

He said their criticism hung over his marriage like an ominous sampler framed on every wall: "Is this what you call taking care of our son?" He remembered the question with every wifely misdeed—not the big things but the little ones, small acts of marital kindness that even women with doctorates do for sick or tired husbands. And then one day he had to tell his parents she was gone, had left him for a woman; how they'd been right about Iris Lambrix-Vaughan: she wouldn't be taking care of him or any other man.

3

Better Dresses

For a few months last year—after I'd welcomed her enthusiastically but before I had slipped on the ice that was the core of her character—I appointed Libby my closest friend. She certainly fit the bill as a single woman of roughly the same age, hometown, and retail mission; and there was nothing overtly wrong with Libby Getchel that would disqualify her for close friendship. Just the opposite. She was perfectly pleasant; she reciprocated my confidences enough to create the illusion of, if not intimacy, the kind of friendship there ought to be between people who worked in abutting shops. Looking back, I was misled by the geography of it all, and the convenience—not unlike Iris Lambrix finding her way to Brookhoppers because Dennis Vaughan, on paper, was just the man she thought she needed.

*   *   *

We'd have coffee together late afternoons when classes got out at MacMillan and the college girls were in the mood to try on dresses. She was often barefooted in the shop, which was carpeted in a thick bedroom rose. Libby promoted the idea that she was an eccentric artist, often wearing odd clothes which had no resemblance to her own full-skirted, party-dress signature look—Capri pants in flowered chintz with rope for belts and Fruit of the Loom pocket T-shirts one day; schoolgirl woolen jumpers the next, which only proved that a woman with Libby's looks and her wide bones could make the oddest combinations look like fashion.

Yet the dress business was slow. I blamed the town and advised her to be careful: she was an artist, an unquestionably attractive woman, a blonde, a maker of fashion statements. Customers could be intimidated by such a package—not so different from high school, when you think about it, confusing artistic expression and a tendency toward aloofness with being stuck up. Don't get me wrong, but was she sending out the wrong signals?

"I wish I could be more like you," was Libby's answer, one of the occasional comments from left field that seemed sweet, even endearing, but not yet out of character.

Libby could only be referring to my superficial charm. I do attract people: customers, waiters, cashiers, road crews, pizza delivery men, wrong numbers. But not for the reasons that parents, guidance counselors and marriage-minded men find admirable. I have always been outspoken and not particularly concerned with pleasing grown-ups, the kind of little girl whose desk was moved frequently in the hope that a new location would improve her deportment. I favored boys, and developed my own brand of tomboyism—scorning girls' games and girls' silly alliances—which was just another form of flirting. Around sixth grade, the girls in my class began to like boys and to develop their own strategies for coyness and popularity. I had a following finally. My report cards began to speak of "leadership ability."

And now I was grown up, back among friends and relatives, their questions about California unasked because the answers were self-evident: No, Melinda LeBlanc did *not* find fame or wealth or a husband there, or why would she be back behind the counter at a hometown flower shop?

I sensed that my life was a source of satisfaction to girls I had ignored and boys I had treated badly, not to mention the many mothers who had suffered my early successes. I *had* had a charmed life: decent grades, too many boyfriends, a name that sounded as glamorous as any model's in *Seventeen*. But what had that gotten me? Some might say poetic justice, returning to the scene of my crimes, sentenced to design wedding bouquets for the dull girls who had hated me, who blossomed after high school, who filled out or got thin or got contact lenses; whose failure to make even the pep squad at Harrow High School didn't matter one iota in the end.

My friendship with Libby inched forward, beyond Main Street to home visits outside business hours. She lived by herself in the small gold Victorian on Adams Street which she inherited from her parents, even though they were still alive. They stayed in Harrow and lived in an elderly "community," the kind for healthy old people who can take care of themselves but get low-salt meals in a dining hall and low-impact aerobics in the rec room. They loved it there, away from the drafts and the broken window sashes and from the curling asphalt shingles on the roof. When Libby moved back to Harrow from New York, she took over the guest room with its high double bed and chenille bedspread. Her old room was too small and too girlish; the wallpaper was white with green sprigs she had picked because it reminded her of Scarlett

O'Hara's dress fabric in the opening scene of *Gone With the Wind,* a Tarleton twin on each arm.

She turned the dining room into a messy studio and the living room into storage for the bolts in her far-flung fabric collection. A dress designer's house should be like an artist's house, I thought, full of visual surprises, of ordinary objects grouped in startling ways. This was mess without charm, not fringed antique lamp shades on Victorian floor lamps but 1950s living room suite in aqua sateen and smelly garbage bags piling up in the kitchen.

Libby's parents had been MacMillan fixtures as Perry Hall cook and a campus landscaper. Their job categories separated her from the sons and daughters of professors, the ones who had grown up in the large white Victorians bought with family money. Libby knew all the faculty children. They came in large sets and all played stringed instruments; their mothers dressed them in matching Easter coats with velveteen collars, arranged them in a line in descending order for an annual photograph. It's not that they weren't nice to Libby—with their going to Highland Day School they didn't have the opportunity to be either friendly or unfriendly. It was just that MacMillan distinguished between its faculty children and its staff children. There were two different Christmas parties and two different Santas; different cookies and different grab-bag gifts; spiked eggnog for the parents at the Faculty Club and cartoned eggnog for the less fortunate at the Campus Center cafeteria. Libby knew about the segregation because Martha Schiff, a public-school classmate, the daughter of a Marxist professor–father and a department secretary–mother, went to both parties and liked to expound on the indignities of what she labeled "academic bullshit."

It was a dividing line that was wide and deep, Libby felt, like servants' children and children of the great house. And the Getchels, happy employees, were contented working for MacMillan with its liberal vacations, health insurance, free tuition for qualifying children, use of the olympic-size pool and tennis courts June through August.

Even if she had studied hard enough to get into MacMillan, she couldn't imagine sitting in a classroom, hearing students on both sides laughing about last night's floury chicken pie at Perry Hall. Or seeing her father—lanky and gray-blond, uniformed knees caked with dirt, dunking his doughnut at the next table in a campus coffee shop. Lots of sons and daughters did it, accepted MacMillan scholarships and went to college free. There was even an award, named after a dead botany professor who had been a townie, given out every Honors Day at Harrow High to the son or daughter of a MacMillan employee with the highest grade-point average. Martha Schiff won it the year Dennis and I graduated, and accepted with anything but an obsequious handshake: for the first time in recent memory, an employee's child with the highest grade point average turned down free tuition and would be taking out loans for Yale.

I imagine that Libby, like me and a percentage of every graduating class, believed she would not return to Harrow once she'd escaped. She belonged in a big city where people didn't care what job titles your parents held; where people judged you on your own accomplishments. That's what we townies thought in our storybook, Hollywood versions of going to New York or to sunny California to make our names.

It took a while, but we discovered that people in big cities also cared what your parents did, but their questions didn't even have the veneer of kindness, the *noblesse oblige* we thought we hated. Libby's answers—"gardener at MacMillan College," "cook at Perry Hall"—didn't evoke the smiles of recognition they earned in Harrow, no compliments about the flowering perennials of that nice Miles Getchel or the famous tomato-soup cake of that dedicated Mrs. G. Maybe people were nicer than she gave them credit for in Harrow; maybe it was Martha Schiff's cynicism that made her sensitive where none was due. And hadn't Martha herself returned after graduate school to teach psychology at the very college that had oppressed her?

New York was hard on Libby. There were many other tall women with good bones who had a style and a walk they thought distinctive. Everyone was pretty and eccentrically dressed. There were out-of-work actresses and models and fine artists working alongside her, lured as eventual apprentices for a name designer, but drafting and cutting and tacking in a department so far down the ladder and so far removed from glamour that Libby might as well have been sewing pillowcases in a Taiwan factory.

Next she tried sales—Human Resources at Lord & Taylor said there were opportunities among their sales force for informal modeling and a management training system whereby their girls became assistant buyers. She started out in Accessories and four months later moved to Moderate Sportswear; something opened up in Better Dresses just after her one-year anniversary. Human Resources said they had confidence in her—while they were chatting would she consider small heels and hose and a look that was slightly closer to the Lord & Taylor image? Had she taken much advantage of her employee discount?

Libby said she made all her own clothes, but bought her underwear and outerwear from the store, of course.

The woman didn't say, "You *make* these unusual clothes, these signature dresses? These are *your* designs? Would you bring your portfolio in tomorrow and we'll sit you down with our head buyer?"

Instead she said, "You sew? Can you do alterations? We'd love to have someone who speaks English in that department."

Libby said, "I'm a designer. I'm not a seamstress. I worked for Albert Nipon before I came here. If I'm working temporarily at Lord & Taylor for any reason it's to learn the retail side of fashion."

"Still," said the woman in Human Resources, "I'm making a notation in your file. It's my job to know these things. It would very quickly become a supervisory position."

"You don't think my dresses are appropriate for the floor?" Libby asked.

The woman smiled diplomatically. "You look marvelous in clothes. Why not use yourself as a walking mannequin; why not boost sales by having a customer fall in love with what you're wearing?"

"A 'walking mannequin'?" Libby repeated.

"As models! Role models for our customers, as representatives of a look. I wouldn't be doing the store any favor to hire an ill-kempt, unattractive sales force. That's hardly earth-shattering policy in the fashion business." The woman smiled kindly. She herself wore a suit Libby recognized from the New Yorker collection—black-and-royal-blue houndstooth, boxy jacket, loose weave; handsome art nouveau onyx pin on her lapel.

Libby inched her chair closer to the woman's desk. "If you didn't work here and could buy your clothes anywhere, where would you go—I mean, what kind of shop would you be drawn to? Small? Friendly? Dresses only? One line? Many lines?"

The personnel woman seemed to like the question; her manual said that employees should be encouraged to confide their dreams. "You mean, kind of an ideal shopping situation? Not one that actually exists somewhere?"

"That's right. An ideal dress shop."

The woman bit her lip, smiled naughtily and let her eyes rest on the ceiling for dramatic effect. "Okay. I would like it to be small, but not too small, because I want a wide-ish selection. I'd like to see a range of dresses, from business outfits and casual dresses to something appropriate for a black-tie affair. I want the salespeople to be frank when something doesn't look good on me, even if it means they lose the sale. I don't want to be pressured. . . . Oh—and this is crucial—I want there to be only *one* of each dress; not one dress in each size, but one of each. I want to know that if I buy it, I am getting something unique. And"—she lowered her voice—"I know this sounds peculiar, but I don't want it to be cheap. I want the prices to define a certain clientele. I don't want students and . . . and—"

"Salesgirls?" Libby supplied.

"You know what I mean. Classic. Good fabric. I don't mind paying a bit more for something that's going to last." The woman asked, "Are you thinking about looking for work in another shop?"

Libby wanted to shake this stupid woman. Was she so pathetic as an employee, so unlikely a person to dream of her own business, so terrible a designer of dresses that even with these crystal-clear questions, this personnel specialist thought it meant she was looking for another *salesclerk* job? She said coldly, "I was asking you because I'm doing research on going into business for myself."

"On your own?" said the woman. "A franchise of some sort?"

"No. My own shop."

Thank goodness she confided in me, the woman's expression seemed to say; thank goodness I can save her the heartbreak. She said carefully, "You know that it takes a great deal of money to open a shop in New York. Hundreds of thousands of dollars. And contacts. It's not a matter of liking to sew and having a few years of retail experience under your belt. It's backbreaking work. Heartbreaking work. So few survive."

Libby looked at the woman and wondered what she could say that would adequately convey how insulted and patronized she felt. After a long pause she pronounced carefully, "I can see you have no idea what I'm talking about."

"Of course I—"

"I worked in the business. I know what it takes to do something like this. Do you think I haven't done any research or talked to anyone? You don't think I listen to my customers and have a sense of what might make it and what might not?"

"Which is a wonderful quality," said the woman, unhappy to have voices raised in her cubicle.

"You think New York is the only city in America where a person can open a dress shop?" Libby continued, noting that in her indignation her plans were taking shape.

She was twenty-eight. She had been an outsider in New York City for ten years. She was an FIT graduate who hadn't gotten her break, who was working her way up a career ladder of dubious achievement. Better Dresses was the place she'd be allowed to serve if only she agreed to small heels and a Lord & Taylor look.

She said to the woman in the black and blue suit, "What is it that you require, two weeks' notice?"

"Elizabeth," she said soothingly, "you don't want to leave us and we don't want you to leave. I'm going to pretend you never said that."

"I quit," declared Libby. "I'm going home."

She had been sleeping on a friend's couch since her last set of roommates asked her to leave. Libby had promised Felice it was temporary, and did read "roommate wanted" ads in the *Village Voice* every week. Two months passed. Felice said she wasn't going to turn her out, and she did appreciate the extra money, but Jesus Christ, did she ever consider doing laundry before the hamper was overflowing? Had she ever washed a dish within twenty-four hours of its use? She wanted to be able to bring a friend home without connoitering the apartment first.

What exactly am I waiting for? Libby wondered, and the day she quit her Lord & Taylor job she knew: she was holding out because she didn't want to stay there, to sign a lease that would commit her to another year in the city. She had no job, no place to set up her sewing machine. In Harrow there was a whole house, her green and white bedroom, the dining room table. Her mother and father would only be too glad to have her and feed her and refuse her financial contributions. Harrow was different now: last time she was home she had had scrambled eggs with andouille sausage at the renovated Mapleleaf Diner. Retail space was manageable, if her parents were willing to help. She had two thousand dollars saved and she'd get loans; she didn't need much square footage or any employees. She'd splurge on the bags, get ones with handles and swathe all purchases in gorgeous tissue paper. People would love being inside her shop. It would be luscious, pastel, warm, with flattering light and deep wall-to-wall. Mirrors would make the store look larger and the customers thinner. The curtains covering the dressing rooms would be pink moiré, and there would be many hooks—for the customer's own clothes, for store garments, a yes hook, a no hook, a maybe hook. It would be part of the new Harrow, like the Mapleleaf Diner with its glass blocks and its art deco hardware. She would call it Rags for Sale, the name she'd had picked out since FIT. It was what her father used to chant when she was little, when he picked her up and carried her around sideways on his hip or upside down over his shoulder, calling musically to his buddy groundskeepers, to passing students, showing off his little girl: "Ra-a-gs for say-al."

4

A Client Wedding

For the sake of clarification, I will say this one time that Dennis and I slept together before Libby moved back to Harrow. We don't discuss it—Dennis and I don't, that is—because it was just a case of dancing with each other at a client wedding and getting carried away after too much champagne. Weddings do that, certain kinds, where the bride and groom have been engaged for a short period and are still romantically inflamed. It was his sister's wedding, in fact, so my gate-crashing was official, and Dennis was dancing with me to make me feel less like an interloper. Then this wonderful lead singer stepped forward, all sweaty and sincere like Paul McCartney singing "Yesterday" on the "Ed Sullivan Show"; the lights were dimmed and it was just him, spotlit, backed by the saxophone player and an acoustic guitar, singing, "Darling, you-oo-oo send me" as good as Sam Cooke ever did.

You've seen it happen: People who aren't dancing take the floor; soon others are kissing their dance partners' necks, and husbands whisper to wives that if they had it to do all over, they would. The song ends, but the band continues in that vein as if it were make-out night at a CYO hop.

We kissed finally in Harrow Inn's parking lot at 2 a.m., a kiss that had been building all evening through successively closer dances, and he knocked me out with the way he finally did it: hands gently holding my face; hands touching my hair; the champion all-around kisser for combined excellence in artistic and technical achievement.

At some point he murmured, "Come back to my place?"

"I've got my car . . ."

"But you want to?"

I nodded and we touched foreheads. "You can leave your car here or you can follow me to my place."

"Follow," I said.

"You're sure?" he asked, but grinning with such sweet happiness that it knocked me out again.

My purple strapless dress was uncomplicated: one long zipper down the back which allowed it to fall away as if engineered for this purpose by a Hollywood prop department. Dennis encircled me in his arms, eventually leaning down to kiss my shoulders as if they had called to him all evening. You can imagine what my hormones were doing—months without love, and now this, Dennis, beautiful in his white tie and tails, refusing to let his lips leave my skin while he struggled with his tie and shirt studs and cummerbund; worked his way out of his suspenders, his trousers, his underwear, as gracefully and poignantly as he danced.

And only when he'd led me to his bed, had shut off the lights, lit a candle on his bureau, had he carefully removed his eyeglasses, one flexible earpiece at a time, so that the myopic, dreamy face above mine would not too suddenly be a stranger's.

He had a wrestler's body and little chest hair; what there was was uneven dots of black fuzz on his incredibly smooth, brown skin. His hands reminded me that he made his living carefully tying loops and knots, a job which demands patience and a kind of passion.

I spent the next day at home recasting my life: Saturday nights and New Year's eves spoken for. An understanding. A commitment. A cascading bouquet of bleeding hearts, stephanotis, freesia, Casablanca lilies and porcelana roses.

I even told my mother: Remember how I've been saying it was a mistake to move back here? No men to date, hardly even a single man in my peripheral vision?

Well, maybe I'll stay after all, I said. Maybe all those pathetic Friday nights at Buddy's fending off underage farmers, and the Saturdays pretending that client weddings were a legitimate form of social intercourse were leading up to this, so I'd appreciate it when it happened; so I'd say to my children, "and all along I was denying the attraction because your father was nice to everyone in a nonexclusive kind of way, and I was afraid to assume too much even though—"

"I know they're a nice family," she said halfheartedly.

"But?"

"Maybe you're not thinking things through. Or maybe you're very lonely."

I said, "It's your house, so I can't ask you to leave. But I am asking you never to say anything like that again."

She said I had misunderstood; other people, not her. She wasn't—

"I don't need your blessing," I said.

33

A nervous Sunday night. Then Monday—no sign. Not at work.

Monday night. I went home immediately after work to fret by the telephone, pretending my evening's goals were a hot oil treatment and a new issue of *Floral Elegance*. My mother broiled me a lamb chop, baked me a potato, offered explanations: He fell asleep early. He's helping his mother haul gift wrapping to the recycling center. He's driving relatives to the airport. He doesn't like talking on the telephone, and he knows he'll see you tomorrow at work anyway.

Tuesday. My mother called at noon to see if he'd come by or telephoned.

"Didn't I promise to let you know?" I snapped.

She asked if it could be, you know, racial? Maybe not what his family had in mind for him?

"Ma! You don't know what you're talking about."

"Just a thought I had," she said. "Men get nervous, even in the best of circumstances."

Then just before I left, standing on the other side of my work table, was Dennis, somber behind prescription sunglasses. He'd like to talk to me—in private, at Brookhoppers? The guys leave at 5:30.

I said, "Why don't you just say it now? You've already stuck the knife in my gut and I'd just as soon not walk around with the handle protruding for another half hour. Twist it and finish me off."

He did, sadly. To the tune of, "It's not you. I can't be with anyone right now. I don't have enough distance on my divorce. I can't see or feel things clearly. It's my problem. It's about me, not about you."

I returned to the spool of blue ribbon I was holding, and began fashioning a bow, the finishing detail on a new-baby arrangement. Dennis watched me loop and snip, and for a time we were both silent.

"It's nothing you did," he repeated.

"It's your idea, then? You're not being talked out of anything?"

"Who would do that?" he asked.

"Your mother. I saw her face at the wedding. She got your ear and said, 'No flighty white shopgirl is going to get my son. Thank the lady for the dances, and tell her you need someone more like your mama."

"They don't want me to get hurt again."

"You think my mother feels any different? You think she wouldn't prefer a potato farmer from Stepney to some guy who murmured things in my ear then lured me home?"

"It wasn't like that."

"I envy you," I said quietly. "You must have quite the full life if you can throw this away."

"I'm not saying that."

"And don't expect me to be your friend. Because I know the routine, and I know that's your next offer: 'We were such good friends; let's not destroy our friendship.'"

"Melinda—"

"In other words, 'I'd be happy to fuck you, but I'm too vulnerable for anything else.' You should have sweatshirts printed up for your catalogue."

I couldn't see his eyes through the dark glasses. He stood there, one hand flat on my work table as if he weren't quite through. Finally, only—"Will you be all right?"

I said, "Don't worry about me."

"I couldn't be more sorry," he said, hesitating at the door, but leaving just the same.

Libby returned to Harrow a month later with that look in her eye and that peculiar smile which I interpreted as retail ambition. I made a beautiful arrangement of French tulips in whites and pinks with a card that said, "Welcome to the block." The day after the opening was quiet, so I visited her with coffee after my morning rush. That was when she told me the story of her and Dennis at Harrow High School, how he formed a bridge over her shoulder and signaled to Libby that he had a different interpretation of their corridor friendship than she had.

"Have you been in touch at all?" I asked.

"Not directly," said Libby. "I knew he went into television after college, in Boston. And my mother sent me a story from the *Sentinel* when he opened Brookhoppers."

"Uh-oh," I said. "You didn't move back here because of him, did you?"

"No," said Libby without much conviction, motioning that I should follow her back to her sewing machine and talk to her while she worked.

I asked her if there hadn't been other men. She was twenty-nine years old, after all: college, jobs, New York. No attachments that had helped a two-minute high school brush-off shrink down to its rightful proportions?

"A few."

"None that went anywhere?"

"One man was an Iranian businessman who spent several months a year in the States, but didn't live here and wasn't going to, obviously."

"Not a great scenario," I said.

"He was very cosmopolitan and very good-looking," said Libby. "It's not like he was some fanatic."

"Probably had a couple of wives already."

"He graduated from Georgetown in the fifties," said Libby.

"Not young."

"Not very good at staying in touch between visits," she said.

I nodded sympathetically; after a polite interval I asked, "Who else?"

36

"A guy from Andrea's apartment," she said, as if I knew these people or had seen a movie of her life.

"Andrea?" I repeated.

"Two roommates ago. In New York. Andrea was the one who had lived in Alaska."

I was still in the discovery phase of my friendship with Libby, which is to say I dismissed the occasional odd remark, the strange dropped name, as either my inattention or her quirky charm.

"I don't know Andrea," I said.

"It was her brother."

"You and Andrea didn't get along, I take it?"

Libby shrugged as if to say, Who does?

"Was it, like, openly hostile?"

She was feeding a long, straight seam under the needle's foot with amazing speed. "There wasn't as much feeling on my side as there was on his—he was younger than us—so she disapproved."

I said that seemed a little unreasonable to me. After all, one person's protecting her brother was another person's meddling, right? Being Libby's roommate gave this Andrea a front-row seat to an event she wouldn't ordinarily have gotten a ticket to at all.

"That's right," said Libby. "And I did like him."

"But it didn't work out?"

"He went back to an old girlfriend, who had been waiting in the wings the whole time."

"And that's when you decided to make your move back here?"

"Not because of that."

"Because of Dennis?"

The sewing machine stopped. Libby looked directly at me. "I came home just like you did." She rose from the folding chair and hung the half-finished garment on a padded hanger.

I asked what was left to do, meaning what would help this project look less like a cotton print house dress. She said she might do jet shank buttons up the front; very 1950s on a fitted bodice.

"Have you ever slept with Dennis?" I asked. "Not that I want to pry; I just want to get a handle on what we're dealing with."

Libby said, "When would I have slept with him?" She didn't ask, "Have you?" because Libby, I was learning, often let a conversation drop after it had covered her own particular needs.

Maybe I should have confessed then; maybe I should have said, "I have. A mere six weeks ago. I had a whole night with Dennis, not some two-minute racial incident that gets billed years later as true love. But of course I didn't: I felt sorry for Libby, sewing her own inventory at a mortgaged, computerized machine with a hundred and ninety decorative stitches in its memory; my pink and white tulips the only sign that someone had noted her return.

"Has he been in to see you?" I asked.

"Not yet. I walk by Brookhoppers ten times a day, so I've seen him from a distance."

"But you haven't just marched in there to announce your return?"

Libby smiled mysteriously.

"You've been waiting for him to do the neighborly thing—new merchant on the block and all?"

She nodded solemnly. "I've been open six days. I think he should make the first move, don't you? I know he knows I'm here."

So this is what I've come back to, I thought: my past. The boys and girls of Harrow High, circa 1978.

I looked at my yearbook that night for the first time since moving back. I leafed ahead past the head-and-shoulders shots to the group activities, to the cheerleading squad specifically. And there I was, all in white as captain, except the maroon "H" on my chest, up on a metal folding chair at the crux of a V-formation, my chin resting coyly in my hands, my elbows on the co-captains' shoulders beneath. Mocking me from the opposite page was the

National Honor Society, standing proud and alert, chins raised like a small, prizewinning glee club. Martha was in the front row, looking as zealous as ever. And there was Dennis, smiling too broadly in the back row, the way athletes do to say I'm still a regular guy even if I'm posing with the brains.

I turned back to my formal graduation picture, a dramatically lit shot of me staring down my left shoulder at the lens. Beneath it, the words which the yearbook staff had chosen to sum me up—words I had adored at eighteen: "Circled by the topaz sand, kissed by the diamond sea, O to dance beneath the moon, with one hand waving free." In other words: wild, popular, good-looking, fast.

I settled down with the yearbook and a glass of bad white wine from the refrigerator, reading the poems beneath other girls' names, trying to find one that missed by as big a mile as mine.

5

More About Me

It helps to know that my parents came from farming families—asparagus and cukes on her side; tobacco and cukes on his: pickling cukes to pickle companies; wrapping tobacco to cigar manufacturers. That's the split here: either you come to Harrow from a good Ph.D. program, or you come from a farm. My maternal grandfather in retirement did a little corn on the side, which provided enough for him to sit in an aluminum lawn chair by the side of Route 6 with a cardboard sign that said, "Butter and sugar corn, just picked." Six days a week from the first runty ears of July to Labor Day I sat with him and made change. He paid me two cents for every ear I bagged, a quarter for every dozen to make the arithmetic easier. We averaged four sales an hour, more on weekends. I read Nancy Drew between customers or wrote letters to my pen pal in Vasteras, Sweden. Out-of-state customers in expensive cars from good school districts liked to see me read. "Smart little girl you have there," they'd said to my grandfather. "Does she go to school?"

"Of course I go to school," I'd answer indignantly. "I don't go in the *summer*."

Papa Jan (I had a Papa Mike on the other side, my father's side, who backed away when his son left us) invariably said, "She gets all A's"—I didn't, but he paid me fifty cents an A, so those stuck in his head. I didn't contradict Papa Jan in front of customers. People were incredibly sappy, I thought, amazed and touched that a farmer's granddaughter out in the country went to school and got A's.

"She read all the time," Papa Jan would say proudly. "She smart as vip." He could say it twelve times a day and never need to roll his eyes at me after they left. I was his favorite grandchild, the only child of his only daughter, smart as a vip.

I had another specialty, on top of counting ears and change: I gave directions. To MacMillan. To the state park. To the nearest restrooms, diner, county fair, to I-91, to the Mohawk Trail, to downtown Harrow and any number of establishments on Main Street. To farms along 6—the Siaccas', the Uszynskis', the Tymkowiczes'; to a farm stand which *did* sell tomatoes and maple syrup and cider. They found me amazing, the way I reeled off directions with the confidence of a gas station attendant. I supplied landmarks, too. I believed in landmarks and positive reinforcement. "Then you'll come to a blinking yellow light with a grange hall on your right and a flea market on your left. Keep going. . . ." I was rarely stumped. When I was, I looked at my road atlas, our stand marked with an *X*, Route 6 traced in black felt-tip. I kept a phone book with me, too, for exact addresses.

41

Later I realized that I experienced every stripe of customer those summers selling corn from the back of the pickup: the mistrustful ones who said, "Not so fast, little girl. How many you up to? These the freshest you got?"; the friendly chatterers: "Bet you get a little bit tired of sittin' here all day countin' ears of corn. You pick this, too? This your daddy?"; the city slickers: "Give me two dozen, no four. I've got a freezer in my basement so we blanch them in boiling water and have them all winter long. We marinate steaks, too—soy sauce, garlic, lemon, olive oil and throw one on the grill when we get unexpected company; any antique stores up ahead?"; the cheapskate: "A dollar! If I came by when you were closing up would you be willing to give me a better price?"; and still my favorite after all these years—the big shot: "A buck? That's it? Here, this is for you, a tip. Buy yourself an ice cream soda," the man in the nice suit would say, folding the dollar lengthwise and putting it into my hand cryptically as if Papa Jan pooled our tips.

I did it for seven summers until I was fifteen when my younger cousin Roger took my job. I was too embarrassed to be bagging family corn in high school. Boys rode by and honked; boys I knew. I wanted a real job; I wanted to be a mother's helper and spend a summer on Martha's Vineyard with a faculty family, or waitress in a coral uniform at a muffin house. Roger was a poor substitute on all counts. He turned lost drivers over to Papa Jan for directions; he was hungry and thirsty and had to pee more frequently than I; he went crazy when a yellow jacket came near him, even in the middle of a transaction. Once in a while on Roger's day off I'd help my grandfather out, and he'd confide to me about Roger not being good company—a nice boy, he wasn't saying that he wasn't nice or not good in school, but not smart in the same way I was.

"I'm older than he is. I know the ropes," I explained, dismissing the praise. I didn't want to outshine Roger, an act which might have resulted in a family conference with Roger getting sent to 4-H camp and me getting my old job back.

"The peoples ask me, 'Where's the little girl, the one who always reading?'"

"Exactly," I said. "I didn't pay enough attention to the job. I made a good impression and everything, but Roger's a better bet."

Roger *was* a better bet. He didn't quit at fifteen but built a real stand of old two-by-fours and scrap lumber, expanding the line to cukes, cabbages, potatoes, rhubarb, tomatoes, pumpkins, and raspberries, all surplus from aunts' and uncles' gardens. Roger stayed here. When I came back to Harrow from California, no happier or richer than when I'd left, Roger hired me with some grace, as if he and Robin hadn't been coaxed by the family to take me into the business. They said I brought a certain California color sense, a Japanese influence, to their arrangements, and besides, Papa Jan, God rest his soul, would want it this way.

So I returned to work for Roger and Robin, the cutest couple in America. They had met at voke school, fallen in love, gone to the prom, graduated as valedictorian and salutatorian, and with utter seriousness sat down with a perpetual calendar and made a ten-year plan that included the exact months of their pre-engagement, engagement, marriage, the opening of their business, the purchase of their starter home, the conceptions of their first and second children.

The amazing thing about Roger and Robin is that they stuck to their plan. They went to college—different campuses of the state college system so that their detractors would say they had a chance to test their love across time and distance, even if it was only forty-two miles. She majored in business administration and he in horticulture. They had sex once they were pinned, and loved it;

43

thought they were the only couple on earth with this trick in their pocket. The formal engagement was announced at graduation—Roger's, which was one day after Robin's. And then the shop: Forget-Me-Not, a name as cute as anyone could stand.

They were utterly sincere as bosses, too, and I almost enjoyed Robin's heart-to-heart talks with me about my work performance and my attitude. She would pull up a stool and say how they valued my work, really they did; and they knew that I'd developed a following in Harrow, particularly among people who care about style and, you know, the latest fashions. And they knew I was dedicated and they could count on me to get a job done. But, sometimes they'd like just a little more consideration with the small stuff, the things that have to be done that aren't glamorous —helping out behind the counter without having to be asked, seeing to the wire service orders. . . .

"You're right," I told them. "I get so carried away with designs—"

"And you're the best," Robin would say, using some psychology she learned in an organizational development class. "It's just that we don't always know where you are, and even though we think we're liberal employers and we're family, Roger and I work fifty-hour weeks and we need a hundred and five percent. Sometimes you're supposed to be here and we don't know where you are."

"I'm having consultations with clients. Maybe I should wear a beeper," I'd say, pretending to be earnest.

"Is there a reason why customers can't come here for consultations?"

"I'm going to ask the *president* of MacMillan to come to me when I need to see the drapes and the rug and the room where the function is? When we're billing them something like five hundred bucks a month?"

"Well maybe not MacMillan," Robin would say. "But the brides. They can certainly come down and talk to you here."

"I have to see the church, don't I? I don't do stock arrangements that would fit in anywhere. That's why people come to me. I thought you knew that."

"I do know that," Robin said, biting her lip at not having made any progress beyond her last pep talk with me. She smiled, her forehead still worried. "Maybe just tell us where you're going? Leave a number if we have a question." She lowered her voice. "And Roger would appreciate it if you kept your coffee breaks down to five or ten minutes. He gets annoyed but never says anything."

"Except to you, right?"

Robin shrugged and smiled, almost my conspirator.

"Maybe you could install a time clock."

"See! You're getting the wrong idea!"

"I'm an artist, not a clerk. I stay up late one night making sketches—on my own time, which I accept happily—maybe I can't even get to sleep because I'm worrying whether Roger will be able to get what I special-ordered. So if I come in the next day and I need to relax a little by having coffee with Libby or Dennis before I start, I think I've earned that."

"You have," Robin cried. "I agree with you—"

"But it gets Roger's goat?"

"I'll talk to him. You know he worships you."

I smiled my artiste's smile and said, "I count on it."

Once in a while an old customer from the corn stand comes into Forget-Me-Not. They don't remember me but I remember them as they were along Route 6, women in their house dresses, men in their swim trunks and Saint Christopher medals on their hairy chests, on guard, half-shucking each ear, corn experts in

45

search of God knows what. They don't recognize me, so they have no way of knowing what I am judging them on: how they treated a little girl and an old man who sat by the road all day, not interested in cheating anyone, selling delicious corn picked that morning at a perfectly fair price.

6

Some of My Problems

It keeps coming back to one thing, and that's what I do for a living, or what I *didn't* do between the ages of eighteen and twenty-five when every other Harrowite with half a brain was earning a couple of degrees. Not that this town respects only professors and doctors and lawyers, not by any means; we love our craftspeople with their craggy faces and graying hair, but it helps that they went to Bennington before they started stitching sandals and throwing pots.

Even Martha Schiff-Shulman, friend and no snob, revealed her bias during our standing Friday supper, arranged in the weeks following the Dennis debacle to give me a semblance of a social life. I was in the process of asking her husband, Stephen, his version of how they had met. (Martha's version: they met in graduate school, hated each other, were thrown together alpha-

47

betically as lab partners, still hated each other until their study group had a potluck dinner at Stephen's apartment where Martha found, looking for the spare corkscrew in his kitchen junk drawer, a picture of herself asleep at a study carrel. She claimed to know instantly that Stephen was, if not in love with her, something close to it.)

"Didn't she tell you we met in graduate school? She asked me out."

Martha, at the open refrigerator, answered with a loud "Ha."

I said, "But then what? Martha said you started off hating each other. Yet here you are living together, married, happy. I need to know how these things work."

"We just thought we hated each other. Luckily Martha had the first inkling that our extreme dislike was extreme something else."

"He's so full of shit," said Martha. She turned to Stephen. "I found the picture in your kitchen drawer, which announced in no uncertain terms that you were in love with me. Correct?"

"Ask her how long it took her to fall into my arms after I confessed."

I asked Martha: *did* she go from hating him one minute to being in love with him once he'd told the truth?

"Slight exaggeration," said Martha, "but enough like a *Good Housekeeping* short story on the face of it to be embarrassing."

I asked what happened to the photo.

Stephen grinned. He slid his wallet from his back pocket, opened it, and smiled fondly at a picture of a wild-haired Martha sleeping sweetly on a stack of books.

"How could I *not* fall for such a sap?" Martha asked. Stephen squeezed her shoulders, and landed a kiss above her ear. Martha rolled her eyes as if public affection didn't suit her, knowing it was hard for me to witness their devotion. It did raise a painful question: Could a man hate me so strenuously that the weight of it would flip itself over and come up again as love?

"How about you?" Stephen asked. "No nice eligible bachelors shopping for flowers these days?"

"No eligible bachelors, period. Nice or not nice."

"And she's awfully busy with work," offered Martha.

I said she'd been married too long if she believed *that*. Work was no substitute for love at my age, and anyone who thought so should let her subscription to *Ms.* magazine run out.

"No old flames kicking around town?" asked Stephen.

"I keep telling her we should have a Harrow reunion as a way to assess exactly that," said Martha, "but she says it's too much trouble for very little return."

"I'm not in the mood to do the work it would take," I said. "I'm not even in the mood to form a committee to *delegate* the work it would take."

"Look," said Martha, "we'll go through the yearbook and send letters to everyone's home address with the hope that parents forward the letters, skipping the undesirables and the known marrieds."

I said to Stephen, "It's a trick. She thinks that addressing envelopes and licking stamps would give me something to do on weekends. She's prescribing occupational therapy."

"Flower arranging is occupational therapy," said Martha. "This is cultural anthropology."

Enlightening: Martha, never famous for diplomacy, was demeaning what I did for a living. "I think you just said that flower arranging is occupational therapy."

"Not the way you do it. *Categorically,* the way I might say that basket weaving is occupational therapy while at the same time I'd spend two hundred dollars for a hand-dyed Hopi melon basket."

"You think any dope can do floral design, basically. It doesn't take an advanced degree; in fact it doesn't take any degree. The only one you can get is from a community college, and you're not impressed by certificates. Would you say that sums up your attitude?"

Martha looked at me evenly. Stephen announced he'd clear away the dishes and, um, correct some midterms if we ladies would excuse him. When he had disappeared, Martha said calmly, "What's the real issue here?"

"The real issue is that you think I'm wasting my time doing something brainless, that you don't understand what it involves— that you probably never distinguished between one of my arrangements and some hack's arrangements, and that your mind is made up. Which is very sad, because I respect what you do and I thought you respected what I did."

Martha said carefully, "Sometimes I think you don't respect what you do."

"I don't respect the fact that I have to work at a place called Forget-Me-Not and that I have to answer to The Stupids instead of being my own boss."

"Okay, then," said Martha, "maybe that's what I'm responding to."

"But you're a psychologist. You're supposed to have insight. You're saying you can't distinguish between my self-esteem over what I do and my irritation over working for Roger and Robin? That doesn't say much for your powers of observation."

"Can I say something?"

"What?"

"Can I make one small observation without your biting my head off?"

I shrugged: go ahead.

"Yes, you are a gifted artist; yes, you design gorgeous flower arrangements—and yes, I certainly do know which are yours; I can tell from across a room that an arrangement is a Melinda

LeBlanc. However: do you want to exercise other parts of your brain? Are you ever sorry that you didn't go to college? Is it too late?"

Well, that's it, I thought; the end of a nicely emerging friendship. I was really glad you moved back to town and I had a free therapist and a spy on the campus, but this is the moment of truth. Good-bye and fuck you.

"You're angry," she said.

"Shouldn't I be? Suddenly out of nowhere you insult my career—oh, sure, you throw me a bone about my artistic talents—but that doesn't count for shit in your book. Not really. You're an academic. What counts is degrees, not IQs. I know people who teach with you, tenured professors, heads of departments, and I know I'm as smart as they are. But so what! I didn't choose to go to college. I only deal with the real world. I work on Main Street. I don't have office hours. I don't even have an office. I must be sorely deficient in brains or else I'd be a college professor writing papers that no one reads."

Martha looked at me, a long psychiatric look, then metered out a sly smile. "Feel better?" she asked softly.

"Fuck you."

"I'm sorry. I think you're as smart as anyone I know—tenured, not tenured."

"No you don't! This has been bubbling around in your brain since you moved back here."

"Maybe I'm jealous. I want to have a beautiful product sitting in front of me at the end of every day."

"Oh, please."

Martha chewed on her lower lip. "I'm sorry," she said.

I shrugged: okay, forget it.

I had this boyfriend, Seth, for four years in California. He supposedly loved me, and his friends thought I was a breath of fresh air, which is what the graduate-level educated (cell biology, U.C. San Diego) say about the high-school educated if the latter is pretty and the former wish they were sleeping with her, too.

We met while I was waitressing at one of the ice cream parlors that had an extended menu of soups, sandwiches, and salads, and didn't mind its patrons sitting around for hours over four-dollar dinners, refilling their coffee cups, switching to decaf after 8 p.m. Seth left 50 percent tips: two bucks for a $3.98 chicken salad plate. Besides he was cute for a scientist: sandy hair and eyeglasses of a yellowish tortoiseshell. I made the first move: Where was he from originally? Connecticut! Holy shit—I was from Massachusetts. . . . Melinda LeBlanc. . . . Harrow. . . . Just temporarily while I was earning some money for college. . . . Where have I applied? Nowhere, officially, until I establish residency. Maybe Santa Cruz? *Maybe the moon?*

Seth talked about this in subsequent conversations, which turned into dates, into making out on the beach, into me moving into his rented house on a flat street of boring basementless houses with carports in otherwise gorgeous LaJolla. He loved to talk about my plans for college; he'd work it in to introductions when his lab friends met me for the first time. *Lest you think she's a clerk at a flower-packing business; lest you can't judge her intelligence by yourself and need some credentials like "will be going to college next year"; "is thinking about applying to the enology program at Davis. . . ."*

The fact is, I understood his apologies: I wouldn't live with someone who had my level of ambition, either. I wrote away for applications to San Diego, Santa Cruz, Davis, Santa Barbara, Sacramento State and MacMillan back home, where they were obliged to give me, as long as I claimed 114 Woodrow Avenue, Harrow, as my permanent address, free tuition.

Receiving the fat application forms was one thing; filling them out with no motivation behind it, and on the basis of someone else's ambitions, was practically impossible. Seth was baffled that I had taken the bare minimum of tests—only SATs but no Achievement Tests. What kind of high school *was* this! Now look what you'll have to do.

He brought home a Dictaphone from the lab: I could speak my essays into it; an oral first draft. Why not talk about growing flowers and how you've grown through that. They'll like that working with your hands/working with the earth stuff. Maybe tell that story about the guy who didn't speak English and you couldn't speak Spanish and didn't know anything about flowers at first so you called them all by their Spanish names; couldn't figure out the orders, never realizing—

"They're not looking for idiots," I said.

"That's not the point of that story. The point is something multicultural. It's saying that flowers transcend cultures and languages and that there's no absolutes with flowers. His 'lirio' is your 'lily.' And you, the English-speaking American citizen, were the one who was at a disadvantage, as if the flowers were the great leveler. It's a good anecdote, and funny. They love when you use humor to make a point."

Years later, when I heard Dennis's radio commentaries, his life lessons drawn from fish and fake bugs, they reminded me of Seth's sappy idea for my college essay. I said no, forget it; I wasn't going to turn working alongside Carlos and identifying flowers by their Spanish names into a college essay which proved It's a Small World After All.

Seth hadn't known someone like me, since he grew up in Connecticut and went to prep school. Not that prep school underachievers all went to college; the few who didn't traveled around Europe with plans for deferring their education for one year. Nobody just moved away aimlessly. If they took dead-end jobs it was for Life Experience and tuition money. Nobody got sidetracked and kept the dead-end job for four years. "You would have known people like me if you'd gone to the public high school," I pointed out.

Seth conceded that I was probably right. There probably *were* smart kids who didn't automatically go to college—first-generation kinds of patterns, parents who hadn't gone either. Seth could imagine this world about as well as he could imagine there were families out there where fathers abandoned mothers, and mothers remarried traveling salesmen and handed out coupons in supermarkets. I was a refreshing change for Seth, a walk on the wild side—or at least on the working-class side—and I knew it would be my floundering around that got to him in the end. His class notes from Dartmouth didn't only say that somebody married this Liz or that Katherine, but identified them with "Williams '84" or "Yale '85" so the groom's classmates could approve, without picture or personal acquaintance, on the basis of one proper noun.

What could Seth have said about me: Part-time waitress? Flower picker? Future college freshman?

After enough time had passed to make me a California resident, after the dates passed when my applications were due, after I failed to write to Harrow High and ask Mr. Alberghini the list of questions I was supposed to ask him about references and transcripts, Seth said he didn't get it at all: Did I *want* to pick flowers in the hot California sun until I developed skin cancer? Had I been lying to him all along about my goals?

I said sure I wanted to have a degree and a profession, and God knows that was the only thing that counted in his book especially now that his sexual needs were under control. He'd realized that what you appreciated in a girlfriend wasn't necessarily what you wanted in the mother of your children.

And I knew he'd call it something else.

I got home from the fields, as I liked to call it, one night soon after that, and there he was wearing a dish towel tucked into his belt as a half-apron.

"Sit down," he said grandly. "I have a treat for you." I slid into the breakfast nook, quite enthralled with this gesture—Seth acting out the role of a television-commercial mate having dinner ready for his working woman. Then he put a dinner plate down in front of me. The meal was slime and mold, literally—the stuff I'd put in plastic containers weeks before and forgotten. There was something long and watery brown that might have been scallions —there was a small red rubber band at one end. Another lump on the plate might have been goulash—now completely penicillin. Something else was a furry gray: old canned fruit cocktail? And the remaining thing, now peachy-orange, was a mound of elbow macaroni that had retained the shape of its home for the past few months: a margarine tub.

"A balanced meal from the four mold groups," Seth said.

"Very funny," I said.

"I was looking for the grated Parmesan and I found everything *but*."

"And you decided you'd teach me a lesson?"

"I can't live like this," he said.

"If you're home more than I am, why am I responsible for what grows in our refrigerator?"

"I'm not the one who saves a tablespoon of goulash. When do you think you're going to use one tablespoon of goulash? What are the odds?"

"You're exaggerating. I save *portions*."

"To what end?"

"All right," I said. "Enough. This is harassment. You've made your point."

"I threw out a garbage bag full of stuff that was inedible. There were a half-dozen bottles with a dribble of relish in each one. That's not me. *You're* the condiment queen."

I picked up my pocketbook and walked out. He asked where was I going and I said, "You're too chicken to admit what the real reason is, so this is how you're breaking up with me."

"I didn't say anything about us breaking up."

"Why? You can't live like this, remember? I'm a stupid, terrible person because I let mold grow in your refrigerator. If I'd gone to college this would never have happened. Isn't that what you're saying?"

I was out the door by now, and heading for the driveway, not running, not very fast at all. He had time to yell an apology; he even had time to stop me and throw his arms around me. But he didn't try. He had found a reason to send me back where I'd come from, something other than the Yankee warnings he'd been raised on about coming from different worlds. And in the version he told our mutual friends later, *I* was the unreasonable one, the one who couldn't take a joke. They probably all listened and nodded and agreed, "Melinda can't take a joke," then rushed to fix him up with graduate students they knew who they'd been keeping in the wings; women with degrees who kept boxes of baking soda in their refrigerators.

Imagine someone dropping out of your life like that, so glad to be rid of his mistake that he doesn't even bother to mouth platitudes about staying friends. I moved my stuff out when he was at the lab, and left my blank college applications in the bathroom wastebasket where I knew he'd contemplate them good and long.

I've regretted that act of throwing away my applications, not because I wanted to apply anywhere, but because it would prove his point—that Melinda was not college material: five years after graduating from high school she's done nothing toward improving herself. If I needed a name to put on my new motivation, the one that makes me angry with myself for working for boring Roger at a place called Forget-Me-Not—it's Seth, and knowing I was smarter in some ways than he was. That he didn't know the name of any Marx brother except Groucho; didn't know until the age of twenty-two that Baja California was Mexico, or that olives grew on trees; didn't know that everyone has moldy food in the back of their icebox; that *he* was the one who couldn't take a joke.

I stayed there, moving north to Orange County. I waitressed at a dockside restaurant where tanned, blond men pulled up in boats. I began to think of myself as a New Englander again; remembered how no one in my hometown had a yacht or used the Atlantic coast as a drive-in restaurant. I began to think fondly of potholes, of toll-takers on the Mass. Pike wearing fingerless gloves; of being indoors listening to snow cancellations.

Everything from New England began to take on character, while things Californian, from mayo on burgers to earthquakes, seemed foolish and foreign. I decided to return, to declare myself a sturdy, salty, thrifty New Englander, who wanted her unborn children—for surely they'd come in my thirties—to experience the four seasons, to shovel snow, to vote Democratic; to know smart and accomplished people who drove beat-up cars, on purpose, proudly.

7

Table for Three

I was a witness to the big reunion, not difficult because it happened at Francesca's take-out counter, my second home.

I walked in—Francesca's is long and narrow with a marble counter running along the left wall and bistro tables along the right; Dennis was second or third in the take-out line. Libby was standing behind him. Not doing or saying anything. Wearing a long, navy blue knife-pleated chiffon skirt and lacy stockings. Her blouse was pale yellow linen with a middy collar.

I had planned to take a table and read the *Sentinel* before plunging into the morning's orders, but this called for a closer inspection. I took my place in line behind Libby and said quietly, "Now's the perfect time." She checked behind her and returned immediately to her self-hypnosis.

"Just say hello," I prompted.

Dennis heard murmurs behind him and turned around, propelled by good business instincts and his natural friendliness. With all the ease in the world he said, "Libby Getchel. I heard you were coming back." He cocked his head slightly to one side and said, "Hi, Melinda."

I said hi.

"When did you hear I was coming back?" asked Libby, and immediately, "Why don't we get a table?" It was a step away to the eat-in side. I took one of Francesca's trademark wire bistro chairs from another table to make three. Libby carefully rolled up the sleeves of her blouse two turns. One of Francesca's stringy-haired waitress daughters asked from the counter, "Menus over there?"

"Coffee for me," I said. "Half French roast and half hazelnut. Milk no sugar."

"French roast, black," said Libby.

"A pot of English breakfast," said Dennis.

"Anything to eat?"

We checked with each other politely. We shook our heads, a consensus. "Just the tea and coffees," Dennis answered.

Libby returned to her microscopic examination of Dennis's earlier remark. "You knew I was coming back?" she repeated. "You knew I was opening up next to you?"

"I heard it was someone originally from here," said Dennis, "and I saw the name on the building permit during the renovations, but I must have been thrown by the 'Elizabeth.' It didn't register right away that it was you."

I winced for her with that disclosure: she leaves New York, starts a new life, throws herself into a new store two doors down from Dennis—no accident, I'm sure—obsesses about her old grievance and what she can do to turn back the clock. And now this piece of news: Dennis, who she's sure has been avoiding her because of the magnitude of their history, announces that he hadn't figured out that Elizabeth was Libby. Hadn't thought about her at all.

Libby turned to me. I could see that her question was not in earnest, but an excuse to twist her mouth into an irked smile at his answer. "How did *you* find out I was coming back, Melinda?"

Dennis laughed at her question; something of a snicker, but an affectionate one. I knew what he was saying: Melinda finds everything out. She's all ears, town crier, president of the grapevine. I said, "My mother saw her mother at Caldor's and told her Libby was opening up a dress shop next to Forget-Me-Not." I made a face at Dennis: anything wrong with *that*?

Dennis waited for the next exchange with a pleasant, open expression on his face. Does he have a clue? I wondered: Libby designs her career around this man and he doesn't have a large enough memory store to cover the stretch from "Libby" to "Elizabeth"?

The daughter-waitress brought the mugs of coffee and Dennis's pot of tea. She was the surly older one, Angelique of all things; the nice daughter came on for lunch.

"So where have you been?" Dennis asked Libby.

She smiled; a question with promise. "New York. Learning the business. Enough to know I wanted my own label and not sell other people's clothes."

"Libby's only selling her own stuff in there."

"Impressive."

"A lot is going to be by special order—designing along with the customer for special occasions. I'll have a relatively small inventory which I'll do myself between jobs."

Dennis nodded appreciatively. "What kind of stuff?" he asked.

"Dresses. Big dresses."

"Big like . . . big?" He twirled his hands in the air.

"Wedding dresses, prom gowns, cocktail party dresses . . ."

"What's a cocktail dress?" asked Dennis.

"You know what that is," I said. "A dressy dress you wouldn't wear to work. A fancy dress. Not down to the floor, but a party dress for nighttime."

"I know what you mean; like the dresses people wore to Diana's wedding, the ones who weren't bridesmaids," said Dennis.

"That's right," said Libby briskly.

"Didn't you wear one of those to Diana's wedding?" he asked me.

I said yes, I had.

"Purple, if I recall correctly."

Purple indeed. Purple shirred crêpe de chine, strapless, fitted, short. I had already given it away to Robin. "Yes," I said. "It was purple."

"Where'd you get it?" asked Libby.

"From a Victoria's Secret catalogue."

"Ah, catalogue shopping," said Dennis.

"I understand you're doing direct mail," said Libby.

"We do a quarterly catalogue plus Christmas."

"It's everywhere," I said.

"Have you seen it?" he asked.

"Excellent," said Libby. "I was going to ask you who did your photography."

"A guy in New York does the studio stuff, the flies, the equipment, the accessories. Someone else, a guy from here who I think is really talented, does the outdoor shots—the guys kneeling in the streams holding the trout. He's expensive but worth it."

"Is he the one who did the poster of you?" asked Libby.

Dennis covered his face with his hands, to show he was too modest to dream up that kind of exhibitionism himself.

"And he hates when people order it," I said.

"Wasn't my idea," he said.

"You're a cult hero. You might as well face it," I said.

"The shot of me was on the back of the catalogue so that

61

people coming into the store would know me—recognition factor. Then we got some calls asking if it was available as a poster. Lester said it would cost almost nothing to run off a thousand. So we did."

"It's his humility they love," I said to Libby. "Nobody wants an arrogant cult hero."

He took off his glasses, held them in front of his face, squinted into the lenses, put them back on. "I'd like to hear your definition of 'cult hero,'" he said to me.

"Easy: People recognize you and stop you on the street. You're very nice—concerned, kind, approachable. It's a talent; it looks like friendship, feels like friendship, maybe even more, but it's purely professional—just the personality people look for in a mayor, or an internist."

Dennis smiled uncertainly.

"Did you know he's on radio?" I asked Libby.

Libby murmured no, she hadn't realized that. What station and in what capacity?

"The trout report," Dennis said. He widened his eyes, as if requesting my complicity or, at the very least, my silence.

"Seriously?" asked Libby.

"What time do you get up?" Dennis asked.

"Early."

"How early?"

"Seven," said Libby.

"Too late. They air it at five a.m. otherwise fishermen will already be out the door."

"Do they pay you to do it?"

"Sure."

"A lot?"

"Enough to make it worth my while."

Libby shook her head and smiled faintly.

"I didn't believe it myself until I heard him," I said, "but some guys won't leave their house until they've caught 'The Vaughan Report.'"

Dennis said in a pleasant, talk-show voice, "Enough about me. Tell me some more about cocktail dresses."

"I think we've exhausted that topic," I said.

Libby turned her bistro chair a few degrees toward Dennis. "You'll have to come into the store and see what I've done. The interior's completely renovated, recessed lighting; all pinks, but architectural, not girly."

"It's really beautiful," I said.

"And how are these dresses of hers?"

"Gorgeous. Unfortunately I can't afford them."

"Sure you can," said Libby. "I'll give you professional courtesy and you'll be sure to tell people it's one of mine when they compliment you."

"Which they will," said Dennis, raising his teacup to his lips and putting it down again—empty. "Guess it's time to get going," he said.

"Come over on your next tea break," said Libby. She meant him; I took coffee breaks, and I needed no invitation.

"I peeked in when the finish carpentry was being done," said Dennis. "Very, very nice."

Libby said, "But you haven't seen it painted or carpeted?"

"Just in passing."

"I think it's a wonderful space. I'd like your opinion."

He smiled a smile I had seen him grant a thousand times before in acknowledgment of customer flattery. I listened carefully and I watched. I saw him reaching out to pull me into their dance, and I told myself it was all for Libby's benefit; that Dennis's peculiar mood today, his refusal to take up the gauntlet Libby was offering, had only to do with his high school grudge, and had nothing to do with me. With us.

* * *

"He's still angry. That's obvious," said Libby.

"He seemed pretty much like usual."

Libby pressed her lips together and smiled as if to say, Well that's your opinion but I know him better than you do. "What did you think of that stuff about him not realizing it was me moving in next door?"

What was I supposed to do now? Say, Maybe he hasn't given you any thought over the last twelve years.

"What are you thinking?" Libby asked. "That I'm mistaken?"

I motioned to Angelique to bring more coffee, waving two fingers in the air to remind her, French roast *and* hazelnut.

"He wouldn't say anything in front of you," Libby continued, "so I shouldn't really count this in any way."

"That's probably true."

Libby said she'd take more French roast. Angelique asked for the second time, "Want anything to eat?"

I said she could wrap me up a grilled bagel, butter no cream cheese, to go. After all these months, I should have been able to say, "the usual."

"When was his sister's wedding?" Libby asked.

"Two months ago, end of June." The night of the twenty-ninth and the morning of the thirtieth.

"Did he bring someone."

"No."

"Did his ex come?"

"Are you kidding? They hate her."

"What did he wear?"

"Tails. White tie."

"White tie?" She looked troubled.

"You know—the works. It was a night wedding. The ushers wore tails and top hats."

Libby blinked.

"What's wrong with that?"

"All those women in cocktail dresses if it was a formal wedding? Seems strange."

"Just the wedding party was white tie. The guests were a mixed bag—the usual Harrow costumes."

"That's what I'm up against," said Libby. "Women who wear whatever's in their closet to a formal wedding on a Saturday night."

"I bought a new dress," I said brightly.

"How did he look?"

I said fine—you know how flattering formal dress can be.

"Was it a rental?"

"I assume so."

"Did he ask you to dance?"

"Dennis? Sure."

"Is he a good dancer?"

"You never *danced* with him, either?"

"When would I have danced with him?"

"In high school?"

"I didn't go to dances in high school."

I said I went to every one; might even have danced with Dennis back then, but didn't really remember. I said okay—he was an okay dancer, as if I'd danced with better in my life. As if I could barely recall my time, in my purple dress, in Dennis's arms.

8

Con

I knew on some level about the man shortage before I returned to Harrow, but I ignored it. Certainly there had to be *some* men around, even if they were a summer influx of master's degree candidates (library science, social work) who walked around campus in sandals and black socks, dazed by the ratio of one man to every fifteen women. How many did I need, after all, but one—one permanent guy to fall in love with and marry?

I bring this up by way of explaining Conrad, a local musician and friend, thirty-five, with whom I have a horizontal relationship.

We met at a client wedding, naturally, at our only synagogue; open bar, sushi bar, taco bar, chefs whipping up custom plates of pasta, carving roast beef and deconstructing huge whole poached salmon to suit our individual appetites. I had veered toward the high-end Hawaiian theme, decorating with birds of paradise, anthurium, orchids and ti leaves.

Conrad plays vibraphone for his quartet, Like A Ghost, which mixes jazz with just enough new age to require a flutist and just enough rock 'n' roll and oldies to make dancing possible. He is tall and skinny but in a way that makes his billowy clothes hang just right. His hair is straight and dark, jawbone length; olive skin, dark eyes, intense looking but good-natured.

It is a successful relationship because we have it clearly defined: we see each other at weddings and if it has been a slow couple of weeks for either of us, sexually, we go back to his place.

It's not as clinical as it sounds, and Con answers some questions I'd always had about how you make love to someone you don't love. What, for example, do you both murmur after the act if not, "I love you"? Con strains and perspires, all the while looking transported and murmuring physical compliments. I look forward to these sessions, and I use them in my fantasy life up in my attic room when it's just me, the bathtub and a carefully aimed stream of running water. I told Conrad as much, and he was flattered. It added a new theme to our intercourse—him pointing out the equivalent of mental freeze-frames for future conjurings.

It's a decent system, one I recommend with the right partner: no dating, no expectations, no jealousies; just two adults with certain drives and certain talents which happen to intersect at consistent intervals.

Granted, the first time we consummated the friendship I had the usual boring questions about what it meant and where it was going, et cetera, but we discussed it on the spot.

"Didn't you enjoy it?" Conrad asked. "You seemed to."

I said of course I did—God, who wouldn't?—but women had a way of turning sex into a relationship seminar, and I had tendencies in that direction, too.

"Well, what do you think this is?" he asked.

"Two consenting adults finding release?" I answered.

"Certainly that."

"A one-night stand?"

Con said no; one-night stands were for undergraduates. He and I were colleagues in the wedding field and had an ongoing professional relationship. Only a complete asshole would screw that up. He hoped that he and I would be intimate friends—friends who were intimate, so to speak—one man and one woman who didn't regard the sex act and the viewing of each other's naked bodies as so sacred an occurrence that henceforth no normal social intercourse was impossible. Sex was the most fun two people could have, right? Better than dancing, better than eating out in a restaurant over a flickering candle, better than renting a video or even better than hearing a major label at a small club. Man and woman with no clothes on, the blood pounding, the juices flowing, the parts throbbing, oh man oh man. Why not do that when you felt like it? Cut through the other stuff and fuck each other's brains out. We're designed for it, you know. We're meant to be doing this. We're animals, basically; why shouldn't something this natural be considered wholesome? Why this *stigma* about it being sacred and . . . and an incredibly big deal? Think about some of the stuff you'd do on a date that you don't enjoy a fraction as much—watching football games, seeing a bad movie. It's a fucked-up world where you say, 'I'll get in the car and drive with him to Foxboro to see some third-rate, Neil Diamond talent—two hours there, two hours back, two hours of so-called entertainment with a guy you maybe—*maybe*—had a drink with once."

So all and all, it suits us fine. We fill a gap. We satisfy each other. He likes long, curly, unruly hair. I like men whose bare shoulders and neck smell like the Tide their undershirts are washed in. We can depend on each other in certain situations—a healthy kind of predictability; we're honest with each other, we do the job, we're kind to each other, and we're available.

No one knew about Conrad's and my arrangement except Martha, who never misses a trick. Even though she was trained to be unmoved in the face of raunchy confessions, she told me point-blank that she didn't think I should be involved with such a type, meaning a musician/fast talker even in my present social vacuum. I countered by playing on her liberal guilt.

"You have a husband and presumably a regular sex life. How can you, with a straight face, sit there and tell me I shouldn't sleep with someone you haven't even met?"

Martha stood firm. "Do you see yourself in this relationship five years down the road, having sex at the whim of some bride's having booked you as the florist and Conrad as the entertainment? Because frankly it doesn't seem to be based on much more than that—coincidence and convenience."

"*And*," I said. "*And . . . ?*"

"Do you think he cares about you?"

"Yes," I said calmly, "in the context of when we're alone together, he's extremely giving."

Martha snorts.

"You're very old-fashioned, you know. Very traditional."

Martha didn't fall for that insult, but smiled as if to say Nice try, Melinda. "Old-fashioned is in again," she said. "Or haven't you heard?"

"We're very careful."

"He's probably high risk."

"I don't think so. I think his sex life is fairly unexciting."

"So how do you come in?"

I said, enunciating slowly, "When we run into each other, which is more often than not at a wedding, we talk, eat, drink some champagne, then, if it's indicated, he gives me his house key and I wait for him there since he's virtually the last one to leave the reception."

"Where does he live?"

"He has a condo on Roosevelt."

"Nice?"

"What you'd expect—huge speakers, shag carpet, aquarium room divider."

We laughed, the conspiracy of two people sitting in a living room such as hers, on her beautiful tufted couch, an antique chaise reupholstered in bottle-green velvet. It was a dark, leafy, Victorian room, with leaded stained-glass windows filtering the room's scant light. "So this is for fun, for laughs, for sexual release? Am I representing your attitude accurately?"

I said she was. Yes.

"And it's not interfering with your forming other relationships in town; for example: you meet someone nice at a wedding, someone's nice male cousin from out of town, eligible, whatever. Conrad is providing the music and giving you the signal—" Martha demonstrated with leering eyebrow contortions—"but you're interested in this new guy, who's dancing with you and asking you questions about your work, your life, all very appropriate. Would you be able to say to Conrad, your great good friend and sexual surrogate, 'Not tonight, buddy; there's an opportunity here for a real-life relationship'?"

"Absolutely."

"And he would be gracious?"

"He'd be disappointed. I'd be disappointed if I'd psyched myself up for one of our dates and *he* canceled . . . but not for reasons that had anything to do with emotional expectations."

"I see."

"What are you trying to get me to admit—that we use each other? Or that I'm substituting a superficial sexual relationship for something deeper? Because I will admit that we use each other.

70

And frankly, it's great sex." I stopped there, counting on Martha's thirst for elaboration and detail.

"How so?" she asked after a nonchalant pause.

"You know."

"Technique?"

I smiled. "That too."

"I don't even know what he looks like."

"Skinny, dark, intense. Sort of looks like a condor."

"Condor?"

"In an attractive sense. Deep-set eyes, beaked nose."

Martha thought this over, then pursed her lips comically as if to say, Sounds horrible to me, but this is America.

"To get back to your basic argument, if no one else has entered the picture and I'm still in need of the occasional outlet then I can see myself doing this in five years. Sure."

"Aren't we cool," she said.

"I happen to think this is a good thing. It might even be a healthy thing. Isn't it my prerogative to view sex as seriously or as casually as I see fit? And isn't it refreshing when two people's view of it meshes?"

"So why don't you marry this guy?" said Martha, in her devil's advocate style. "You're so compatible in every possible way. What's keeping you from taking this into the realm of reality, which is to say, seeing each other on a more normal basis?"

I smiled slyly, nudging her elbow with mine, and asked if I'd failed to mention he was something of a jerk.

9

The Way Men Act

Libby, Dennis and I all belong to the Downtown Merchants Association, which has two factions: the shopowners who have been here before Harrow was fashionable, and the newcomers who brought the fashion. Each think they know best about the directions downtown should take: the old guard wants it to be a place where you can buy vinyl handbags and molly screws and quarts of milk. The newcomers want more of the places they like to shop in and eat in—pastel cafés and coffee roasters. Libby, Dennis and I have one foot in each group, sociologically with the townies but aesthetically with the trendies. Dennis's two hats are particularly valued here: the old guard remembers his glories in the name of Harrow athletics, and the Artisans' Loft crowd knows exactly how many out-of-state license plates are attributable to the lure of Brookhoppers, how many customers pop their heads into Loft stores to ask directions to that place that sells trout flies.

Dennis talks with men at the DMA social hours. Works the crowd. Spreads the Gospel. All it takes is one customer, one fly fisherman with the realization that Dennis Vaughan, demigod, is standing by the cookies socializing merely with two women merchants, of all the lucky breaks. So it begins:

"Dennis? Jim O'Rourke, O'Rourke Opticians, one-thirty-two Main? Could we talk a little shop? Do you ladies mind?"

Dennis smiles and shakes the man's hand. Libby and I wait to see if "talking a little shop" means a topic of concern to all us downtown merchants, or whether this is another trout fanatic. As always, it is the latter. Libby and I slide away, excusing ourselves as if they'd notice. This was not who I had come to socialize with, not the Jim O'Rourkes whose spectacle shop was paneled in knotty pine and on the second floor of the Hildreth Building, as yet ungentrified.

At the last meeting, we drifted toward the coffee urn, supplied this time by Adrian's. A laminated index card was propped behind the spigot announcing, "Decaf choc. hazelnut." A pink place card among the cookies said in a different hand, "Mandelbrot and ruggelah by Sadie's Table."

"Maybe we need music," I said to Libby. "Stop fooling around and get right down to it—a dance. The Downtown Merchants Association's Dance, first Tuesday of the month."

"Nobody would come," said Libby.

"They'd have to. Attendance would be mandatory or your business would be blackballed. And you couldn't bring a date. Strictly stag. We'd have a snowball dance. One couple could start, and when the music stopped, they'd have to ask someone else to dance, and so on until everyone was dancing."

I noticed Libby looked at Dennis then, an involuntary glance that suggested cutting in.

"We'll let Roger and Robin start," I continued. Then: "Of course, they'd have to break apart to dance with someone else, which would violate their marriage vows." I laughed at my own joke, expecting Libby to join in.

"Why do you say that?" she asked without a smile.

"You know—going steady since tenth grade. Mr. and Mrs. Perfect Picture of Marital Devotion."

"Oh," said Libby.

"You knew all that."

"I guess I did."

"But . . . ?"

"Nothing," said Libby. "I have nothing to add to that."

I stared severely, nudged her a few feet into a more private corner and asked, "Roger or Robin?"

"What do you mean?"

"Which one do you have the goods on?"

"Neither," said Libby. "Really."

"They're right over there . . . ," I said, faking a start toward them.

"It's nothing concrete," she said quickly. "It's just a sense I've gotten."

"I know it's Roger."

"Forget it," said Libby.

"He came on to you?"

She didn't say anything, but looked around to see who was within earshot.

"What did he say?"

"It might have been my imagination. It wasn't really what he said—"

"I love it—Roger!"

"It was just a distinct impression I had that he was asking me out."

"What did he say—'Libby, will you go out with me?'"

She shook her head.

"I know: 'Libby, will you go out with me, my wife doesn't understand me?'"

She laughed.

"What?"

Surveying the room before answering, she said, "He came into the shop just as I was closing—he never comes in the shop alone—and said, 'I'd like to talk to you sometime about our window displays. They're side by side and I thought maybe we should coordinate some things.'

"'Fine,' I told him. I wouldn't have thought much about it but he was turning bright red and looking back over his shoulder, watching the door. Then he said, 'I mean dinner sometime. Would that be all right?' I said, 'I don't think so, Roger.' Instead of saying, 'Well, fine, do you have a moment right now to discuss the windows?' he just slunk out, and every time I've seen him since then he pretends not to see me."

"And you think you might have been imagining that was a come-on?"

"I suppose not."

"He could have made it clearer, of course. He could have walked in holding his pecker."

Libby smiled wanly.

"And you didn't tell me until now?"

"I thought you'd enjoy it too much, or that you'd say something to him or to Robin."

"Because you thought you owed Roger some discretion?"

"I thought I should just forget it ever happened. Our stores are side by side . . . I might have been reading too much into it. I thought it might be playing God to tell on him."

"Were you tempted at all to say yes?"

Libby gave me a reproving look. "Hardly," she said. "No offense."

I told her no offense taken.

"You're not going to say anything, are you?"

"Oh, God. Am I going to have to take an oath here?"

"It was just ten seconds out of Roger's marriage and I'm sure he regrets the whole thing."

I shrugged and nodded, went for a refill of decaf. When I returned to her side I made a testimonial speech: I couldn't have kept quiet. It shows what kind of character you have. I mean it. If I were you I would have run over to tell me so fast that I'd have gotten there before Roger. I'd be dying to tell someone. I never would have been able to keep it to myself.

Libby said, "Maybe if you'd only been open a few weeks, and you felt your business would suffer if you couldn't keep a secret—"

I shook my head slowly, back and forth, smiling cynically, back and forth, the whole time she talked.

"No?" said Libby. "Even about yourself? Nothing you've done has gone unreported?"

"Sorry," I said blithely.

"With men?" she asked. "No secrets? No married men?"

"Oh," I said. Then, "Not technically."

He had been my boyfriend in eleventh grade, after Danny Acciaioli, before Wally Routhier, and he had walked into Forget-Me-Not on business years later engaged to Candee Conlon. They arrived beaming with her mother who pretended to be *so weary* inspecting the parade of caterers, dressmakers, bandleaders and now florists. I was sure Mrs. Conlon remembered me from high school, probably even remembered I had dated Billy Riley while Candee was organizing bake sales for the Future Teachers of America, and had now come to rub my unmarried face in it.

I was gracious, professional, and it wasn't an act: even as a sixteen-year-old semi in love with him, I had seen Billy Riley's limitations. He had been cute certainly, and nice in a goofy way, the kind of kid who passed you in the hall and tapped your far shoulder so you'd look in the wrong direction. Now he was grown up and "Bill," a gym teacher at the junior high.

I asked them if they had been going together all these years.

"Oh, no," Candee said. "We ended up in the same M.A.T. program last year," speaking slowly so I wouldn't miss the reference to their advanced degree. "I mean we knew each other from high school, but never really *knew* each other."

"You're a teacher, too, then?"

"Guidance," she said proudly.

She wanted a bouquet of daisies and miniature carnations. She had a picture from her cousin's album. Pastel ribbons, baby's breath. Ugh. An off-the-rack bridal bouquet. I hated to do them, hated to have my name on something so mundane.

"And for you?" I asked Billy.

Mrs. Conlon said with authority, "Carnation."

"Stephanotis is handsome against a black lapel. One stem. Very elegant."

Candee looked at her mother then back at me. "I think carnations are more suitable for men," she said. "Besides, the tuxes are powder blue."

Then there were the tables, the church, the altar. Kentucky Derby–size bows to match the yellow of the seven teacher–bridesmaids' dresses and picture hats. Each to carry a single daisy. Cute.

I knew Candee didn't wish me well, and that her patronage was calculated to put me in my place. She never once said, "What's going on with you, Melinda?" Or, "Why don't you come to the reception? There's a very nice usher who's dying to meet you." She obviously loved things the way they were, or at least the way she saw them: Melinda LeBlanc, alone and lonely, waiting on Candee Conlon, bride.

I hadn't known Candee well in high school. She had been chirpy and busy, the kind of person I would have called studious if she had been smarter. As I recall, she ran for things— secretaryships of school clubs; class vice-presidencies—and lost to more popular kids. For a time she had dated Chuck Krysiak, who had lived next door to me and pretended every day for four years that our leaving our houses at the same moment for the bus stop was an amazing coincidence. Chuck had been in Candee's crowd. She would not have been asked out then by Billy Riley, who for all his goofiness, did have letters in track and golf.

What I remember most about my few months of dating Billy were his exceptionally lame arguments in favor of letting him go all the way—that if I let him do it once he wouldn't ask me again; or that if he wore a rubber it didn't count. Saturday night after Saturday night, parked in his father's maroon Bonneville, he had hoped that with all our rubbing and probing I wouldn't notice another appendage getting lost in the melee. On some equally lame principle, I held out. Later, after the breakup, I wondered what I had ever seen in a dullard like Billy Riley. I was almost thirty before I realized that women don't have a category for recreational sex and that we specialize in calling hormones love.

A couple of days after their first wedding consultation, Billy called me at home. "I just wanted to say it was great seeing you again," he said.

"Same here."

"Bet you were surprised to hear who I was marrying," said Billy.

"Actually not. My mother clips engagement notices of people I know and sends them my business card with a note."

"Good thinking."

"Every once in a while it gets results."

"You must of been surprised to see me walk through your door, though," he tried.

"Not really."

"Recognize me right away?"

"Instantly."

"Even though I'm much better-looking now, right?" He laughed self-consciously, saving me from an answer. "You look pretty great yourself," he continued.

"Thank you."

"Made me wonder what you ever saw in a guy like me. . . ."

"You were always popular," I said noncommittally. "You always had some pretty girl on your arm. And now Candee," I added quickly. "She's so attractive."

Billy murmured his agreement.

I thanked him for calling and, for good measure, sent a message to Candee: I was waiting for the picture of the altar. A Polaroid would be fine. Whenever it was convenient. Congratulations again.

I called Candee to tell her Robin had priced everything out and our estimate was ready.

"I can't talk to you right now," she said a little breathily.

An hour later she called back. "Sorry," she said, "but Bill and I were making love."

I should have said, "Do you think I care what you were doing when the phone rang? Do you think I'm *interested?*"

79

But a whole hour to call me back? I gave her the estimate and got off quickly. Go find another florist; go find cheaper carnations, you asshole.

To a middle-aged customer who looked as if she'd cluck along with me in disapproval I said, "A client just told me she had to hang up because she was making love."

"Did she say to whom?" the customer asked, instantly engaged.

"My old boyfriend," I said.

Being my customer gave Billy the idea that we were now close friends. He called the shop mornings from his office behind the gym. I'd answer with the usual, "Forget-Me-Not!" and he'd always say, "Hi" in his popular-guy voice; just "Hi," a boyfriend's verbal shorthand.

On principle I'd ask, "Who is this, please?"

"Bill!" he'd say, sounding wounded. Monday mornings were his particular favorite: What had I done over the weekend?

"Work. Why?"

"C'mon, all weekend?"

"I don't discuss particulars. I'm very discreet."

"Did you have a date?"

"Does Candee know you call me like this?"

He said nervously, "Sure."

"I doubt that."

"C'mon," said Billy.

Finally one day in person I said it: Did he or did he not have an unnatural interest in his florist's private life? Was he going to deny he was coming on to me?

"I didn't plan on this happening," he said after a pause.

Let me guess, I said: Everything's okay, you're in love, finally got up the nerve to propose, not the all-time great passion of your life but you're hitting thirty and people are starting to tell you that nothing's ever perfect—

"Gee," said Billy. "Exactly."

"Then some woman comes along. It's not like you want to throw everything away and start over 'cause who knows how this one will turn out and a bird in the hand is worth two in the bush, but all the same you feel . . . nervous."

A pause that means: yeah, I'm listening.

"So you don't do anything overt, but you think to yourself, I'll run it up a flagpole and if she salutes, it'll be a sign that I shouldn't rush off and marry Candee Conlon."

Billy chewed on his bottom lip, watching me, trying to figure out if I meant "Yes."

Mostly, it was flattering. Billy continued to call and to drop by the shop alone. I supposed I had to take a moral stand sooner or later, especially when the wedding got closer. And who knows— if Candee hadn't been so smug, playing the gracious winner to my unloved loser in a contest of her invention, I might have stopped him cold.

But I'm only human. One day when Robin and Roger were both out, I said yes. We went to the back room, after turning the sign on my door that said, "Be back in a few minutes. Please wait."

We agreed it would be recreational sex and not result in any upheavals; we also agreed that after this one time, we wouldn't do it again—the very negotiating card he'd used thirteen years ago in Mr. Riley's Bonneville. We confessed beforehand that the prospect of consummating an old, unconsummated relationship was good material for our fantasy lives, and that we'd leave well enough alone.

We went ahead anyway, and that was that. It was nice; quick and nice—but nothing to change either of our histories. Billy didn't renounce his engagement, and I didn't fall in love. Not that Candee deserved any charity from me, but I sensed that Billy was getting married in peace, having used up the symbolic condom he had been saving with my name on it.

They came into the shop together, the new Mr. and Mrs. William F. Riley, after they'd returned from their Disney World honeymoon. Candee had a wedding picture for me which showed off her bouquet and her army of attendants. What a twit she was, with her matched rings and her textbook etiquette. "I'll put it in my portfolio," I lied.

Billy stood a few yards back from the counter instead of hopping up on it to sit and talk. He asked me how business was; if flowers were harder to get in winter; how many miles we had on our van—formally and piously, the way men act to let you know it was all a large mistake.

You don't have to be nervous, I wanted to say: we did it finally and got it out of our systems; we made an agreement and I wouldn't dream of spilling the beans. I'm not interested in ruining your little marriage.

They paid with a check from their new joint account. Candee had signed it and had written "Thank you!" across my bill in her upbeat teacher's script. *Thank you!*

At least I enjoyed that, the sheer irony of her good manners: her dragging him into Forget-Me-Not to pay their bill in person; Candee and Bill—two cute names on a napkin—*thanking* me for a beautiful job.

I rang it up and said rather grandly that what I had done was nothing, nothing at all.

The DMA meeting was over, and Libby and I were walking west up Main toward the college. After the quadrangle, Main Street would fork and we'd separate. "Do you ever see him?" she asked.

"From a distance. He'll walk by the store and look in if he's

82

alone, but keep his head down if he's with Candee." Borrowing the proper note of regret from countless television scoundrels I said, "I'm not proud of what I did."

"I think you are, a bit."

"Because I told you?"

"Because you got back at Candee Conlon for gloating over Billy Riley."

"I didn't get back at her because she doesn't know. You don't get back at someone if they don't know what you did."

"I suppose that's true."

It was a particularly dark night and I could see Libby's face only when we passed a streetlight. We continued to walk, the fork just ahead of us, and I thought she was smiling. "What?" I asked.

"I think she came into Rags looking for a wedding dress. Her mother didn't like anything, and it didn't seem to register that if I advertised as doing wedding dresses how come I didn't have something right there on the rack for her to try on."

"That sounds right."

"A loser," said Libby.

"But not every loser deserves to have her fiancé serviced by the florist just because he asks nicely?"

Libby didn't answer: her mysterious-lady behavior.

"Don't worry. I'm basically good deep down, even if I'm not nice. Luckily I'm in the back room doing designs, and I get humored or at least tolerated because I do it better than anyone else in Harrow."

After a few moments Libby said, "I'm considered nice."

"I'm sure you are."

"Even people who think I'm strange would say I'm nice."

"True. You're not that strange, either."

She asked me if I'd like to keep walking and have some decaf at her house.

There was no other word for her kitchen than squalid. I knew I couldn't eat here; I didn't even want to boil water here. Trash was barely contained in a large garbage pail, the metal kind you put out on the curb for pick up, and the overflow was being caught in two stained grocery bags. Her kitchen table was covered with dirty cereal bowls with milk dried to a yellow skin as if she never cleaned up or washed dishes until the clean ones ran out. The smell emanating from the sink was of old gray sponges.

Libby looked around as if seeing the state of her kitchen through my eyes. Every surface was painted the drab green of frozen lima beans, cupboards included, and the floor was a speckled linoleum that my mother had ripped up two renovations ago. "It's not very appetizing, is it?" she asked.

I offered to put the dirty dishes in the still-dirtier sink if she took out the garbage. Libby looked around then said, "I think you're right."

I also offered to make the coffee, too, while she did the outdoor job.

"I only have instant. Is that okay?"

"Or tea."

I wondered what Libby's mother thought of the condition of her former kitchen; retired cooks must have standards of cleanliness; wondered if they still had a key and dropped by as if it was still their house. When Libby returned I asked how her folks were.

Libby turned. She had a bulging bag in each hand for another trip to the garage. "Happy," she said. "A little bored. My dad misses the gardens at the college. He even putters around over there for free."

I asked if her mother missed the cooking.

"Not at all. She's thrilled to get three meals a day served to her. Twenty-something years, cooking breakfast and lunch for ninety. She hated it, and she wasn't any good. Perry Hall had the reputation for the worst food, which wasn't really true because

84

they all had the same budget per student, but she never introduced any fashionable foods without a fight. They petitioned for a salad bar, and then they had to petition for the stuff they wanted on it because she was so unimaginative. She wasn't really bad, just very much from the shepherd's-pie school of cooking."

I told her about my mother's food phobias and prejudices: no condiments; no pickles or things pickled; in restaurants she'd only order things that were whole: small fish, shrimp, potatoes, string beans, peas, baked apples. And worse, she'd *ask:* Are your salad greens torn? Are your cherry tomatoes halved?

A red aluminum teapot, which Libby had put on for tea without changing the old water, whistled. She took it off the stove with the grimiest potholder I'd ever seen.

I told her about Seth and me and our breaking up over rotting Tupperware contents.

"And that was really it? You never heard from him again?"

"Nope."

Libby didn't say anything until she had matched cups with saucers and we were both sitting at the table. "What *is* it with these men? Their lives are so great that they've never needed to look back? I don't get it! They're all so happy, married to their little sweeties from the wife pool—you know the type—former teachers, good mothers—"

"Candee Conlon," I said sourly. I told her I knew the type and I didn't understand it either. The supermarket checkout line was filled with women who hadn't dated in high school, who had earned their B.A.'s in early childhood education, then met guys who, amazingly enough, decided that this person in front of me at the register with the big chuck roast, the Juicy Juice and the toddler in the pink snowsuit, was the woman he wanted to marry; the woman he had chosen from all the women in the world to spend the rest of his life with. I couldn't get over these women with their tiny diamond engagement rings and thin gold bands and their coupon collections, writing checks and always finding their courtesy cards.

Why them instead of us? I asked.

"My mother used to say, 'Every pot has its cover,'" said Libby. "She believed that, too. She didn't meet my father until she was in her late thirties."

"Every pot does *not* have its cover, or there wouldn't be unmarried people walking around still looking. Or you find a cover, marry him and it's the wrong one." I told her my mother and father had gotten engaged after knowing each other six weeks. Six weeks! They were madly in love—*trembling* with love—couldn't wait to get married. Twenty years old. You should see their wedding pictures. You can see what was going on: young, madly in love, horny; couldn't wait for the honeymoon, which actually meant something in their case because they both had lived at home with fathers who made bedchecks at midnight. They spent seven days in a motel room on Lake George—still smiling in all those Lake George honeymoon pictures—and when they went back for their first anniversary my mother was hugely pregnant and my father kept driving to a phone booth a mile down the road to call a MacMillan student—do you believe it?—who he was seeing on the side. He'd never dated a college girl, he told my mother. Never in the years he was single. And then this girl from New Jersey was hitchhiking on Route 6 one day, said she was going to visit her boyfriend at UMass; tall with streaked hair, tanned legs. A senior. Bold in a way he'd only dreamed about. She made the first move. Was *so* interested that he'd grown up on a farm. Laughed at his picture of Jersey as the garden state. He drove her all the way to her boyfriend's dorm, waited outside while she told him she had other plans, came back to the car and stuck her tongue in my father's mouth, just like that. He didn't even tell her he was married, which worked out fine because MacMillan still had curfews, no overnights, and it was the custom to fuck your boyfriend in his car and then get dropped off at the dorm by one. At least once a week he'd say he was going out, wouldn't be home for dinner, or he'd come home from work, shower and change and go out again.

"After I was born he reported every detail to my mother; told her he was too young to stay with one woman for the rest of his life. He had made a mistake. Not that this MacMillan senior was necessarily it. But that was the point: he had to find out! He was too young not to follow it through; too young to be tied down and not able to fall in love over and over again."

"*Was* she it?" Libby asked.

"Are you kidding? She graduated and left town and never looked back. She was a fast rich girl, the country-club kind who dates college guys when she's in tenth grade, and married men when she's in college . . . likes to shock her rich friends—the first one in the pool to skinny-dip at the country-club dance. She didn't love my father, except for his talent for being able to keep up with her sexually, apparently. And the most disgusting part was her name was Linda."

"They named you after her?"

"No. My mother liked the name and they had agreed on 'Linda Louise' and then he picked up the New Jersey Linda and didn't have the strength of character to talk my mother out of it. Can you *imagine?*"

Libby asked me what happened to my father when Linda took off. I said, "He moved back in with his parents. They just took him back in. They didn't seem to get it: none of their other children got divorced for stupid American reasons like running around with other women. My other grandfather used to go over to my father's parents' farm every month and ask Papa Mike for a check.

"This old guy, no judge or lawyer backing him up, would drive over in his pickup and say, 'My daughter vant some money'—he was Czechoslovakian—every month. Didn't call first; didn't say, 'How about if you send her a check for the same amount the first of every month so I don't have to come over?' He just did it. Didn't say anything more. Didn't insult anybody. Papa Mike would disappear for a few minutes, come back with a check made out to Mrs. Joseph LeBlanc, my mother, and give it to Papa Jan. No words from him either, just grunts from two old guys whose kids had embarrassed them by marrying for love."

Libby shook her head sadly, then said, "MacMillan."

"It would have been someone else if she hadn't come along."

"Maybe not. This Linda sounds pretty aggressive—thirty years ago hitchhiking; throwing yourself at a townie in a pickup—"

"Actually, it was a regular car. Papa Jan had the pickup."

"Still. Mind-blowing I would think to a young guy, newly married after a short engagement. Maybe he wouldn't have gone so crazy over just a regular flirtation. It sounds as if it would have taken a Superman to resist."

"No it wouldn't have. It would have taken someone with some character. He didn't have any."

"Did you know him?" asked Libby.

"I went to his funeral," I said—the challenge I always offered when people asked about my father.

"When was that?"

"Nineteen seventy-six. The Bicentennial accident?"

"I don't remember," said Libby.

She should have. My father's car had been demolished by a freight train—his fault completely. The engineer had testified that the driver ignored the duly flashing signal; the driver appeared to challenge, no, to *race* against the train. No evidence of vehicular distress. No skid marks. It had been front-page *Sentinel* news for days: three men killed gruesomely. The newspaper wouldn't let go of the story. Even after the funerals and the investigation, *Sentinel* subscribers had to turn it into an editorial-page debate over truth in photo journalism versus good taste. Even now, the accident was noted annually under "On This Date in Harrow."

"You don't remember the accident when we were in high school? Three men killed? Right at the end of the school year?"

Libby half-shut her eyes and stared over my shoulder at the lima bean walls. After a few moments, she said, "Sorry." She added more hot water to her cup and offered me the same. I said no thanks.

She sighed with what I thought was sympathy or at least resignation—until she spoke: "I think Dennis's marriage and divorce did a lot of damage."

I said I was confused. Weren't we talking about my father's death?

"Exit relationships," she said. "I would be his and they're doomed."

That was it, her universe. A father killed in a public death? His estranged teenage daughter finds out about it from the newspaper, and sees him for the first time at his wake? Not much to discuss there, I guess; not compared to Libby's life in the here and now.

I said, "I'd forget about Dennis if I were you. He's not ready to get involved with anyone so soon after his divorce."

"She was a *lesbian,*" said Libby.

"So?"

"He's not going to want to go back to her. And I doubt very much whether he's still in love with her."

"He's confused. Who wouldn't be after that? Everyone in town knows what happened to him. I'm sure he wants to lay low until people forget."

People? her eyes seemed to ask; what people? People knew about his divorce? . . . There was a bad train wreck that killed three men when we were teenagers?

I didn't scold her. I didn't even respond. I must have thought on some level, for reasons I can't fathom now, that this blankness meant she didn't care what people thought, and that was an admirable trait in a friend.

10

We Save Georgia

It was the Friday before Thanksgiving week, and snowing hard. The public schools had closed at noon, sending Robin scurrying to meet the school bus. I asked Roger if I could leave early—of course I don't expect to get paid for the *hour* or so he'd be without my services.

"You can go," he said nobly. "I'll consider it comp time."

I had noticed a car parked in front of the shop when I'd arrived just before 10. Smiling at the woman sitting in the passenger seat, I jangled my keys as if to say, "I made it finally. Come in. We're open." She hadn't smiled back, but had looked away quickly. Not a customer, I thought. A young woman, college aged, running the motor of a new yellow Rabbit, waiting for something else.

I stepped into the snow and noticed that the Rabbit's motor was still running, but the driver was gone. I walked to the curb: The girl was slumped sideways across the gearshift. I didn't yell. I considered for a few seconds how embarrassing it would be to yank open the car door only to find that the girl was sleeping. I walked to the window and knocked lightly with one knuckle against the passenger window. The second time I knocked harder; I took my woolen mitten off and pounded. Nothing. Dead. Like teenagers parked on lover's lanes who leave the motor running and get carbon monoxide poisoning. As far as I could squint into the snow, there was no one else, no other Good Samaritans to enlist. I ran into Brookhoppers and yelled, "Dial nine-one-one. Tell them there's a car parked in front of my shop with a dead woman in it. I think!"

Dennis ran past me as if he were the lifeguard on duty and I was a nonswimming bystander. I dodged the counter, found the telephone and dialed 9-1-1. "This is Melinda LeBlanc," I yelled, "three-thirty-one Main Street. There's a woman slumped over in a yellow Rabbit in front of Forget-Me-Not. I think she's dead. The doors are locked but the car's running. Dennis is out there now." They all knew Dennis. I didn't have to identify him beyond that or say anything more to make the call legitimate. I hung up and ran outside, flipping Dennis's specially designed "Open" sign to "Closed."

Dennis, his plaid flannel shirt-sleeves still turned up neatly, was running back into his store. I yelled, "I called them," and he said, "Get out there so they'll spot us!"

I hurried to the Rabbit and looked in the passenger window. The girl, I thought, had shifted slightly. Gravity might just be dragging her head lower. Or rigor mortis. Great red hair, I noticed. Full-length raccoon coat. In seconds Dennis was back, brandishing a small hammer. I barely saw the tap of the hammer's head on glass. Without a crack, it crumbled undramatically into pellets, leaving a small hole that Dennis enlarged with more taps. He stuck his hand through and unlocked the door. In seconds, leaning into the front seat, he had shut off the motor and placed his fingertips on one side of the girl's neck.

He patted her face. "Sweetheart!" he yelled. "You have to wake up!"

I had opened the passenger door by now. A few people had stopped and were watching nervously. Dennis slid the girl onto the cold sidewalk. A woman bystander said, "I don't think you're supposed to move them until help arrives."

"She's not injured," said Dennis, still trying to rouse the girl, who was murmuring nonsense. "She's unconscious."

"She'll catch pneumonia," the woman said.

"He knows what he's doing," I snapped.

"Look in her purse," Dennis commanded. "Find out what her name is."

I found a small leather purse the size of a tobacco pouch on the front seat. I also found an empty brown plastic bottle. The prescription was for Valium, made out to Georgia Root.

"Suicide!" I yelled. "She took a whole bottle of Valium."

"What's her name?"

"Georgia."

"Georgia!" he yelled, kneeling on the wet sidewalk, lowering himself so that his words were yelled into her ear. "Georgia honey, wake up."

"I'm getting some blankets," I said. I ran into Libby's store—dresses, fabric, wool, anything—one door away and yelled for her. She said she had no blankets; would her coat do? Here. And bring her inside, for God's sake. Let her lie on the carpet rather than a cold and wet sidewalk. I ran back outside, Libby following me.

Dennis said no, the cold was helping her come to; then yes, Jesus Christ, he was freezing to death. To the small crowd he said, "The ambulance should be here any second. Have them come into Rags for Sale and don't touch anything in the car." He had the girl, Georgia, in his arms by then. His hair and eyebrows were white with frozen snow. Sirens finally sounded. Dennis hesitated then moved toward the store.

"Does he know her?" an onlooker asked.

"I found her," I announced to no one in particular. "I thought it was carbon monoxide poisoning."

"Not out in the open like this," someone said, "unless the tailpipe's blocked."

A cruiser arrived, its rear end fishtailing on the unplowed street. One officer jumped out.

"In there," we yelled and pointed. "With Dennis. She's alive."

"We need an ambulance," I shouted. I repeated Dennis's orders to the crowd—send them in; don't touch anything. I was still holding the empty prescription bottle. Like a good detective, I took the purse from the front seat and went into Rags for Sale.

Georgia Root was vomiting on Libby's rose carpet. She'd pause, moan, roll her spine down to the floor and cry. Libby was pacing, and Dennis was chanting, "You're going to be all right. You're going to be all right."

I appointed myself the spokesperson and strode over to the officer, the empty pill bottle evidence that this had been no frivolous call. "I found this on the front seat when we broke into the car," I said.

He took out a small notebook and asked my name. I introduced all of us, including Georgia Root. I said, "The doors

94

were locked and we thought she might be alive so Dennis broke the window so we could get in."

He made me repeat the sequence of events, and echoed my answers in a way I was sure he had learned at the police academy. He was looking for me to contradict myself. I was patient, though. I knew he usually dealt with low-lives who murder their wives, lock them into cars and call it suicide. I was patient. He was young, and cute in a high school track-and-field kind of way. As spokesperson and observant good citizen I told him how I had left work early—floral artist, Forget-Me-Not—and observed a young Caucasian woman in said vehicle, motor running, who I had discerned at an earlier point in time sitting upright. This time, though, she was slumped over. I thought you could get carbon monoxide poisoning from sitting in a running car for a long time—was I wrong about that?—so of course I presumed her to be deceased. I ran to the shop of Dennis Vaughan to place a call to 911; this Dennis Vaughan responded by taking the said measures to secure entry into the vehicle and to then administer first aid in the form of yelling and slapping her into consciousness. I checked the front seat of the car for her pocketbook to ascertain the victim's name, whereupon I identified this empty vial as the—

The cop stopped me by striding over to Georgia who looked fully conscious and composed enough for his purposes. "Miss?" he said, kneeling carefully on one knee. "Would you like to tell me what happened?"

Dennis stood up and went into Libby's back room. He returned with a paper cup of water for Georgia.

"I hate water," she said, accepting it anyway and taking a small sip, eyes on Dennis. Turning back to the police officer she said, "Will this be in the paper?"

"I'll take care of that," said Dennis. Newspaper editors and publishers tended to be fly fishermen.

Libby said, "I need seltzer for the rug. And I'd appreciate some help with the cleanup."

Georgia, still sitting, said, "Where am I?"

"In Harrow, ma'am," said the police officer.

"I know that. I meant *where*."

"In Rags for Sale," said Libby.

"I thought so," said Georgia.

"You parked out front," I said.

"And these folks most likely saved your life," said Officer Scott T. Frappier, whose name was engraved on his badge.

"I noticed you sitting in your car when I opened," I said. "So naturally I was surprised to see the car still running hours later with no one sitting in the driver's seat; no one visible, that is."

"I was unconscious?"

"I thought you were dead."

"I took pills," said Georgia.

"How many?" asked Officer Frappier.

"The whole bottle. However many were in there."

Officer Frappier wrote something in his notebook.

"I can call the pharmacy and see how many the prescription was for," I volunteered.

"That's my job," said Officer Frappier kindly.

"What kind of pills were they?" Dennis asked Georgia.

"Valium."

"Miss?" the officer began.

"Did you find my note?" she asked.

"I didn't see a note," I said.

"Did *you*?" she asked Dennis.

She reached into the pocket of her jeans and extracted a folded piece of white lined paper. She handed it to Officer Frappier and said, "Here. You must be collecting evidence."

Libby and I looked at each other over the heads of the kneeling men and the seated, red-haired Georgia. We acknowledged what any woman would have noted but these men seemed to be missing, that this rather attractive Georgia was using us to make her point, to send her message to some party who had wronged her.

"Are you taking her to the hospital to have her stomach pumped?" I asked the officer.

"No!" said Georgia.

"You might not be out of the woods, miss," he said.

"I threw it all up!"

"You should go," I said. "At the very least to talk to a shrink."

"Where the hell is the ambulance anyway?" asked Libby.

"My car is right out front," said Georgia.

I stepped closer to her and said, "What about your parents? Are they around? You can't just drive away as if nothing happened. You almost died."

"I won't do it again," said Georgia.

Officer Frappier went back to his notebook. "Can you tell me exactly what happened from the time you first noticed the car parked outside your shop."

I repeated the chain of events. Georgia, cross-legged, listened as if she were enjoying my story. When I came to the part about Dennis pounding on the glass to rouse her, then breaking her window she said, "I wasn't faking. I really didn't hear anyone knocking on the glass."

Libby said, "How'd you happen to pick this stretch of Main Street to commit suicide on?"

None of us shushed Libby; her rude question sounded just right for this rather too-chipper Georgia Root. "I just picked the first parking space I came to this morning. I needed a place to sit and think. If it hadn't been snowing so hard or if I had snow tires I might just have ridden around. I do that when I need to sort things out."

Officer Frappier nodded solemnly and made a few scratches on his pad. He seemed to appreciate all our initiatives in asking the victim questions. "Is there anyone you want me to call?" he asked after flipping back in his notes and then forward again.

"No," said Georgia. "No way."

"Who was the note to?" I asked.

"Ma'am—" interrupted Office Frappier, "the young lady might not want to discuss any—"

"Professor Kornreich. Feel free to read it."

Officer Frappier opened the note and scanned it. "You're currently enrolled at the college?"

"You can read it out loud," she said. "I'm beyond feeling self-conscious at this point. These people have seen me half-dead. They've wiped up my vomit. I'm so numb I couldn't even feel embarrassment over a suicide note."

"That's really not necessary," said Dennis.

"If she wants us to hear it . . ." I said.

"Go ahead," Libby said to the officer.

The officer read it in a monotone. "Dear Ian: You will lose your job after this. You will be unable to get a job at any college in the United States. You will have to move to a part of the world where they don't read newspapers and have never heard of MacMillan College. You might as well stop sculpting. No one will want to own an Ian Kornreich unless they are scumbags too. I talked to the Dean of Students this morning and told her everything— places, times, dates, promises. She believes me. As God is my witness, Georgia M. Root."

I said, "Well, I guess that spells it out."

"A professor?" Dennis asked.

"Sculpture and drawing," said Georgia.

Libby and I exchanged more looks: we knew about students who fucked their professors and vice versa; and all of us townies knew the chronic divorcing and once-in-a-decade marrying that came out of these affairs.

"And guess what happened when I went to the dean? Guess what she said?"

Officer Frappier poised his pencil as if the answer was going to be part of the official record.

"She said, 'Thank you so much, Georgia. We like to keep track of these things so that if we get future complaints about Professor Kornreich we have a record of some kind to refer to.' So I'm like, 'In other words, you don't believe me,' and she goes, 'I am taking down everything,' and I go, 'But if you believed me you wouldn't just wait around for the next student he seduces to come in here crying. You're protecting him instead of me.'"

"You said that?" I asked.

"More or less," said Georgia. She turned to Officer Frappier. "I probably should have gone to the police or to the college radio station instead of her. She doesn't want it getting out because parents freak and the admissions office gets complaints for the next five years from parents of girls applying—"

I interrupted. "And the male faculty closes ranks and says, 'Professor Kornreich is a respected member of this community and the female student in question is a known liar and fornicator.'" I held my hand out. "No offense. That applies generically."

Georgia said, "Do you guys know Ian?"

"We don't have to," I said. "We know the way the system works."

Dennis put one hand on Georgia's shoulder. "You need to go to the hospital and you need to talk to someone. I'm not comfortable with us discussing these things so casually."

I huffed to myself, annoyed at the reproof. Aloud I said, "He's probably right."

"He's right, miss," echoed our policeman.

Dennis helped Georgia to her feet. He transferred her two-handed grip to Officer Frappier, who guided her by her raccoon coat's elbow to the door. Georgia looked back at us, at all three of us, and said in a shaky voice, "Thank you, Dennis."

11

An Early Night

Any normal routine was out of the question. We had saved a life and even Dennis would close his shop. The snow was still swirling; the barometric pressure was still falling. Winds from the northeast, Libby's radio announced. Dennis invited us across the street to his apartment for an early supper.

Libby asked if he was sure. I thought: not everyone lives in a pigsty and has to disinfect before inviting friends in.

Dennis said he was sure. He wanted to talk about what had happened. The adrenaline was still pumping—us pulling her out of the car like that, thinking she was dead. And her being still alive.

"You were quite the Eagle Scout," I said. "You seemed to know instinctively what to do."

We hung around as Libby closed up and rang out. I couldn't help but notice there hadn't been one sale. She put a black velvet opera coat with rhinestone buttons on over her checked balloon pants; she slipped off her ballet slippers and pulled on her L.L. Bean hunting shoes. Her hat was a knitted band of fluffy white angora, circa 1959, that she tied into a bow under her chin with straps that ended in pom-poms. He answered by saying, "That's all it was, instinctive. You feel their carotid artery, you see if their pupils dilate. If they're unconscious from pills or fumes you try to wake them up."

"Poor kid," said Libby.

"Poor little rich kid," I said. "Comes to MacMillan with her own new car—"

"What kind of charlatan would give a young girl a prescription for Valium?" said Dennis. "Her parents must be idiots to let her go away to college with a bottle of pills."

"Do you know where she's from?" Libby asked me.

"Of course," I said. "Ridgefield, Connecticut."

"Her parents could get up here in a couple of hours," Dennis said quietly.

"They could fly up in minutes on their own private jet," I said.

Libby said, "We have to cheer him up. He saved someone's life and he's bummed out."

"It's a big responsibility," he said. "Someone wants to be dead and they wake up alive because of you."

"She parked her car on *Main* Street," I said. "And she left her motor running. She did everything a person does when she wants to be found."

"I can't believe you two," said Dennis. "This could have been a *tragedy*."

Libby in her velvet coat put her arms around Dennis and patted his back. I thought he would push her away after a short, polite interval, but he didn't.

"It's television," I said. "It dilutes the effect of tragedy. We don't know how to act when it happens in real life."

We walked three abreast, down one block and across the street to Dennis's place. We huddled and shouldered our way into the wind. The snow stung our faces and darkened the afternoon sky. "There will be no school, all schools, all day in Harrow," I intoned. Libby picked up my chant, stomping our feet to its rhythm, a phrase that still made me happy after all these years as an adult: "No school, all schools, all day, in Harrow."

Dennis's condominium had been a fire station in another life. He said the hole in the floor with the sliding pole was added during renovation for atmosphere. Each unit had one. It was a beautiful place, multilevel—a half flight up to the two bedrooms; a half flight down to Dennis's sunken studio; a loft in the A of the cathedral ceiling, the store's no-nonsense gray/beige carpeting throughout. The kitchen was freestanding between the living and dining rooms; copper pots hung above the kitchen island. The kitchen floor was a rectangle of high-gloss blond wood, pegged and fashionably scarred under its shine as if recalling heavy black boots and large Dalmations.

I waited for Dennis to utter one syllable acknowledging I had been there before. Libby cooed about what a showplace it was, how she had guessed he would live like this, neatly, architecturally, casually yet elegantly.

"It looks bigger than I remember it," I said, "which may be because I was here at night."

"When was that?" asked Libby.

"Before you moved back."

Dennis went through a few silent, in-from-the-cold gyrations, blowing into his fists, rubbing his hands, feeling his wet socks.

"It was just a little get-together after Diana's wedding," I said. "It didn't last long."

Libby unbuttoned her velvet coat and handed it to Dennis. "You entertain?" she asked.

"Occasionally."

"He rotates the guest list. Everyone gets a turn eventually," I said.

Dennis's cynical smile was lost on Libby. He changed the subject by asking if we were hungry, thirsty, warm enough, dry enough?

"I didn't eat lunch," said Libby.

"Let me see what I have." He opened the refrigerator and called out, "Eggs. Turkey baloney. Blue cheese. Beer. Milk. O.J. Dr. Pepper." He took out a deli container, checked under its lid and said, "Never mind."

"Throw it out if you're not going to use it," I said, smiling at Libby, reminding her of my history.

"Something hot would be good," she answered.

He opened the eye-level freezer compartment. "Pork chimichangas. Lasagna. Chicken à la king. Pepper steak. Turkey pot pie, two of them. French bread pizza. And mystery care package. Pea soup—I think. Could be corn chowder."

"Doesn't Mummy label it for you?" I asked.

Dennis looked at me and said smartly, "No she doesn't, Melinda."

"I'll have that, with a beer. If you don't think she'd mind."

"Soup sounds just right," said Libby.

He put the large rectangular container in the microwave; hesitated over his choice of power levels, then hit "defrost." He passed around matching cloth napkins—fish on batik—from a basket centerpiece and we sat down at the glass dining-room table.

"You did all this yourself?" asked Libby.

He shrugged. "I vacuum when it needs it. A MacMillan student comes in twice a month to undo the rest of the damage."

"She meant the accoutrements," I said.

"Cloth napkins, copper pots, this table, the whole look," said Libby.

Dennis paused. "Wedding presents."

I said I noticed many were in a fish motif.

"Still," said Libby, "it isn't you exactly, or what I think of as you. It's more urban"—pressing as if she wouldn't be satisfied until the words "Iris" and "wife" had crossed his lips.

Dennis smiled. "I think I'm pretty urban. Besides, I don't want to come home to a place that looks like Brookhoppers."

"I suppose not," said Libby, "but if it were me I wouldn't want any reminders."

Dennis stood up, saying he'd get the beer. I suggested he rotate the soup a quarter-turn.

"It's on a carousel."

Libby asked if the microwave had come with the condo. Dennis said it had; a lot of the stuff was thrown in when they were negotiating, like the icemaker.

"Negotiating the purchase, or the divorce?"

"The purchase."

"Did it cost a fortune?"

"More than it would cost in today's market. We bought at the peak."

"You must do very well," said Libby.

Dennis laughed.

"Is it the mail-order part? Is it, like, *half* of what you sell?"

"Sixty-eight percent last year. Sixty the year before. Thirty-plus the year before."

Libby and I shook our heads and exclaimed over his percentages. Libby asked him how many dollars he generated per square foot and if his salespeople were on salary.

I saw him hesitate over the first question. I jumped in and said, "This is depressing. Let's talk about something else."

"Like Georgia Root?" Libby asked.

"Let's call patient information and see how she's doing," I said.

Dennis shook his head. "She won't even be listed yet. She could still be in the emergency room waiting to be seen."

"She was perfectly fine when she walked out of Rags," said Libby, "even if she was playing it for all it was worth."

Dennis looked startled; I knew he hadn't seen a trace of Georgia's dramatic talents. "Melinda found her unconscious," he protested. "The car would have run out of gas eventually and even if the Valium couldn't have killed her she would have died of exposure. They would have found her outside the shops tomorrow morning."

"No," I said. "She already had one ticket on her windshield. The meter maid would have noticed something amiss if she had to write a second ticket for a car whose motor was running. Even a meter maid would have called for help. She was not going to die today. Her number was definitely *not* up."

"Which isn't to say it wasn't hugely traumatic," said Libby, now sounding careful.

"You weren't there for the worst part. You didn't find her and think she was dead like Melinda and I did."

"That's true," Libby murmured.

Dennis ladled his mother's pea soup into three earthenware bowls and served us. I said it was delicious, a lie.

"I've only seen green pea soup," said Libby.

Dennis shrugged. He had taken his glasses off at the table, which gave his eyes a softer, sadder focus. "You and I experienced it differently than she did," he said to me.

"And maybe I experienced it differently from you."

"It's the snow," said Libby briskly. "It's very cinematic. It's reminding us of Jimmy Stewart's suicide attempt in *It's a Wonderful Life*."

"I wouldn't say that," said Dennis. He asked if we wanted crackers; he probably had some somewhere.

"No, thanks," I said.

"Can we sleep here tonight?" Libby asked suddenly.

Dennis took another spoonful of soup, then wiped his mouth carefully with his batik napkin—buying time, I thought. "Do you want to?" he asked.

"We can't very well walk home in this."

"Melinda too?"

I said no, it wasn't necessary. The storm was letting up.

"I have room," he said.

I said no thanks, I had to work tomorrow. Two guests were too many. Besides, it takes me such a long time to recover from these overnights. But Libby should stay if that was mutually convenient. Roads would be treacherous; why put her at risk if he had an extra pillow and the urge to entertain?

"Why put yourself at risk?"

I said I was parked in a snow emergency lane and that I'd be towed. I added, making it up as I went along, that my mother was scared during blizzards the way some people are during thunderstorms. But Libby—you earned every second of this, brother—had no car and no live-in mother. Why should she have to worry about mine?

12

Nothing Happened

I walked the mile and some fraction to work the next morning, layering my clothes like the weatherman suggested, wearing sunglasses against the glare, scarf up to my nose and green rubber Wellingtons. I arrived by 9:30, a half hour before most of the shops on Main opened, and rewarded myself for such pioneer spirit by ordering a grilled bagel and mocha latte at Francesca's. I saw Libby walk by, head down in the wind, wearing last night's opera coat over last night's balloon pants. I asked Angelique to pack up my order, caught up with Libby as she was unlocking the door and said, "Well?"

She invited me in. We both stomped our feet on her mat and she locked the door behind us. There was a faint smell remaining of Georgia Root's vomit, and a new swirl to the pile of the rose carpet where Libby had scrubbed with club soda. "I'm going to change into one of my dresses," she said.

"You're going to have to air the shop out before you open," I said. I followed her into the small office in the back and talked as she put on a long-sleeved brown velvet dress with leg-o-mutton sleeves.

"Can you sell that if you've worn it all day?" I asked.

Libby shrugged.

I must have looked distressed because she added, "If it gets dirty, I call them 'models' and I take off forty percent."

"Good idea." I opened a window, hoping the cold air would circulate into the showroom so I could eat without gagging. "How'd it go last night?" I asked after a few bites.

Libby told me as she rooted around the back room for stockings and changed into pink acrobatic slippers: Nothing.

She had stayed over in Dennis's guest room. They lost power while watching the news on TV just after eleven, too late evidently to inspire anything romantic like a candlelit game of Scrabble or cognac in front of a flickering fire. Libby told me Dennis found his flashlight—of course it was a Black & Decker industrial type, fully charged and mounted on a wall just where it was supposed to be; he checked the fuse box, hit a few circuit breakers, looked out the window at extinguished street lights and announced, "Pretty good timing, though. Bedtime." He had a second working flashlight for Libby and explained that his clock radio was on a backup battery so it never stopped; they'd be awakened at the proper hour—seven for him, okay? He showed her to the spare room, which had its own full bath and linen closet. He closed the door behind him without an awkward or lingering or wistful last word, without the slightest hint that he wished it could be otherwise.

I asked if she was positive; couldn't he have been lying low, waiting naked in bed, for her to make the first move?

"You don't think I know the difference between a man who

wants to sleep with me but is restraining himself and a man who doesn't?"

"He's hard to read," I offered.

"Not to me," she said. "Not last night. This was a sleepover at your grandmother's house—a wake-up knock at seven-thirty. Fruit Loops and orange juice by eight. We didn't even walk to work together. He wanted to get in early to write and I figured there'd be no one here all day so I went back to bed and let myself out."

"I'm sorry," I said after a few moments.

"So am I," said Libby.

He was writing when I got there, his radio commentary, which he taped on Mondays. "Want me to come back?" I asked.

He said no, he could use me for inspiration since he was writing about Georgia Root's suicide attempt and how nature had forced a neighboring shop owner to close early, thereby discovering what would have gone unnoticed and saving what would have died.

"Me?"

He nodded. "Do you mind?"

I said no, not at all. But what did that have to do with fly fishing?

"I'm branching out. It sort of fits—nature, the elements, life and death. People will make a connection even if I didn't intend one. The station doesn't care. I'm their only commentator of color. They get a grant for having me."

"Read me what you have."

Dennis began to read in the croon he used on air: The snow, the feeling of calm and peace he had felt at work—the store empty, his associates sent home. Being in a warm, dry, bright, safe place while the snow and wind raged outside.

"I get it: fish underwater—*their* bright, warm safe place with the dangers lurking outside: Us, right?"

"Not really," said Dennis, "but that's what they'll think."

"Go on."

He read: "She was young, still a teenager, with hair that bubbled from her smooth—"

I shook my head and he stopped. "Hair doesn't bubble," I said.

"Men will understand what I mean. It curls but it's long. The curls keep on going."

"But 'bubble' used to be a haircut." I described it with my hands, short and teased.

He rubbed his own head, exasperated.

"Never mind. Leave it. I see what you're getting at. Tell me the rest and I won't interrupt. I just want the gist of it."

He paraphrased, sounding less enthusiastic. "Then I say how we thought she was dead, but we couldn't leave it at that; we got her out and she was actually alive. And within minutes she was walking and talking and worrying about her car."

"And," I said, twirling my index finger like a TV director with a commercial approaching: *so what's the point?*

"We played God," he said solemnly. "We changed the course of someone's life."

"Oh," I said. Then: "Isn't that a little . . . self-congratulatory?"

"I thought of that, so I changed it to the third person. Besides the point is that she walked away and out of our lives—that we made the difference for her between life and death, about the irony of it being completely over now. We'll probably never see her again. She'll live her whole life separate from ours, and we'll always wonder what happened to her, but she'll just go on about her business not wanting to be reminded of what she did . . . Human catch and release."

"You don't know that. She might keep in touch."

Dennis shook his head.

"She might send us Christmas cards every year." I smiled. "She might send you a hugely expensive arrangement of out-of-season flowers next week."

111

"I called the hospital this morning. She wasn't even admitted. Her parents came up and got her and took her home."

"Don't you think that's good? She didn't have a beef against her parents. It was against that professor."

"I guess," said Dennis unhappily.

"Cheer up. I'm sure if they came to get her in a blizzard it was because they didn't trust the psychiatry department of a hick community hospital. They want her under the care of an expensive private shrink in Fairfield County. She's in good hands. She'll always be grateful. Her parents are going to be calling me any second for an FTD thank-you basket. I'd better get over there in fact."

"I wish I could use her name," said Dennis. "There's something so fitting about 'Georgia Root.' So basic."

"You know what I think? I think Georgia Root opened her eyes and developed a little crush on her hero. I wasn't going to say anything, but I think you're responding to that in some sublimated way. Libby and I picked up on it. We didn't exist as far as Georgia Root was concerned. She found herself in the brawny arms of an obviously concerned citizen—generally regarded as cute—and recovered pretty quickly. You're responding to that on some level. And it's a dramatic way to meet someone, certainly. Romantic. Swashbuckling. You might as well have carried her out of a burning building. That's what your story is really about. Carrying a cute redhead in your arms and waking her up. It's a Prince Charming story."

Dennis looked at the piece of paper as if my translation might be there in black and white for him to study. Finally he said, "I'd hate to think I'm that transparent. I honestly think it's something more."

"It's sexual. I was just as involved, and Libby to a lesser degree but neither one of us was so dazed by it. I think I'm as sensitive as the next guy, but you're clearly having a different response. You rescued her, which I think is key here, what you really want—no assertiveness on her part, no overt sexual response, but a damsel in distress—and every movie you've ever seen requires you to carry her off into the sunset and take care of her."

"Take care of her?" he repeated, as if it was the most ill-conceived idea ever spoken.

I turned his rough draft toward me, reading silently, irritated because my hair was at least as long and curly as Georgia Root's. Without looking up from the pages I murmured, "Heard you were a perfect gentleman last night."

He pounced as if he'd been waiting to strike at the first nocturnal reference. "You and your girlfriend don't have a subtle bone between you!" he cried. "You cook up this plot to maroon Libby at my apartment, assuming I'm going to go along with it, and then you breeze in here demanding an explanation."

"I did *not* breeze in here and I did not demand an explanation. You invited us back. The roads were treacherous. I barely made it home alive. Some people had to sleep at civil defense shelters."

"I doubt that. You're playing cupid for some asinine reason."

"You invited us—your fellow lifesavers. When would we have had time to invent a plan?"

I waited while he rang up a customer's book purchase; waited still longer while the customer, an elderly man in a navy blue beret, read the first page of his new fly-fishing novel happily to himself at the cash register.

"Besides," I said when the man finally had left, "why would I want you to sleep with Libby?"

"Because you know I'm not interested in her, and it's a weird, masochistic form of punishment."

Libby would die if she heard herself classified as punishment. "If you're not interested in her, you'd better tell her outright. She moved here to pick things up with you."

"Pick things up?" he repeated.

"Libby told me what happened."

113

He rapped the side of his head as if it were an unresponsive appliance.

"In high school? When she told you she only liked you as a friend and she didn't want you to get the wrong idea?"

Dennis's eyes closed to a squint. After a few moments of recollective effort, he relaxed his features and said, "Sorry."

"You don't remember? It wasn't this huge racial incident by the lockers that scarred you for life?"

Dennis laughed. "Apparently not."

"I don't believe you."

"Then don't."

"But I thought it was this big unresolved . . . thing."

"Guess you were wrong."

"It was to Libby."

Dennis said, "I can't help that."

"I mean—she thinks you're avoiding her to this day because of it."

"I never went out with Libby."

"That's the whole point. You wanted to, right?"

"I think I had some ideas in that direction—I mean guys in high school are always trying—but I never acted on it."

"Well, you'd better tell her."

"Me? You're her coconspirator. You tell her. You started it."

"She wouldn't believe me, even if I *was* inclined to do your dirty work. Her brain only receives selected messages."

Dennis moved a step closer to me along the display case. "Does she know?" he asked quietly.

"About what?"

He checked to see if anyone else was within earshot. "About us, after the wedding."

Oh, that, I said; no, I hadn't told her. Surely he trusted my discretion.

"I knew that," he said.

114

I assumed my front-desk voice. "I'm glad you brought it up," I began. "I've decided you were right—ruining a cordial business relationship because of one romantic detour would have been a mistake." I continued: "Consider it a mutual decision. Don't feel guilty. None of this takes anything away from the experience, which was wonderful, even unforgettable, but is certainly not compatible with friendship."

When I finished my speech Dennis said, "You told me you didn't want to be friends after what happened."

"It's a small town," I said.

"That isn't new."

"If I stay mad at you, you'll start avoiding me and things will be even more awkward."

"I won't," said Dennis. "I mean, I don't."

"Then we're friends?"

He nodded. I put out my hand for him to shake, and after a long pause, he did.

13

Ian Kornreich

The harness bells hanging inside the front door of the shop rattled their awful noise, signaling me to come out from the back and wait on a customer. It was a Wednesday morning, the day Roger went to Boston for special orders. Robin was doing errands early so she'd be back for the late-morning crush.

It was a guy, fortyish, in blue jeans, a collarless white shirt and red suspenders. His hair was thick and almost all gray, cut by a good barber. He wore tortoise-shell glasses walking in, but took them off as soon as I appeared.

"I'm looking for Melinda LeBlanc," he said.

I said that was me.

"I'd like to talk to you."

"And you are . . . ?"

"Ian," the man said, almost wincing. He held up his hand in defense as if expecting banishment or protest.

The harness bells jingled as another customer entered, a stout woman in a plaid winter coat clutching her pocketbook at her belly with both hands.

"Go ahead," said my visitor. "I'll wait."

"Can I help you?" I asked the woman.

"How much are those lavender roses?" she said, pointing.

"Five-fifty a stem."

"Are you kiddin'?" she said. "That's what roses go for?"

"These ones do because of the color and they're extremely fragrant. The red are less and the sweetheart roses are lower than that. We can do cut flowers—"

"I wanted them to be roses," said the woman, "but I didn't know they were that much. I was kind of hoping for a dozen long-stem roses."

I said, with this gray-haired man watching me, in a kind voice like Roger and Robin employed, "How much would you like to spend?"

The woman brightened. "Up to fifteen?"

"And you want to make a statement, right? You want that message you get with roses, right?"

"It's for my boyfriend."

"Okay! I take one perfect sterling rose, long-stemmed. I put it in a bud vase with some baby's breath and some leather leaf, and a pretty silver bow and we deliver it to your boyfriend—twelve-fifty."

"For one rose?" the woman said.

"No. One sterling rose is five-fifty. If we turn it into a statement, put it in a reusable milk-glass bud vase and deliver it, twelve-fifty. There's a design fee involved with a bud vase."

"I would love it," said the gray-haired man quietly. "I'd actually

117

prefer the simplicity of a bud vase to a whole dozen roses, if you're looking for a man's opinion. Less is more."

"Really?"

"Absolutely."

"You wouldn't think it was faggy?"

I laughed. The man said earnestly, "I'd probably propose to you upon its arrival. I'd certainly be charmed."

"Well," she said, "maybe I'll do the bud vase." She clicked open the clasp of her black vinyl pocketbook and took a ten-dollar bill and three ones from a change purse.

"Do you mind?" I asked the man, pantomiming paperwork.

He shook his head.

"It'll take a sec to write it up."

"Are you gonna take care of it right away?" asked the woman.

"Immediately. He'll receive it between three and four today." I scribbled the order quickly, smiled at the man's name—Ziggy Swift—and rang it up.

"Can I watch you make it?" she asked.

I said she couldn't. Sorry. I had a few arrangements to do ahead of hers; first come, first served, but hers would go out on the very next delivery and I'd pick the most perfect rose in the cooler.

"I hope so," she said.

"Good luck," said the man. "I hope everything works out."

"Me too," said the woman.

"Me too," I said lamely.

"What about a card?" said the man.

"Jeez," said the woman. "That's right, a card." She looked at me as if my incompetence had been certified. *No card? You call yourself a florist?*

"I'm not usually the one who writes up the orders. My cousins usually take care of the details. I'm the floral artist."

The woman was inspecting our rack of cards, finally choosing one with two crossed champagne glasses and falling confetti in the lower right corner.

"That's usually for anniversaries," I said.

"Does it have to be?"

"No."

"I like that one, too," said the man, smiling at me.

I handed her a pen. She wrote something quickly, his name probably, then paused to consider the meat of it.

" 'I can't stop thinking about you,' is always good," said the man, "or 'Darling, last night was unforgettable.' "

"I couldn't say that in a million years."

"Why couldn't you? Isn't that what you're thinking?"

"I don't know. Maybe. It seems kind of . . . what's the right word?"

"Clichéd?"

She shrugged.

"Turgid?" he tried.

"It's like a card that comes with flowers on TV, not what I would ever write."

I stepped in. "How about, 'Thank you for dinner.' It was dinner, right?"

"That's it!" cried the handsome stranger.

The woman pressed her lips together, then wrote something on the card. She put it in its envelope, licked it shut and handed it to me. I said, "I'll get right on it."

The man repeated, "Good luck."

The customer left, doubts unspoken but expressed in the set of her mouth and the double grip of her pocketbook. Before she was out the door I mouthed thanks to the handsome man.

Alone I asked, "What can I do for you?"

"A bud vase, please," he said, his eyes blinking innocently. Before I reacted, he laughed and touched my hand with the briefest of taps. Only kidding.

119

"Thank God," I said.

"I'm Ian Kornreich," he said again.

"I think I'm supposed to know who you are."

He hesitated before saying, "I teach at MacMillan." He took a newspaper clipping from his wallet and laid it on the counter.

Ian Kornreich. The villain. The addressee of the suicide note. "Oh fuck," I said.

Ian's expression hardened. "I wanted to talk to the people who found her to set the record straight. I've been accused of something I didn't do."

I hadn't meant, Oh, fuck—you criminal. More like, Oh fuck—I thought you were flirting with me and now I find out you're a bad candidate for what I had in mind. "I have nothing to do with Georgia Root," I said. "I don't expect to hear from her again. Not even a thank-you."

"I've been wrongly accused," said Ian. "I don't even know Georgia Root."

I took the clipping and reread it—my mother had collected extra copies of the paper from our neighbors—and I hadn't recalled any mention of Ian's name. "You're not in the paper," I said.

"I'm on leave for the rest of the year," he said grimly. "Not by choice. I'm trying to exonerate myself. The police have the note on file, and the college was sent a copy. I'm trying to re-trace her path and set things straight with the people she lied to."

"You don't *know* her?" I asked.

"She answered an ad I put in student employment for a life model. Not for my sculpture class but for my own work."

"Oh, God. You have students as models?"

"Yes! I always have. I do it through student employment so it's completely . . . correct. I don't sidle up to people at the student center and slip them my phone number. What would you do?

Take out a personal ad? I also put ads in the *Sentinel* and *ArtWeek*."

I knew this wasn't any of my business, but I couldn't stop now. "Did you hire her?"

"Yes."

"So you *did* know her."

"She didn't show up for the first session. I left a message on her answering machine reminding her, then sent her a follow-up note. She came next time, wearing boots and a long coat—raccoon— and she had no clothes on underneath. I thought it was strange, but I also thought that since she hadn't done it before she didn't know the protocol. I probably should have said right then on the spot, "I don't think this is going to work out for this particular project. I'll pay you for today." But she had this great Medusa head of hair that just snaked down in these red curls, with this ropy texture . . ."

"Everyone notices that hair," I said.

"Anyway, I just wanted her head so I told her she could drape herself if she felt more comfortable, just expose the shoulders. But she said, no, why not get used to the sensation of nudity in this context. I told her where to sit, and she did, but then after a while, maybe a half hour, she started touching herself."

"Uh-oh," I said.

"You're not kidding *uh-oh*. I froze for a minute, looking down at my sketch, hoping I wasn't seeing what I was seeing; hoping that she had an itch and when I looked up she would have scratched it. I finally looked at her again, maybe fifteen seconds had passed, and she was most definitely masturbating. A performance. Making little noises. I stood up and said, 'Please stop that.' Of course she didn't. I turned my back and said, 'You can't do that here.' She asked, 'Even if I don't move my head and shoulders?' I walked to the door of my studio, still not looking, and said, 'I want you dressed and gone in one minute.'

" 'No you don't,' she said.

"I left and stood outside the closed door. It was the strangest few moments, to stand there and know that inside your door is some adolescent fantasy of a beautiful naked woman performing a seduction in no uncertain terms . . ."

"Aren't you the angel," I said.

"I was! I have a code of ethics: I don't date students. I don't kiss them; I don't let on I would like to. I don't sleep with them. I don't encourage their advances. I tell them explicitly when they're stepping over the line."

"Your wife must appreciate that."

"I'm not married."

"Were you ever?"

"No."

"How old are you?"

"Thirty-six this month."

"Have a girlfriend?"

He shook his head no.

"Heterosexual?"

"Yes."

"What would happen if you had a student and you fell head over heels in love with her and you felt pretty sure that she reciprocated. You wouldn't work something out in private, begging her discretion?"

"I'd wait until she graduated," he said.

"I don't believe you."

"No one else does either."

"What if she was a freshman? You'd wait four years to ask her out? You'd wait until you were forty then go up to her at graduation and say, 'Are you doing anything next Saturday?' "

"That's the point. I don't act on these crushes. That's all they are. Little flare-ups, aggravations of the nerve endings. They pass. I remind myself of past infatuations that disappeared as fast as they arrived. I ask myself if it would have been worth losing my job over Stephanie Barnes or Marjorie Fine or any of the dozen others who moved me profoundly but whose names I can't even remember now."

"So what happened inside the studio?" I asked.

Ian looked up at the wall clock behind me. "I feel bad about taking you away from your work."

"In twenty-five words or less."

"She didn't leave. I could hear her in there, still . . . performing. Louder and louder, obviously for my benefit, until she—" he paused, looked pained, looked behind him toward the front door—"climaxed."

I was still holding the bud-vase order in my hand. I looked at it, pretended it needed a notation, then smiled politely, embarrassed for how totally engaged an audience I was.

"You don't believe me," he said quietly.

"I'm getting very nervous about my orders. The owners are going to be back any second—"

"I'll buy some flowers. I was going to anyway. And I'll decide quickly. What smells good?"

"Are they for you?" I asked, the automatic question, the handsome-man, is-there-a-woman-in-your-life census.

"I like cut flowers in my studio. As a special treat. What besides roses? I've already heard your roses spiel."

I said by all means, freesia, the most beautiful scent on earth, and right here in my cooler. Priced by the stem.

"Fine," said Ian. "I'll take—what?—six. However many makes up for taking your time."

"Don't buy them for that reason."

"I do want them. I'd also like to convince you that I'm not such a terrible guy."

I was too vain to say, "Why bother convincing me? I have nothing to do with this incident. I'm not your judge and jury." I knew Ian Kornreich had come in for stupid reasons, thinking he had to clear his name, assuming I had given Georgia Root's story a first or second thought. But now things had changed. There was an oddly sweet desperation in the way he looked, pained, trying to please, when he explained about Georgia Root's sex act; the way he sought my approval.

He believed what he was saying, and he wanted me to know the rest. We made plans—quite civilized, polite, dinner plans, to talk further.

In other words, yes, I made a date with a reputed wrongdoer and smoothie, a handsome artist raconteur recently suspended for malfeasance or worse. Of course he had lied to me. Why shouldn't he? He had nothing to lose.

But I was thirty years old, living with my mother, working for my cousins, and he was a man who said he could be moved profoundly. You don't act sensibly and nip things in the bud. You don't listen to the voice inside you telling you you're crazy or desperate or both. You say yes, you give him your address, and you hope.

14

I Do It Again

I didn't mean to keep Ian's visit secret from Dennis, but it seemed I was having trouble telling him. I wasn't hesitating out of shyness, because I would have enjoyed relaying Ian's claims about Georgia's funny business. I wasn't squeamish about sex in mixed company; I'd have no trouble repeating Ian's story with all the flourishes. But I knew Dennis would take Georgia's side and imply with a certain set of his face that I was shallow, disloyal to my sex and easily bought off with dinner. I would say it was just a suspicion I had, from the first sentence Georgia Root uttered in Libby's shop, from the first lasso she threw around Dennis, that she was more ruthless than I was, and certainly crazier. Men have another view of these things, and wouldn't think an allegedly dying woman would turn the moment to her social advantage. It came down to this: I wanted to believe Ian; I didn't want to hear how stupid I was to have dinner with him; I didn't want to hear Dennis's diatribe about my need to side with any handsome man who implies that he finds me attractive.

Instead, I confessed to Libby over coffee the next morning, she at her sewing machine, wearing a cotton kimono with the name of a Japanese hotel imprinted every which way. I repeated every word Ian had used to describe Georgia's quasi-public sexual practices.

"I knew it," said Libby. "I knew it."

"Can you imagine—eighteen years old? Where does a freshman in college get the balls to seduce her professor? Don't forget he's more or less our age, but to her someone who's thirty-six would be old. How promiscuous do you have to be to start something like that with no provocation?"

"Or how immodest?" asked Libby. "You have to be unbelievably comfortable with your body to do that. If it's true."

"I think it is true. I think if he was making it up, especially if he was guilty and had seduced her, he'd have put a little more actual sex into it to cover all bases."

"What does he look like?" Libby asked.

"About five-ten, five-eleven. Nice build. Prematurely gray hair, good haircut. Sort of boyish. Blue jeans and suspenders . . ."

"What kind of jacket?"

"Bomber. An old one. Leather cracking to a fashionable degree."

Libby squinted to conjure up Ian Kornreich. "I think I've seen him," she said.

"Where?" I asked.

"Just around. At Francesca's maybe. The gray hair and bomber jacket sound familiar."

"He has acne scars. I find that quite poignant."

"Me too," said Libby.

126

"He asked me out," I said quietly.

She took her foot off the floor pedal and looked up. "And?"

"He wanted to talk more about Georgia Root. It seems important to him that I believe him."

"Did you go?"

I said that I was going. Hadn't even hesitated.

"Does Dennis know Ian turned up?"

"Do you think I should tell him?"

Libby smiled, acknowledging Georgia Root's hold on our friend; a smile that said, "Are you crazy?"

Well, I didn't have to tell Dennis anything because Ian took himself to Brookhoppers and asked if he might speak to Mr. Vaughan. It made perfect sense: he had come to me, a name listed in the newspaper story of Georgia Root's rescue, so naturally he would seek out Dennis, too. I got the account of their conversation from Ian during our dinner the following Friday. We went to a new Cajun seafood restaurant that had opened in the unlucky spot where a string of parents-taking-out-their-daughters restaurants had tried to break the jinx but hadn't.

Dennis had been strangely hostile, according to Ian; had obviously believed everything Georgia wrote in her suicide note. "I'm not interested in your side of it," he had said.

"My side is the truth," Ian had pleaded. Dennis had all but stuck his fingers in his ears when Ian tried to tell him what Georgia had done. It was as if he wanted to believe her, as if he had something at stake in her telling the truth—

I interrupted and said, "Dennis is a little bit in love with Georgia Root even though he won't admit it. This rescue of his knocked him for a loop. Libby and I—Libby from Rags for Sale?—were there for practically the whole thing and it's as if we had parallel experiences. We did what we needed to do and that was it. We got

127

over it. Dennis was in a daze. Still is. He became Prince Charming and now he doesn't want to hear that he rescued a disturbed princess."

"Has he seen her?" Ian asked.

I said I didn't know, but didn't think so. Which was part of his blue funk. No thanks from Georgia, no calls from her family, just a two-inch story in the local paper.

"What's he like?"

"Perfect," I said automatically.

Ian raised his eyebrows.

I explained: Smart, successful, good at a lot of different things. Has a cult following.

"Married? Single?"

"Divorced."

"Is she black?" he asked lightly.

"You might know her. Iris Lambrix? Teaches business at MacMillan? Tall, black, hair pulled back tight like a ballerina; an attitude?"

"Really beautiful?"

Iris? Not the one I was thinking of.

"Does she teach management?" Ian asked, sitting up a little straighter.

I said she did. He knew her?

"I've seen her," he said, the nonchalant way a man says it when he means he's noticed her but *good*.

I asked what the woman he was thinking of looked like.

"Oh," he said. "Tall, prominent cheekbones . . . kind of a shy smile?"

Now this was interesting: another man's take on Iris Lambrix.

Then Ian asked how I knew her as if the vision of Iris had burned out his pathways, erased our conversation. I said, "Dennis Vaughan. She's his ex-wife."

"Oh, that's right."

128

" 'Ex-wife' because she left him for a woman."

He pondered that as if sorting out the pronouns. "You mean she's gay?"

"Looks that way."

"But she was married."

"It happens all the time. Then they say they hadn't been tuned in to their bodies and their sexual politics."

"I didn't get that sense from her," he said, his eyes reflecting some heterosexual sparks he must have exchanged with Iris.

"Maybe she'll convert back," I said. "That happens too."

He forced a smile— So! Where were we?

"I never heard the rest of the story: Georgia Root is inside your studio pleasuring herself and you are outside the door, listening. Did you finish telling me what happened?"

I watched Ian closely to detect any sign that he was concocting a sexual fantasy or, if telling something close to the truth, relishing it too much. I became convinced that he wasn't doing either. He spoke as if he were a reluctant witness testifying to an embarrassing crime; no joy in the retelling, just a civic duty to be performed. I could have fallen in love with Ian Kornreich, watching him chew his lower lip. I silently blessed his parents for not correcting the slight overlap of his two front teeth.

"I waited until it was quiet inside the studio," said Ian. "I didn't go in but I yelled through the door, not *yelled* but in as loud a voice as I could without attracting attention, 'Get your things and get out or I'll call the campus police.' She came to the door wild-eyed, a whole other affect. Furious—"

"Dressed?"

"Yes. But furious. She had miscalculated, and I'd have to be punished for witnessing her mistake."

"What did you do then?"

Ian said flatly, "Nothing. I did nothing."

"Even though you thought she'd try to ruin you?"

129

"That was in retrospect. After she went to the dean of students, then I looked back and remembered the look on her face as she walked past me and realized that it meant revenge. At the time, stupidly, I thought she was a young kid who was angry because she was embarrassed and would go back to her room and throw things and hope she never ran into me again."

"What did she tell the dean?"

Again, in a monotone, as if any inflection would crack his composure, he said, "That I had ordered her to take off her clothes, to touch herself, to keep touching herself; that I undressed too. That I masturbated watching her."

"And the dean believed her?"

"Enough to set the wheels in motion for a suspension. She called the dean of faculty who called my chairperson and set up an emergency meeting immediately. Without me, I should add."

"Are you fired?"

"Suspended with pay for the rest of the semester."

"And then what happens?"

"Then I either go back or get terminated."

"I'd sue. I'd sue her for lying and trying to ruin your career and I'd sue the school for finding you guilty until proven innocent."

"She's sick," said Ian. "I think pretty certifiably sick. If I can document that, then the job part will work out. In the meantime, the school is covering its ass. If they kept on a professor after there had been a serious charge of misconduct and if it happened a second time, they'd be in deep trouble."

"What about you?" I said indignantly. "You're innocent. This could ruin your life, not to mention your career."

Ian said, "You believe me."

"If you're not telling the truth, you're the best liar I ever met."

He smiled ruefully and said, "I'll take it. I need someone on my

130

side even if she's just being a polite and gracious guest. Even if she doesn't have a vote on the peer review committee."

I leaned closer across the table and said, "I do five hundred dollars a month worth of floral arrangements for the college. I am the personal florist to the fucking *president* of MacMillan College."

"Melinda," he said, a warning if I'd ever heard one. "I wouldn't want you to think I was trying to get you involved."

"I'm already involved. I saved Georgia Root's life and she lied through her teeth."

"That's true," said Ian without enthusiasm.

"I could help, even if it's just as a sounding board. I know the way the college works. Not that you don't, but I've lived here my whole life, practically, and I have friends over there who would never connect me to your case."

Ian motioned for the waitress and mouthed, "check."

"We're not going to eat?" I asked.

Ian looked surprised and asked if I was hungry.

"I assumed . . . you did ask me for dinner."

"Well, by all means, then. If I said dinner, you get dinner." He smiled obligingly, and turned to the chalkboard on the wall behind him.

"Never mind," I said. "The popcorn shrimp filled me up."

"I'm buying you dinner," he said firmly, still reading the menu.

I took out my wallet and put a five-dollar bill on the table. "You wanted an informational interview and I misread the signals. Imagine my thinking 'dinner' meant the actual eating of it?"

Ian sighed a long, sensitive-male's sigh. He winced delicately then began the usual letdown speech, emphasis on his current fragility.

"Okay," I said. "I get the point."

"I can't tell you what it means to me that you believe me, and I'll always be grateful for that."

"Please."

"I'm being as honest as I know how," he said.

"Why don't you just say that college professors don't date flower sellers and, besides, you have the hots for Iris Lambrix?"

"You're hurt," said Ian.

"I'm used to it," I said.

15

I Send Flowers

I did an amazingly stupid thing the next morning, the kind of thing pathetic women specialize in: I sent Ian flowers. A Holland mixture with a card that said, "Don't mind me."

Nothing happened. No response. Our driver Frank, a retired mailman in his seventies, said yes, that a gray-haired man had come to the door and personally accepted the flowers.

"Did he look happy?" I asked.

"Not especially," said Frank.

"Did he look annoyed?"

Frank thought about it. "Not really."

"Kind of neutral?"

"Kind of. You know the guy?"

"I just thought they were extra nice stems," I said lamely. "I didn't have any other special orders today."

"Sure they were nice. I noticed that myself."

"Could've just been an inconvenient time when the doorbell rang. You can't always tell how a person feels from the way they answer the door either."

"I don't know about that. I'm pretty good at readin' people's minds, though. Even the worst sourpusses smile when they open the door and see me standin' there with flowers. And the bigger the better. You should tell people that when they order—the bigger the better. Of course he coulda had another gal there with him when I brought 'em. That's happened. I've had guys send me away and tell me to come back later when the Blue Chevy is gone from the driveway or the porch light's turned off or some such thing."

I said thanks, no matter; silly to get personally involved in deliveries, wasn't it? I left him to his acrostics which he did, jacket and cap still on, between deliveries. Robin, who had listened to our entire exchange, followed me into the back room and asked me what was up. Of course I lied. I said it was Libby's order, a guy she had met. I was looking for some feedback for her. It would have been nice to give Libby a glowing report from Frank, that the guy had jumped for joy.

"How did she meet him?" asked Robin.

"I think he came into the store."

"And she sent him flowers, just like that?"

"They went out to dinner."

"What'd she send?" asked Robin.

"A Holland mixture."

Robin took that in: not an excessive gesture; not really anything she could fault.

"I'm all for it," I said. "You'd be a millionaire if every woman who had a nice first date sent flowers to the guy. You should encourage it."

"Are you going to go over and tell her what Frank said?"

"I'm kind of busy. Besides, there's nothing to tell."

She looked at the order in front of me. "This is for tomorrow. Maybe he's called her by now. You'd like a break, wouldn't you?"

I said yes, all right, I'd be at Rags. But I wasn't going to collect data for Robin's downtown merchants' social file. She should *not* expect a report. Okay? Be back in ten minutes . . . Oh, and could she get a name and number if anyone calls?

I ran next door to Rags without a coat. There, in perfectly pedicured bare feet, in shimmery grape toenails, was Iris Lambrix, frowning at her reflection in the three-way mirror, modeling the dress that had been in Libby's window that morning: a sleeveless flapper dress, milky chiffon over peach silk with a black silk rose on one shoulder and black beading. Looking sensational despite my resistance to thinking so.

Libby smiled and said, "It looks as if it were made for her, doesn't it?"

Iris didn't exactly scowl, but raised her eyes in the mirror to examine the source of this unsolicited personal remark.

"I'm Melinda LeBlanc," I said. "I work next store."

"What do you do?" she asked.

"I'm a florist."

"Your shop?"

I said no, my cousins owned the shop. I was on the *creative* side—I pushed the word out in drawing-room English, which made Libby laugh, and made Iris look grimmer.

"Do you think the peach is too insipid?" she asked.

I closed my eyes and shook my head definitively, as if I wouldn't allow such a word to be used about this dress.

"It's peach, it's seashell, it's . . . it's not melon, not cantaloupe," Libby said.

Iris trusted me now. She didn't want to hear Libby's mewings. "I wish it were a shade more vibrant," she said.

"What's it for?" I asked.

"An awards dinner."

"Black tie?" I asked.

"Optional."

"Do you ever wear flowers in your hair?"

Iris asked squarely, "Why would I do that?"

"With your hair pulled back, a white glamellia behind one ear. It would be stunning."

Iris stared at herself in the mirror; she checked where the dress hit her knee.

Libby said softly, "A pale hose and a dancing slipper in black—small heel and a strap across the instep."

"And great earrings. Find some flapper earrings, teardrop shape maybe," I said.

Iris stared again. After a few moments she began moving her head from side to side, barely noticeable, a very small arc.

"No?" I asked.

"It's not right."

"You look fantastic in it," I said.

"Melinda's right," said Libby.

"It's not exactly what I was looking for," said Iris.

"Are you seriously in the market for something to wear to this awards dinner?" I asked Iris. She walked past me without answering and parted the curtain of the middle dressing room with a decisive backhand.

"Don't," mouthed Libby.

"Because you'll never find anything that comes close to this. It's perfect," I said, raising my voice.

"*Melinda—*"

"Has she ever actually bought anything here?" I asked Libby.

She signaled that I didn't understand, that I was out of line, and that she'd take it up with me later. Iris came out of the dressing room wearing her own clothes, a challis print dress and a wide purple suede belt. "I'd like to think it over," she said to Libby, ignoring me.

"Do you visit Dennis's shop when you're down here?" I asked, just to be difficult.

"Dennis?" repeated Iris Lambrix.

"Your ex-husband Dennis?"

"Are you a friend of his?"

"Quite good friends."

Libby had gone into the dressing room to retrieve the peach chiffon. I could tell from the set of her features when she came out that Iris had not handled it with the proper respect. She turned it right side out and draped it over one forearm like a solicitous valet.

"My store is right next to his," I continued.

Libby went to the front of the store to redress the mannequin in the peach dress. The window had been decorated with hanging silver stars and one crescent moon, which didn't suggest any particular theme to me but looked pretty and romantic. "A night of stars," I said to Iris, pointing my chin toward the window. "Perfect for an awards banquet."

"Why would I visit Dennis?"

"No reason," I said.

"If you're such a good friend, you probably know that we don't have an ongoing relationship."

"I do know that. But you must run into him, even here."

"Here?" repeated Iris.

"Dennis and Libby are friends, too."

"From high school," Libby called from the window.

"Did he ever mention us?" I asked Iris.

"I don't remember."

"How long were you married?"

"A year."

"Not long," I said.

137

"It was a mistake."

Libby came out from the window and went outside on the sidewalk to check the effect. "She's so pretty, isn't she?" I asked Iris as if it were too apparent to escape comment. "We all went to Harrow High together. Everyone knew Dennis, of course. Everyone knew all of us, now that I think of it."

"And why would that be?" asked Iris.

"Dennis was a star—"

"—and because he was one of the very few African-American students, he was not only noticed but aggrandized? That's a pattern."

Libby came back inside and asked, "Do you think the moon is too much?"

"It's the best part of it," I said, "except the dress of course. I think it's one of the most outrageous ones you've ever made."

Libby smiled uneasily, glancing to see if my extravagance was further annoying Iris.

"Look," Iris began, "I don't know what your problem is, but I assume there's no rule here that if you try a dress on you have to buy it. I would buy it if I wanted it, but I'm not positive. At these prices, I would like to be positive."

"I'm sorry," said Libby helplessly. She raised her hand to me and grunted, pantomiming that she'd like to chop me one. Turning to Iris she said, "If you decide that you want this dress I'll take ten percent off . . . and I guarantee that Miss LeBlanc will give you a free flower for your hair."

Iris said stiffly, thank you, she'd consider that seriously. However she had to get back to school, to class. The dress was lovely. The store had lovely things. She wished she could afford an entire wardrobe of Rags.

"Maybe we can have lunch," I said, earning one last cold stare. "Really," I called after her.

As soon as Iris had closed the door behind her Libby said, "What is *wrong* with you? You never cared whether anyone bought what they tried on. I want people to come in here and try things on without feeling that they have to buy something."

"I know."

"So what happened?"

I walked over to the rack of sale dresses and sorted through them without any involvement. "I'm depressed," I said.

"Why?"

"Longish story."

Libby turned her head toward the window. I saw that Dennis was outside talking to a smiling man, being gracious as always, nodding his thanks over the usual compliments—I love your commentary on public radio, I love your store, I use your flies.

I said, "I'm leaving. I'll buy the dress if she doesn't come back for it. It's the least I can do."

"If I ever let you back in."

Dennis came in before I slipped out. Libby and I greeted him. Without returning our hellos he said, "Iris said you were harassing her."

Libby and I exchanged looks, mine guilty and hers worried. I said, "That was fast."

"I wasn't," said Libby, "but Melinda was out of control."

"And why was that?"

"I'm in a bad mood and I took it out on your ex-wife because she tried on this gorgeous dress of Libby's—that one, in the window—and it looked like it had been custom made for her; the length, everything, and she just shrugged and said, 'I don't think so.' She comes in here a *lot* and never buys anything."

"Are you serious?" he demanded. "What the hell business is it of yours what people do in Libby's store?"

"I'm a big mouth. I apologized to her."

"She said you were saying stuff about me."

"Just that we were friends."

"Look. She wouldn't have come running to me with a little insignificant gripe. You must have really pissed her off for her to come into the store to report on this."

"We apologized quite nicely. Libby even offered her the dress at a discount, which to my mind was not necessary."

"I was quite appalled," said Libby.

"She was angry and I don't think you should be pissing people off, especially when they're people of color who have no way of knowing that it's not a racial thing."

"Oh, shit," said Libby softly.

"Did you tell her it wasn't a racial thing?" I asked.

"I didn't tell her anything! I didn't know what went on in here."

"I'm going to call her," I said. "I don't want there to be any misunderstanding. I'll send her flowers. I'll buy her lunch."

"You'd better do something."

Libby said to Dennis, "You thought it might have been *racial?* You couldn't really speak up for us with any certainty, could you, because I hurt you so badly in high school?"

Dennis glanced at me. I turned away from them to slide hangers one way then another along the same sale rack, measuring my distance to the front door. I heard Dennis say, "Can we talk later?"

I said, "You can talk now. I have to go. Robin is going to kill me."

Ignoring me, Libby said, "When?"

"After work?"

"Can't. We're open tonight."

"You don't have to work straight through."

He chewed on his lower lip. "Okay. Between six and seven."

"Where?"

"Across the street?" he asked softly. Very softly. I barely caught it. It took me a few moments to realize that he meant his place.

Not Libby. She knew instantly: Across the street. Fine. Six sharp.

I slipped out.

I began calling her house at 7:05, and she answered at 7:20. . . . Bad news from Libby's perspective: Dennis had announced over take-out pizza that he liked Libby very much; enjoyed her company, admired her work, her designs, her style; very much valued having Rags for Sale two doors away from Brookhoppers for esthetic and commercial reasons—was happy that his customers' wives shopped at Rags while husbands were buying flies; happy they were old friends with roots in the community . . . everything, really; every complimentary thing a man could say about a woman in the context of friendship. . . .

But he didn't feel about Libby the way she appeared to feel about him. He was sorry. He absolutely bore no residual ill will for perceived slights in high school.

There! The air was clear. He felt much better. Hadn't it been awkward, and isn't it better to know where everyone stands? Libby should not be embarrassed. He was flattered. Absolutely. Who wouldn't be flattered by the attentions of the prettiest girl at Harrow High?

"I'm not at Harrow High," said Libby. "That was twelve years ago. I can't believe I've misunderstood—"

Dennis said he was sorry, very sorry. But he knew they'd still be friends.

"What else?" I asked her. "Did he offer any more explanation than that?"

Libby said no. Wasn't that enough? It was over before it ever started; at least he'd made himself perfectly clear.

So that was it . . . almost exactly what I guessed he'd say, but for one discrepancy: I thought *I* had been the prettiest girl at Harrow High.

16

A Kind of Consultant

What do you want with her?" Dennis said when I asked for Iris's phone number.

"I want to explain why I was obnoxious."

"Let's hear it," he said.

I told him I hadn't formulated every syllable of my apology yet, but the gist of it would be my own lousy mood, my basic decency, my general self-improvement campaign, my professional relationship with the college, my concern, first and foremost, that Iris continue her patronage at Rags for Sale—

"No way," said Dennis.

"I acted like a jerk and I'd like to set the record straight."

"I don't want you calling Iris," said Dennis.

"Because . . . ?"

"Because what do you think the chances are of you saying

something inflammatory as opposed to your sincerely making peace with her?"

"I see. If we make peace, we might discover some common ground."

"Is that what this summit is all about?"

"Us, you mean? The night that never happened?" I put an imaginary key to my lips and twisted. "I'm looking to apologize to Iris for the other day. I'm not expecting her to fall all over me when I call—"

"That's for sure."

"But I can wheedle her into accepting my apology, don't you think? I'm pretty good at getting people to soften up around the edges."

"When you want to," said Dennis.

I reached her at her office at school. "Melinda LeBlanc," I explained, "the florist from Main Street? Next to Brookhoppers?"

"Yes?" said Iris.

"I was wondering if you'd like to get together for lunch this week?"

Iris didn't answer right away.

"I'd like to talk to you."

"That really isn't necessary," she said.

"Because you're writing me off as a total asshole?"

Iris laughed and I took the opening: "It's not even a question of being rehabilitated; I'm actually quite agreeable in most situations."

"That's what Dennis tells me." In a slightly thawed tone she said, "I'm done by noon on Wednesdays."

"This Wednesday?"

"What time?"

"A little later? One o'clock? Then I can get my orders filled."

"The Faculty Club at one?" asked Iris.

144

"I can't treat you at the Faculty Club, and I wanted to go someplace where you'd be my guest."

"That isn't necessary."

"I asked you to lunch and I'd like to treat you."

"All right. You pick."

"Do you like Japanese? We could go to Kobe's."

"Kobe's at one, on Wednesday," confirmed Iris.

"Thank you," I said.

Do you believe I *forgot?* I left her sitting at Kobe's for half an hour while I sat in the back room at Forget-Me-Not, thinking it was Tuesday because we'd been closed Monday for Martin Luther King Day, and it felt like my second day at work. Then I saw the date on an order: "for 2 p.m. delivery today, Wed.," Robin had written.

Not an auspicious beginning to my friendship with Iris. I realized in enough time to call the restaurant, explain my gaffe to the maître d' with the hope he'd pass along my profuse apologies to Iris and prevail upon her to sit tight.

I ran the six blocks to Kobe's, impressively out of breath and contrite upon arrival. She was wearing a navy blue wool suit with a short jacket, and looked as if she'd just left the boardroom. I was wearing jeans and an oversized cotton sweater that hung below my parka. "I honest to God thought it was Tuesday," I told her. "The holiday threw me off." On Wednesday—when I thought Wednesday was tomorrow—I had planned to wear a Libby dress and to look smart.

Iris accepted my apology; said she had no appointments this afternoon and had graded two papers while waiting for me.

"You're being a good sport," I said. "I hope it's not because you have such low expectations of me."

Iris smiled politely.

"About the peach dress at Libby's store," I began.

145

"I think we've covered that," said Iris.

"I can't believe I got so agitated over someone else's merchandise."

"My sentiments exactly," said Iris.

"It wasn't really the dress at all—not the sale, anyway. It was something else. . . ."

"It always is."

"It was like a symbol of something to me."

"And what would that be?"

I thought for a few seconds. "My life in Harrow."

"You knew this then, or is this a theory you came up with after the fact?"

"Both. I knew I was reacting to something other than you buying a dress, but it took some time for me to analyze it."

"Let's order first," said Iris. She signaled to our waitress, and we both ordered the same luncheon special: soup, cucumber salad, six pieces of sushi and green tea.

"How do you mean 'the symbol of your life in Harrow'?"

"It's like this: no matter how perfect your design is—whether it's a dress or a wedding bouquet—it still takes someone else to pull it off. Even if it's the perfect dress for the perfect occasion on the perfect body, it takes that customer to validate it. It'll never leave the store if you only please yourself. . . . Do you see what I mean?"

"You're in a service-oriented business. You're in it to design flowers and to design dresses that people will buy. You're not a lawyer or a stockbroker or a consultant—"

"I'm a *kind* of consultant. I could even call myself that."

Iris, in what sounded like her classroom case-study voice, asked, "What's your background?"

"I've been here for a year and a half—"

"Here? Meaning what?"

"At Forget-Me-Not, as floral designer."

"Do you have people under you? Supervisory duties?"

"Roger, my cousin, does some basic arrangements, which I usually check over before they leave the store—"

"Good."

"He's just not that great at arranging, but he still owns the store. I wouldn't say I *supervise* him. I just boss him around sometimes out of habit. I'm older than he is."

"What else do you do?" Iris asked, moving on, her mind made up on supervision.

"I talk to brides and mothers of brides a couple of months before the wedding and scope out the place, the type of affair they want, how much they can afford, the colors. . . ."

"All consulting, by the way," Iris snapped.

"I do some research, find some old photographs in books of period pieces—Victorian, Edwardian. Movie stills sometimes, or sketches of medieval weddings, stuff like that. I keep a file. Lots of times the bride brings in a picture of something she saw in a magazine."

"What else do you do besides bridal consultations?"

"Everything—funerals, bar mitzvahs, bat mitzvahs . . . I do a lot of stuff for MacMillan; everything at the president's house and all development office functions."

Iris looked moderately impressed: People with titles and advanced degrees used me then. "You must be good," she said.

"I'm very good. I'm certainly the best designer in Harrow."

"Good. Don't apologize for that."

"I rarely apologize for anything."

Iris, smiling grimly, said, "Yet you called me up and invited me to lunch specifically so that you could apologize."

"That's true."

"Because . . . ?"

"Because I knew I offended you."

"And you had a reason that you didn't want me to remain offended?"

"Sure. Dennis."

"Did he ask you to apologize?"

"Just the opposite."

"Why?"

"I have a big mouth. I generally say what's on my mind and Dennis knows that."

Iris took a few sips from her miso soup and said from behind the bowl, "What's on your mind that would make Dennis nervous?"

I broke apart my chopsticks and started in on my salad. Iris waited. "Look," I finally said, "I have no hidden agenda. I want to apologize and I want to be your friend."

Iris leaned closer and, pronouncing every word as if I were taking dictation, "You're curious about me and I'd like to know why."

Would you like me to hire a skywriter, Iris? You were married to Dennis and you left him when you turned lesbian? Anyone ever find that mildly interesting before, or am I the first?

"I understand your friend's interest in me," Iris continued.

"Friend?"

"Libby Mitchell. Dennis told me. Her infatuation with him is a little pathetic."

I said, well, that's a pretty strong—

"What is it based on? Some unfulfilled teenage longing, part rebellion, part regret, part fantasy?"

What fantasy? I asked.

"I know the patterns. Dennis Vaughan was deified in high school. He couldn't be an ordinary nice kid . . . good

148

athlete . . . decent student. He had to be a superstar. There's books written on this subject. It's well-meaning racism. And Libby Mitchell happens to be stuck in a time warp."

"Getchel," I corrected.

She turned her attention to the plate of sushi, beckoning for the waitress. "What are these?" she demanded.

The waitress pointed to each piece in turn. "Yellowtail, smoked eel, shrimp, halibut, California roll, salmon."

"I'd like more ginger," said Iris.

"I don't use this much ginger. You're welcome to it."

She hesitated. Germ phobia, I thought; one of my least favorite traits. I decided to test it, rather than walk around unfairly labeling Iris as a fanatic. "I don't have a cold or anything," I said.

"Thank you anyway. I'll need more than that eventually."

"And it's kind of unappetizing to eat off someone else's plate, isn't it?" I prompted.

"Some people don't mind, but I wasn't brought up with that," said Iris.

"Where was that?" I asked.

"Queens."

I'd never been to Queens and had nothing to add. I asked if Geraldine Ferraro had been her congresswoman.

Iris said yes as if it were the most uninspired question ever posed.

"I guess that's like asking someone from Massachusetts if Ted Kennedy is their senator," I said. "When I was living in California people used to say to me, 'How come you don't talk like a Kennedy?'"

No response from Iris. Happily, the waitress appeared with the extra ginger. I asked her to save me a scoop of red bean ice cream. No hurry.

Still trying, I smiled at Iris. I asked in sisterly fashion if she had maintained cordial relations with Dennis's parents or sister.

"No I don't."

"I got to know them when I did Diana's wedding."

"I didn't even know Diana got married."

"She married a white guy," I said tentatively. "They were all very civilized about it, but I had the sense the Vaughans weren't pleased."

Iris shrugged. "I don't know what they thought would happen in this town."

I played with some stray grains of rice on my place mat, making them stick to my index finger. "I think his parents would be really upset if Dennis got involved with a white woman. Both their kids marrying out of the fold might make them feel as if they'd failed in some way."

Iris shrugged. "They probably just want to see him happy."

"Sometimes I wonder if that's the big obstacle with Dennis having a relationship. He'd refuse to get involved with a white woman for reasons that have nothing to do with his feelings, and more to do with the racial stuff, even if it's just to please his parents."

"Is that your theory? That he's cutting himself off from your friend because she's white and he's holding out for a black woman?"

The waitress brought my ice cream stuck with slices of apple and orange. I said, "Not Libby, necessarily. Any woman."

Iris stared at me, then said, leaning a few inches over the table, "I'd just go for it. I wouldn't concoct any theories."

"Excuse me?" I said.

She smiled for the first time. "Do I look like a fool?"

"No—"

"Who've you been discussing your love life with that they don't see through this whole sociology lecture? I'd say fools."

I said carefully, "I think you misunderstood my point."

Iris leaned back into the upholstered banquette and grinned. "I think I understand it more than I'm supposed to."

I tasted my ice cream, using an apple slice as a scoop. Finally I said, "And what if you were right?"

"I told you already—go for it. That's what you have to do with Dennis, serve it to him on a platter. For all his success with the fly-fishing crowd, he's got zero confidence with women. He won't take any risks."

"You talk to him?" I asked.

"Rarely."

"You know a lot."

Iris didn't answer immediately, but looked at me as if measuring the distance traveled today. When she spoke it was matter-of-factly: "I did it to him, marrying him when I shouldn't have been getting married. Screwing up his head—the self-esteem thing, the masculinity thing."

"And now you want . . . what? To help him? To undo the deed?"

Iris picked up her spoon and dipped into my red bean ice cream uninvited. Spoon poised, she asked, "Anything wrong with that?"

17

Nick

Dennis was on the phone, making doodles on a message pad when I arrived at Brookhoppers with my coffee. He rolled his eyes for my benefit as if to say, "Nothing important, just making a customer happy." He returned to the unseen caller with sudden, solemn attention. "You want to balance the size of the fly with the size of the tippet. What are you using?" He bobbed his head impatiently as if he knew this exchange by heart. "Okay. For a fourteen, you're better off using a four-X . . . No, this is Dennis." I knew the caller was saying, "Holy mackerel, you mean I call the shop and I get Dennis Vaughan, just like that? You answer the *phone?*"

"You're welcome," said Dennis. "Any time." He hung up and said neutrally, "Hi, Melinda."

"Hi."

"What's up?"

"I'm taking a break."

He came out from behind the counter and sat down at the fly-tying setup in the window. I followed him there. I said that I'd followed through on my impulse to have lunch with Iris and had found her to be reasonable company. My first impression, frankly, had been cold bitch, but she was a very bright woman, even insightful—

His scissors poised a second longer than usual under the magnifying lense before snipping a thread off the feathery mottled bug in progress. It reminded me suddenly of what I did, in a way I hadn't noticed before. I had just finished an English bouquet, deceptively free looking but each stem actually wired: blush roses, ivy, stephanotis, lilies of the valley each on its own stiff perch just so it could look as if the bride harvested them in a fresh, crisp bouquet, the kind God intended brides to carry, the exact kind that wilted to a limp mess without my intervention.

He batted away the magnifying glass on its gooseneck stem and smiled at the finished product. I asked what it was supposed to be.

"A mosquito. Can't you tell?" He called to Lyman, "Want to take over?"

Lyman did a goofy shuffle in one spot to indicate he was raring to go; a joke of course—none of them liked too long a stint at what they called the floor show.

Lyman, always charming, said, "Does Melinda go along with the job?"

"No she doesn't," Dennis said.

"I think I have my own job somewhere," I said.

Lyman slipped into Dennis's seat. Grinning, he asked, "Did you tell her?"

It had the scent of gossip. "Tell me what?" I demanded.

Lyman mouthed something to Dennis and Dennis shook his head.

I told them they were being extremely rude. Once you say something like "Did you tell her?" you are duty-bound to fill in the blanks.

Lyman shrugged apologetically as if he'd crossed over into the unexplored territory of Dennis's annoyance.

"Can you give me a hint at least?"

"It's none of my business," Lyman began, "except that it sort of is."

I recognized that tone. It was the signal for a speech: best friend of the wronged party speaks up, usually at the end of one aggrieved boyfriend's term. And Lyman fit the profile: confident, loyal, no personal ax to grind except his buddy's well-being.

"It's about Nick, which probably doesn't surprise you."

"Nick?"

Lyman's smile broadened. "You've noticed?"

"I know Nick."

"I mean you haven't noticed his . . . regard for you."

"Isn't he a kid?"

"Twenty-five next month," said Lyman. "Just a year younger than me."

"Do you know something for a fact or are you putting two and two together on your own?" Dennis asked him.

"I know."

I looked toward the workroom. "Would he kill you for telling me?"

"Depends," said Lyman. "Certainly not if you're going to follow it up in a rewarding way."

Nick with the brown beard and the round wire-rims, the one Lyman and Dennis called in—not to charm the customers but for the best clinch knot, for the last word on every fishable inch of the Starkfield—the one who, now that I thought about it, would hold a crush very close to the Velcroed flaps of his vest. "Nick?" I repeated.

"Definitely," said Lyman.

"He's never—"

"He wouldn't," said Dennis.

"I never noticed anything that I'd categorize as a move. . . ."

"You don't notice shy men. You don't have to. There's enough confident guys in this world who speak up first and fill up your dance card," said Dennis—with a little too much conviction, I thought.

That's what they discussed among themselves: Could Melinda *ever* be attracted to anyone who didn't share her loudmouth, be-popular, no-sweat view of life? Certainly not the high school boyfriend composite of Eddie-Brad-Danny-Billy-Wally; certainly none of the handsome men who sauntered into Forget-Me-Not and left rather easily with her phone number.

"You didn't get any vibes about this?" asked Lyman.

"No."

"Would you consider it?"

"Have you seen my social calendar lately?"

"Is that a yes?" asked Lyman.

"What do you think?" I asked Dennis.

He stared for a few beats beyond his usual, easy response time. "Do you mean do I mind if you went out with Nick?"

"However you take it is how I mean it."

"I don't have any say over my employees' love life."

"It's not like it's going to mean you'll be hanging around here any more than you already do," said Lyman.

I looked at Dennis. To Lyman I said, "Sure."

"You hardly know him," said Dennis.

"Maybe I'd like to get to know him better. And maybe I have my own reasons."

"You jumped right into it as if, no big deal, I'll give the guy a break—have to eat anyway . . . why not let him eat his sandwich at the same table."

I curled my lip. "I can see you really have a lot of faith in my character."

"Look," said Dennis, "I have to say this because I love Nick and because this can of worms got opened right under my nose: Don't use him. I'd rather you didn't ask him to lunch if you think there isn't a chance for something to grow out of it. I don't want him hurt. He's not asking for anything and I don't know if you have the kind of relationships where the guy comes away stronger and better for having been thrown over."

"And maybe you've been giving too much advice to your fans and it gives you the idea that you're 'Ask Beth.'"

"I didn't mean to sound judgmental—"

"Is that what the rest of the world does?" I asked angrily. "Comes away stronger and better after getting dumped? Is that what happened to you?"

"If you're talking—"

"Well, if you did it wasn't because your wife was such a fine and good person, because I can testify firsthand about *that*—but because you shouldn't have married her in the first place. If you came away stronger it was because you came away at all."

Lyman put his arm around my shoulders and squeezed, as if he'd suddenly remembered how good they were supposed to be with all kinds of customers and crackpots. "Only a good friend would say something like that, right? He's trying to be constructive. He wasn't trying to be mean. Besides, you say whatever you feel like to him and he doesn't take offense."

"I say things to him which qualify as advice, which is different. I'm not talking about his character flaws."

Dennis said, "I'm perfect. I'm the 1980 recipient of the Paul J. Johnston Jr. Memorial trophy. I thought you knew that."

I smiled begrudgingly. I asked if Nick was out back listening to all of this.

"He comes in at noon. He works till nine."

"And what do you recommend as a first move, as long as you're choreographing?"

"Why don't you just talk to him," said Lyman, still cheerful and oblivious.

"I've talked to him plenty of times."

"Come in when he's here alone so he doesn't think you're looking for Dennis. Make it a natural progression. If you like him enough to spend some time with him outside the store then suggest lunch. Or dinner."

I nudged Dennis's arm with my elbow. "He'll die, right? He'll think he died and went to heaven."

Dennis groaned and asked if I'd ever, even for one minute, experienced a moment of self-doubt.

I returned obediently to Brookhoppers at 3 p.m., a plausible time for a coffee break. Nick was waiting on a customer, a man in a handsome navy blue blazer and gray flannel trousers; a man, I realized, like the others in my unsuccessful history who I'd notice over a calm and flannel-shirted Nick any day. The man was listening—fly fishermen listen to the point of reverence in Brookhoppers. Nick was holding a net and turning the grip in his hand saying, "not because you're necessarily going to hook into such big fish but because it'll help you land it more reliably and stress it less."

Nick looked up at the sound of the door and acknowledged me with a barely noticeable nod. The customer took the net from Nick and made arcs in the air, forehand, backhand, borrowing from his tennis game.

"Hi, Nick," I said.

Another nod and the suggestion of a polite smile. The customer looked over to see who was interrupting the sacred ritual of being outfitted for the sacred sport. It was not a time to take in a woman's presence, even mine. I said, "Sorry."

Nick continued, placing different-sized nets in the guy's hands. This was not a price-tag slave; this guy wanted what looked best, what felt right, what would be recognized on the river as the equipment of an insider. Nail clippers will do the job *almost* as well? What does the job better? This kit, this expensive one, with the scissors and file *and* the clippers? I'll take it. Led by Nick, they moved on: waders, vest, hat, glasses, map, fly-fishing manual, fly box, fly ointment. Nick's patience and attention span were award-winning; he was the Mister Rogers of the sales floor. And the problem with Brookhoppers was I couldn't invent a nonsocial reason for being there: no newspapers for sale; no gum or cough drops by the register. I stood there foolishly while Nick, alleged admirer of mine, explained everything there was to know about taking that first trout on a fly.

Finally I walked to the door. Nick called, "Were you looking for Dennis, Melinda?"

"No, you," I answered and left.

A minute before five, Nick came into Forget-Me-Not. Interestingly, Robin did not alert me or flutter around the way she usually did when a potential husband entered the store. Nick asked if Melinda were there, and was she free. I heard his voice and came out.

"When you left you said you were looking for me," said Nick.

"I was."

"Did you have a question?"

I didn't want Robin involved and I could see she was all ears. I said to Nick, "Actually, I needed a gift for my stepfather. Maybe I'll come by when I'm done here."

"We're open till nine," said Nick.

"I'll do that."

Robin said when Nick had left, "They have nice pullovers on sale at Goldenberg's."

"I don't wear pullovers much," I said.

"For your stepfather. I bought one for Roger and his father to put away for next Christmas. And they gift-wrap free."

"I'm getting him something for fishing. You can't go wrong with a new vest and a few new flies."

"When's his birthday?" Robin asked.

"Next month."

"I like to get these things out of the way, too," she said approvingly.

I went home to shower and change before dropping in on Nick. I put on a black wool jersey dress that Libby had designed. Its long sleeves and longish skirt confused people—how exactly did something vaguely Amish in volume do so much for a body. Nick, I figured, would not even notice I had changed clothes. It would register subliminally and he would think I looked spectacular in an unspecific way. I put on black flats—after all I was supposed to be coming from work and who arranged flowers in high heels?—and fluffed my hair out to evening volume. No perfume; Nick would like the smell of soap as much as anything.

I drove back to the store around eight, refusing my mother's offer of dinner. I told her I was going to meet a customer for a wedding consultation.

"You look awfully nice," she said.

"Oh?" I said. "Am I too dressed up?" I had no jewelry on, after all. And it was supposed to be that all-purpose black dress that could serve in all but the most formal situations.

"Who's the client?" my mother asked.

"A bride."

"Must be a nice wedding," she said.

"Do I look as if I'm trying too hard?"

"I suppose you could be going out on a date afterward. It's not her business how dressed up you are for a consultation." She

159

thought this over and asked if the groom was going to be there, as if she'd hit on an explanation.

I said I didn't think so. Just the bride and her mother, two women who dressed smartly and had progressive ideas about church arrangements.

"That's nice," my mother said.

"I might be home late."

"I never notice such things," she said, rolling her eyes.

I stopped in at Forget-Me-Not to give my lies some foundation in truth. I looked at the next day's orders, put them in the sequence I'd feel like doing them tomorrow from most prosaic to most creative. I tidied up my work table, which would please Robin and Roger, and scrubbed the ancient coffee residue from the insides of two mugs. It was 8:35, a good time to go next door. I could talk to Nick, buy a gift for Gerry if necessary, and be there when he locked up without the appearance of dawdling. We'd go to Buddy's for a drink, maybe even a dance, and I'd take it from there.

There was no one in Brookhoppers at 8:40. Nick was putting many pairs of waders back into their rightful boxes as if his last customer had been hard to fit. "Hi, Melinda," he said wearily. This was not a man excited to see me; this was a man who'd worked too many hours and hoped the front door would not open again before closing.

"Busy night?" I asked.

"Not exactly."

"Tough customers?"

"Sort of," said Nick. "What do you need?"

I had this sudden flash that it was all a mistake, either misreported by Lyman or misunderstood by me. Men with crushes on me were flustered when I spoke to them, but Nick was only tired. He wasn't even being as nice to me as he'd been to customers all day; that banker/attorney type in the morning could have nominated Nick for salesman of the year. Now he was acting as if a nuisance, the chronic social butterfly on her endless coffee break, had arrived to prolong his torture.

"I'm sorry," I said. "You look dead. I won't bother you."

Nick sat down, collapsed down, onto one of the stools his big-footed fishermen rested their feet on to be fitted. He smiled apologetically and said, "No, *I'm* sorry."

"Is something wrong?" I asked. (A coy question. In movies wouldn't the shy suitor say, "I looked up and saw you and, gosh, Melinda, I knew I could never have you, and suddenly it all seemed so hopeless . . ."?)

Nick said, "My dog is sick and I wanted to run her over to the vet's tonight but no one could cover for me."

"Is it serious?"

"She seems kind of weak in the legs. She fell going down the stairs."

"Is she old?"

"Four."

"So it's not old age or anything?"

"No. She's real healthy and she's rock solid on her feet. This scares the shit out of me."

"Are they open at night?"

"Someone's on call. I'm taking her in as soon as I close."

"What are you waiting for? You think somebody's life is going to depend on buying a fly at eight-forty-five p.m.? Get out of here. Dennis wouldn't care if you closed a little early. No one's gonna show up now anyway."

"You showed up," Nick said after a few moments.

"And if the store had been closed? I'd have come back tomorrow."

"I don't know. . . ."

"You go. I'll stay and lock up at nine. If some guy comes in

161

looking for something, I'll distract him." Nick didn't respond to my straight line; didn't smile as if to say, "Boy, if anyone could do that it would be you, Melinda." I added, "I can even figure out which waders go in which boxes. I'll leave them in a stack right on this chair and you can come in early tomorrow or whenever."

"You mean it?"

"Absolutely. I've locked up for Dennis before. It's pretty small potatoes compared to your dog's health," I said, ever magnanimous.

He stood up. "You're right. I'm going. Don't forget the lights and the alarm." At the door, parka hurriedly bunched up in his arms, he said, "This is so nice of you."

Eight-forty-five. Big deal, fifteen minutes on a January night. I punched in the alarm code, locked up, and left.

162

18

The Ultimate Pragmatist

Nick's dog, it turned out, had Lyme disease. The symptoms were classic, the vet said; a blood titer confirmed it and the cure was to give Vivi nine gigantic erythromycin pills a day for one week, which he disguised in a gob of butter. I found all this out because I inquired the next morning, learned first of the vet's hunch and the next day of the confirmed diagnosis. It's not that I had fallen in love or anything, but, given the state of my dance card, Nick wasn't the worst idea ever hatched.

Let me explain what he looked like: All the friendly, brown-bearded, hazel-eyed, twenty-five-year-old men who ever sold you cross-country skis or showed you to your table at a vegetarian restaurant or checked your vise at a U-frame-it shop. He wore long underwear beneath his flannel shirts so that edges of the thermal gray always appeared at his wrists and neck. He wore blue jeans and running shoes in summer; L.L. Bean corduroys and hiking boots in winter, from which you could view two inches of his gray rag socks. Smart, courteous, professional; smiled at your jokes but didn't know how to flirt. Went to college in the country—especially Dartmouth, Bowdoin, Hampshire, University of Vermont—and after graduation in Hanover, Amherst, Durham, Burlington or Orono expanded his job as salesman of things outdoorsy and/or healthy from part-time to full-time, which led to increased responsibility and eventual management. He didn't own a suit or tie and, once promoted, was too democratic to use his office for anything but extra storage. His employees were "associates" or "representatives" or "waitrons." Together they had dogs, four-wheel-drive vehicles, and bike racks; they had plastic honey bears next to their office coffee machines.

In short, not my type.

But there's such a thing as pragmatism. I read an O. Henry story in my high school anthology about this good boxer who freezes when he's in the ring. Walking down the street, he meets a fancy guy and his entourage. They shove him around and the boxer knocks out the fancy guy with one punch. His bodyguards say, "Do you know who this is? He's the world heavyweight champion." The man, our hero, now finds the nerve to call the woman he's loved from afar to confess his love. She tells him to come over, and when he arrives, a starry-eyed younger sister he'd never noticed before greets him—she's the one who answered the phone—and says she's loved him, too, from afar but thought it was her older sister he had a thing for. That's where the pragmatism comes in: he doesn't say, "Oops. I didn't know that was you on the phone; there's been a bad mistake; I thought I was talking to her." Instead, he notices her eyes and hair and her beauty and falls in love on the spot. I was crazy about that story,

"The Ultimate Pragmatist." I didn't even know what pragmatist meant for another five years, and I certainly wasn't the kind of student who looked it up in the dictionary.

Meanwhile, back in real life, nothing had passed between me and Nick that could remotely be construed as personal. He thanked me repeatedly for closing up the night before, and sent medical bulletins on Vivi through Dennis. He kept Vivi with him at Brookhoppers so he could give her the pills every two hours and forty minutes. This was no problem, of course, because fly fishermen love big yellow dogs, particularly ones with bandanas around their necks and an outdoorsy disease. You'd think he'd have brought Vivi around to meet me at my shop, the perfect excuse for a social call, but he didn't. I found myself in the oddest position—worrying about, even pursuing, a man I'd never thought twice about until I'd been informed that he liked me, *really* liked me, and it was my opportunity to prove myself less superficial and uncaring than my adolescent boyfriends would testify to.

Finally, after a week of letting this distract me, even annoy me, I went over to Brookhoppers with a specific agenda, to ask Nick out. Dennis sent me out back where Nick was unpacking a new shipment of books. I said I hadn't seen Vivi out front today. Was she okay?

He said she had finished the course of the medicine and was back at home. A follow-up blood test would tell them if the Lyme disease had been cured.

"She doesn't mind staying home all day?"

"She's in the yard. I built a run for her and there's a shed for when it rains."

"Oh," I said. "I guess dogs like being outside."

Nick's cheeks, I noticed, were turning pink, as our conversation sank downward into self-conscious dog talk. I knew he knew why

I was there; that this was social. There was something about going all the way into the back room, something much more deliberate than conversation out front, that announced my intentions.

"Would you like to have dinner together after work some night?" I asked.

Nick straightened the stack of books in front of him and pushed them away to make room for another title.

"I'd invite you for dinner, but I live with my mother so it's a little awkward," I continued. "I was thinking maybe just Buddy's."

Nick managed only an embarrassed shrug.

"Is that a yes?"

"I don't know."

"Do you want to think about it," I said, still confident.

He shrugged again. "You caught me off-guard."

Paying you all this attention for days? Asking after your stupid dog for a week? "Did I?" I said innocently.

"I'm really flattered that you would ask—"

Flattered? The universal *no*.

"—But I'd have to think about it."

"Is it because I asked *you*? Is that not how you like to do things?"

"No," said Nick. "I like that. In general."

Jesus fucking Christ: He was saying no.

I called Martha Schiff-Shulman at her office and said, "Listen to this."

"Something's not right," she said after hearing my synopsis. "How long ago was this alleged crush? Was Lyman acting on recent information?"

"He seemed to think so."

"Are you attracted to this Nick?"

166

"I could be."

"Which one is he?"

"The beard and wire-rim glasses."

"And the other one's name?"

"Lyman."

"How old?"

"Twenty-five."

"Young," said Martha. I heard a knock in the background and an exchange with a student where she bargained for two more minutes on the phone.

"Do you have to get off?"

"In a sec. What do *you* think is going on?"

"I think there was a break in the circuit somewhere between Lyman and Nick, and Lyman got it wrong."

"Or maybe Nick doesn't want to make the boss angry."

"Huh?" I said.

"You heard me," said Martha.

Roger pouted when I came in and said he'd taken two orders over the phone, both of which could have used my input: one must've been a call from the college; who else would want to know what kind of flower petals were edible?

"What'd you say?"

"I said give me your number and I'd have our expert call you back."

"Be happy to," I said, walking past Roger to the back room. He followed me with pink message slips. I put my pocketbook into the bottom drawer of my file cabinet and put on the short green kimono which I used as a smock. Roger still looked unhappy. I said, "I wasn't goofing off. I was doing customer relations over coffee."

"Morning's not a good time for customer relations," he said.

"I'll be working late tonight, and I have a wedding tomorrow, so if we're talking total hours worked, you're worrying about nothing. "I'll probably be here until eight tonight."

"Whose wedding?"

I gave him the bride's name and added, "Moss Creek Country Club. Big job."

I could see Roger's face release some of its resentment, so I moved in for the final peace offering. "Something else bothering you?" I asked.

"Unh-uh," he said.

"You sure?"

"I'm sure."

"Everything okay at home? The girls okay?"

"They're fine."

I watched him carefully, saw he didn't start back toward the front, but stood there, as if waiting for me to hit the right question. "Everything okay between you and Robin?"

He had no acting ability whatsoever, so even though he said, "Yeah," I could tell this was it.

"Did you have a fight?" I asked.

He shook his head.

"Do you want to talk about it?"

Shook his head again.

"Are you sure?"

"Nothing's wrong," said Roger.

"You can talk to me, you know."

He stood there for a few seconds, then slapped the front of his thighs with a couple of bongo-drum taps as a way of saying, "Let's get back to work." I knew Roger, though, and knew that he was thanking me, that he hadn't been able to hug me or squeeze my shoulder, and that his own peculiar physical gesture was as close as he would get.

Robin came in late—she cleaned their house every Friday morning, a ritual set in stone. She was as cheerful as ever, making her usual irritating observations about the benefits of name-brand cleaning products. Roger remained glum. Robin didn't seem to notice. I concluded that despite his own conversational deficiencies, despite the fact that this was how Robin always carried on, something had happened to Roger and he couldn't stand her anymore.

I was still at work, a half hour past closing time, when I saw Dennis, Libby, Nick and Lyman together, all but me of the 300-block unmarried merchants, walking down Main together, the stride of good friends headed for a pleasant evening together. I wanted to grab my coat and run after them and yell, "Hey, wait for me. I'm coming with you." But I didn't. I wasn't eight or twelve or fifteen anymore or any of those ages where being left behind should feel like this. I was thirty with work to do and some dignity. Was there an explanation for the omission of me, their leader? The three men by themselves might have meant any variation on a business dinner; I wouldn't even have noticed an exclusively Brookhoppers contingent walking by.

But Libby as their centerpiece, one woman and three men? Hadn't anyone thought to include me? Hadn't anybody wanted me along? My friend Libby? My admirer Nick? My friends Lyman and Dennis? Even if they'd forgotten, wouldn't walking by Forget-Me-Not remind them?

Laughing, leaning around each other to direct funny comments to a particular appreciative ear, they were a picture of carefree youth, a college recruitment videotape of handsome boys and girls having healthy, interracial fun between classes. I hated them at that moment for forgetting me and for brazenly walking by the shop. They might as well have stuck their tongues out as they

169

passed the sprayed-on snowy meadow I had designed for the window; might just as well have looked past my white poinsettias, my dwarf birches, my glittery pine cones to me, abandoned and stunned behind the counter, and jeered.

19

More Love on Main

I went home to mope and my mother noticed. She made me an omelette and sat down with me at the kitchen table, expecting to hear something more substantive than friends walked by the shop and didn't stop.

"Maybe they were just walking to their cars," she said.

"They weren't."

"How do you know?"

"I know their habits. They were going someplace together, all four of them."

"I don't get it," said my mother.

I rose to get the bottle of salsa, a culinary habit acquired in California which irritated my mother. She ate her salads dry and her tuna moistened with plain yogurt, and thought salsa on eggs was the moral equivalent of ketchup. I sat down again, spooned a ribbon of salsa across my omelette, and said, "I felt left out. I'm not saying it's logical, but it's the way I felt."

"Are you done with that?" she asked, her nose wrinkling in the direction of the jar.

"I guess."

She tightened the cap and put it back in the refrigerator, a tray on the door where she lined the other untouchables.

"I was pathetic. I had to leave; I was too upset to work after that. Do you believe it?"

"I don't get it," my mother repeated.

"What don't you get?" I snapped.

"What about them walking down the street together upset you? Was it because Libby was with them and not you?"

"Of course! If she hadn't been with them, it would have been just Dennis and his two employees. I wouldn't have thought anything of it."

My mother sat down one chair closer. "Is something else bothering you? Did you and Libby have an argument or anything? I haven't heard you mention her much over the past couple of weeks."

"We've all been busier than usual."

"Are these men married?" my mother asked.

"You know Dennis isn't married. The other two are young."

"Could Libby be dating one of them?"

"No."

My mother was temporarily stumped. "Are they black?" she finally asked.

"No. You've seen Nick and Lyman. They've been with Dennis since the beginning. Do you think only blacks work for blacks?"

"It's a legitimate question if you're trying to figure things out."

"I'm not trying to figure things out! I'm just pissed at myself for acting like I'm in high school."

My mother thought things over while she watched me eat. "Are

172

you expecting your period?" she asked after a few moments. "You could be feeling a little blue."

I shrugged.

"Do you want some tea?"

"Coffee?"

"How many cups did you have today?"

I said I didn't remember exactly. Three?

"Have decaf and I'll join you."

I said okay.

She put the coffee on to drip and sat down again. I told her the omelette was delicious; that I hadn't realized how hungry I had been.

"What did you have for lunch?"

"Tuna on whole wheat with sprouts and a V-8," I lied.

"What time was that?"

"One-ish."

"You should have a little something for a snack midafternoon. You were probably hungry and didn't realize that that was what was making you irritable. You should keep some fruit in the cooler or a carton of yogurt."

"I'm too busy to stop usually."

"How long does it take to eat a piece of fruit?"

"I'll try to remember," I said.

She took away my plate and silverware and got mugs for both of us. I made a gesture toward standing and helping, but she told me to sit; I was tired. She'd get the coffee, the milk, the homemade cookies she had made with no white flour and no white sugar.

When she was seated again, dessert before us, she smiled and said, "This is nice, isn't it? I don't feel as if I ever get a chance to talk to you except on the run."

"It just seems that way."

"I thought when you moved home there'd be lots of nights like this."

"You knew I'd be busy—"

She tapped her forehead with two fingers. "Up here I knew what you were saying, but I had my own view of what it meant to have you as a grown-up under the same roof. I wasn't scared away by that stuff about you coming and going as you pleased without the third degree because I said to myself, 'Good. I don't want to be the matron here. She's an adult. Who needs to concern myself with who she's out with and what time she's getting back!' I had enough of that when you were a teenager. You thought it was freeing *you* up to have some ground rules about coming and going as you pleased, but actually it was freeing *me* up. Except I kept my half of the bargain but you still act like I'm the jailer."

"I have no complaints," I said. "I think you've made it easy for me to be back here."

"I'm an interesting person, you know," said my mother after a pause and a swallow of coffee.

"I know that."

"I think you get your flair and your . . . nerve from me."

"That could be."

"I mean it. People knew who I was in high school. I didn't just get good grades; I was popular with boys *and* girls. Some of it was because of my brothers, but not all of it. Things haven't changed that much between men and women since I was in high school. We thought we were sneaking around and hiding things from my parents; we thought we *discovered* it."

This was not startling news. I'd seen her scrapbooks and her snapshots; I'd heard the story about the senior football captain who came up to her—a mere junior usher—and said, "I just thought I should tell you I've been in love with you for two years and now I'm leaving and it's too late," kissed her cheek, and walked back into the crowd.

174

"I've told you the story about Russell Rousseau—"

"The football captain? About a hundred times. How come you didn't walk after him and say, 'Okay. Now you've told me. Where do we go from here?'"

My mother smiled. "Is that what you would have done?"

"Sure. A guy tells you he's been in love with you for two years then walks away?"

"The truth is, there are football captains and there are football captains. This was no Adonis. This was the big hulking kind, the kind who didn't change his shirt all that often."

"*Now* you tell me."

"He did say that to me, though. And I'm sure it wasn't an easy thing to do, to come up to practically a complete stranger at graduation."

"Whatever happened to him?" I asked.

She laughed at something else, something from back then. I asked her what.

"My brother John played with him. He was a halfback on the same team; very fast. High scorer or close to it. He used to say about Rusty, "He's big, but he's slow." She laughed again. "I really knew a lot about football. I guess I still do."

"What happened to him?" I asked again.

"Farmed, I guess. His folks had a tree farm."

"He didn't get recruited by colleges?"

"Not smart enough. If he hadn't been so big, he would've gone to the voke, but I suppose they got him to come to the high school so he could play football and basketball. In those days you could flunk everything and still play."

"But he must have graduated; that was the scene of the famous declaration."

My mother smiled modestly.

"Do you ever look back and think of someone who you might

175

not have been attracted to then because he was . . . you know— didn't stand out in any way or wasn't your type at the time. And now you wonder how come you never noticed him?"

"Not Rusty Rousseau!"

"I know. I meant someone you got to know later, maybe when you were older and wiser and not looking for flash."

"Why?"

"I'm just asking. It's been called to my attention that the kind of men I'm attracted to have not been so quick to reciprocate."

My mother took one of her unappetizingly healthy-looking cookies and bit into it. I could tell it had no give—that she had cut down on the fat and made them with a few tablespoons of canola oil. Raisins offered the only taste and chewability. "Mmmm," she said. "The wheat germ gives it a nice nuttiness."

I took one and dunked it in my coffee. I knew from experience.

"Lou Schiner," she said.

"Lou Schiner," I repeated. "The fish man?"

My mother nodded.

"What brought that up?"

"You asked me who I admired now that I wouldn't have noticed when I was young and foolish so I answered Lou Schiner."

"I never know which is which."

"Lou is the taller one with the sick wife; Manny has the darker complexion."

"He just popped into your mind?"

"I go there at least twice a week. No one else can touch his fish."

"What else?" I asked.

"We talk. He's been on the same corner for years and years, so he knows everybody. He was there before Harrow was fashionable, when people just wanted scrod and swordfish and a lobster now and then. Now the gourmet cooks come in, these college

176

professors, and special-order monkfish and shrimp with their heads on and squid by its Italian name." She laughed at the pretentious shoppers. "I'm one of the few customers from the old days. I come in after five and he knocks a dollar or two off my fish; he knows I appreciate the stories."

"Is this friendship new?" I asked.

"You won't believe it," she said, clicking into another level of confidence. "We started talking at our reunion. I'd always been a customer, but we hadn't ever said anything besides exchanging pleasantries."

"And then what?"

She looked at me as if measuring something; I knew it had to be how far she could go, how much she could trust me; whose side I'd be on. Children could have funny reactions to things; funny and irrational loyalties to boring stepfathers. She said slowly, "And then we danced."

"I didn't buy that much fish; not as much as I buy now. Your father liked his meat and potatoes so we'd have fish on Fridays only, but not even every week because I used to make tuna casseroles half the time. Lou came to my table at the reunion— there wasn't such a big crowd—and he asked me to dance.

"'You were such a skinny little kid then, Rosalie,' he said. 'Like a little girl, a little bird.'

"I didn't say how I remembered him as one of those extremely clean boys. Reddish-gold hair, very good in school, not interesting, but good. And clean. When you think about it, good qualities for his business.

"I said I guess I was a late bloomer. He corrected me. 'Not at all. You were blooming in high school, too. I'm the late bloomer. I never had the nerve to talk to you then.'

"I said, 'I'm a regular customer, you know.'

177

" 'Thank you,' he said. He danced with his cheek resting on my hair."

" 'Is your husband here tonight?' he asked me.

"I said no, he wasn't. He was out of town. Immediately I was embarrassed. Those words can have a certain meaning if taken a certain way.

" 'Is it a good marriage?' he asked.

"I backed away slightly so I could look up at him. 'Isn't that a personal question?' Lou laughed easily, not at all put off. 'We've known each other thirty-some-odd years, haven't we?'

" 'It's my second marriage,' I said after a pause. I skimmed over it—your father, you. I said I'd remarried quickly. Thought I knew what I wanted; what to look out for. I asked him if he was married.

" 'Three daughters,' he said proudly; not exactly an answer.

" 'Is your wife here tonight?'

"Lou said no, she wasn't. She didn't get out much. An illness. She was sick, very sick; insisted he not miss this, his thirty-fifth, tonight."

I asked my mother what was wrong with his wife.

"It's mental," she said. "She calls it 'nerves.' " Lou says her mother had the same thing—spent most of her adult life in bed calling it nerves."

"Does she see a shrink?" I asked.

"She refuses."

"And he can't make her see a shrink?"

"He says he'd have to drag her bodily. She says it's not mental; she says she has MS."

"What do the doctors say?"

"The doctors say it's definitely not MS. They can't even find the weakness she says she has which keeps her in bed."

"How old are their daughters?" I asked.

"In their twenties. One in college, the other two married."

"Are you sleeping with him?" I asked.

She shook her head no, but without conviction.

"Are you considering it?"

"I don't know how these things work. I can picture us together, but I can't picture the steps leading up to it. Like who says what first . . . where we'd go, getting undressed . . . all the stuff that's automatically taken care of when people have affairs on television."

"Is he sleeping with her?"

My mother lifted her shoulders and held the shrug for a few moments.

"Do you two talk about things like that? Do you see each other away from the shop?"

"We talk on the phone. Long conversations—him from work when the shop's empty and I'm here alone."

"Are you in love with this guy?" I asked.

She looked at me evenly, not smiling, and said, "Am I?"

I said it certainly sounded that way.

"We're both married."

"These things happen," I said, "and more often when you're not in love with your husband and he's got a sick wife."

"Nothing's happened," she said.

"I think you're telling me about this whole thing so that something will happen. I think if you wanted to forget about him you'd have kept it to yourself."

She smiled a small, conspiratorial smile then, a smile Libby might flash for a half-second when Dennis's name was mentioned. "I think about ways we could be together," she said.

"You can bet Lou does too—a guy with a sick wife who spends the day in bed? I'm sure that desexualizes a bedroom pretty fast. I'm sure he's in love with you."

"You don't even know him."

"I know *you*. You're his best-looking customer, I guarantee that, not to mention the best-looking woman at the thirty-fifth reunion."

She touched her short curly hair, dyed the same dark brown as it had once been.

"What about Gerry?" I asked.

She put both elbows on the table and held her face in her hands. "I have to do something about that sooner or later."

I asked her what she was waiting for.

She said to see how things might work out with Lou.

"Look. This thing with Gerry is either working or it's not working, independent of Lou Schiner."

"You don't divorce someone out of the blue just because you don't love him."

"You certainly do! If you shouldn't have married him in the first place? If you're relieved when he's on the road and bored when he's around? Or are you one of those women who say, 'Well he doesn't run around and he doesn't drink much and he doesn't hit me, so he must be a good husband.'"

"He's not a *bad* husband."

"Ma-ah—"

"What would I say? 'Gerry, I made a mistake; I don't love you. I want a divorce. I'd like you to move out of this house, even though you're only here a couple of nights a week'? He'd talk me out of it. He's an excellent salesman."

"Would he talk you out of it because he'd be lost without you and couldn't bear the separation, or because he's got a good thing going and it would be a lot of trouble to upset the status quo?"

"What do you mean?" my mother asked.

"I don't think he's such a great husband! He comes home to this very attractive wife, you fix him these delicious, low-fat meals and do his laundry; he gets sexual release as needed, and leaves

180

with his suitcase all packed and his socks all matched. And I'm here to keep you company so you don't complain about him being on the road and you don't cramp his style."

"His style? You think he has women on the road?"

"Do you?"

"Every wife whose husband is on the road thinks about that from time to time—every time I watch 'Oprah' I see men who have two wives, two families, two houses. They're all salesmen! But it's not the kind of thing I think for very long, because the guys on the talk shows have a different kind of personality than Gerry. They have a get-up-and-go that he doesn't have. It takes a lot of energy to do that kind of thing."

I found myself making a case for my mother's divorce to my perfectly nice stepfather who hadn't done anything to deserve my new conviction in this matter. I was rooting for love in the form of Lou Schiner because I had nothing going on in my own life and theirs seemed sweet, like the love between good, linchpin soap opera characters who aren't allowed to fall from grace, even in their adulteries. I repeated my theory that she was allowing this confession to cross her lips because she wanted to lay it at my feet; she wanted me to encourage her to follow this Lou Schiner thing to its logical conclusion. How long had she been holding this in?

"I was waiting for a night when Gerry was out of town and you weren't on the run so we could talk."

"Would you ever bring him back here?" I asked.

"No."

"Because the neighbors might see him coming in or going?"

"Everybody knows him. Besides he drives the van."

"Have you ever kissed?"

She smiled. "Once."

"A real kiss?"

She nodded solemnly.

"Where did it happen?"

181

"At the market. Nobody was there. Manny was out. He motioned I should follow him into the food locker. And he did it."

"That's pretty kinky," I said.

"It was very romantic."

"Does it happen every time you buy fish?"

"No!"

"Do you think Manny knows?"

"Manny flirts with me, too."

"Maybe he knows; maybe Lou confides in him and Manny flirts with you as a cover. I bet he knows. You pick up that kind of thing when you work side by side with someone."

Love at work reminded me of Nick and Lyman, and Lyman's supposed insight into Nick's inner life. "Reminds me of my troubles," I said. "Love among the downtown merchants."

"Anyone I know?" my mother asked, without the sarcasm she would have used a week ago.

"Sorry," I said. "This is your allotted time; your life we're discussing here. I want to talk about you. I'll get the refills."

"Well," said my mother. "I think I've covered everything."

"And how do you feel? Purged? To get it off your chest and to confide in a sympathetic audience like your only daughter, a war-torn veteran of *affaires de coeur?*"

"Better," she said unhappily.

20

I Check Him Out

First thing Saturday morning, I went to Schiner Bros. Seafood to check out Lou. I went alone, but with my mother's consent, promising to be discreet.

Lou was waiting on a woman from MacMillan; I could tell by the characteristic faculty stare that asked, Who are you? Someone I should know and be nice to? If not a colleague are you at least a gourmet cook such as I or are you here to buy his premade stuffed quahogs?

"Do you know where I can get parchment?" she asked Lou after making her assessment of me.

"Parchment?" he repeated, not yet looking up.

"I'm cooking them in parchment," said the woman.

"Oh, yeah," said Lou agreeably. "I saw it on the menu at Legal Sea Foods in Worcester. I wondered what that was all about."

"Busman's holiday?" I asked.

Lou looked up to see who had spoken in this new, friendly tone. I continued, "You work here all day and you drive all the way to Worcester for a fish dinner?" I smiled. Lou wiped his filleting hand on his apron, back and forth several times to no particular end. "I'm Melinda," I said.

"I know," said Lou, not yet able to resume his task. The customer stared at me as if to say, Should I know who Melinda is?

"I want the skin off," she said, a way to get him back on course.

He held up the small white fillet he was working on. "It's already off." I watched his hands, reddened from being wet all day, fingers thicker than they might have been on another man of his height and slender build. Workman's hands, like the rest of him not handsome but poignant somehow, faithful and competent; nice. A good man whose rough red hands would thrill my mother just the same. He had thinning gray-blond hair and half glasses. Under his apron he was wearing a dress shirt of faded green pin stripes. No watch or wedding band.

"Not working today?" he asked me, eyes on the sole.

The customer's ears pricked up. A key to my identity, my profession; to my last year of school completed?

"I've got a wedding at four."

"Anyone I know?" Lou asked.

"Fontanas and Galganos."

He nodded happily. "Customers. Where's the reception?"

"Moss Creek Country Club."

"Who's the caterer?"

"Fabulous Fetes."

"Good. I supply them."

"I'll give you a report."

The woman sensed that our clubby talk was slowing down her filleting. She said irritably, "My daughter's in the car."

"I'm in no hurry," I answered, the ever-reasonable customer, then said agreeably to Ms. Professor, "You can get cooking parchment at the kitchen shop on the lower level of the Artisans' Loft."

"I can?"

"I'm pretty sure I've seen it there."

"Call from here," Lou offered. "Save yourself a trip."

"I'll run over. I could use a few things there anyway for tonight."

"Don't forget flowers for the table," I said, smiling.

"Her line," said Lou, tilting his head toward me.

Mystery solved: a common flower seller, merely another local merchant. "Which shop is yours?" she asked.

"Forget-Me-Not," I said in the apologetic way I always pronounced Robin's simple-minded idea of a clever name.

"I've heard good things about it," said the woman.

"You've probably seen my work at the college. I do all the president's stuff—receptions, parties, weekly arrangements for her foyer."

"Why did you think I was affiliated with MacMillan?"

"Was I right? Associate Professor? The social sciences?"

"Women's European History."

"That's where she gets it," Lou interjected.

"Sorry?" the woman said to him.

"Cooking fish in paper. Sounds European."

"I suppose it is." She turned back to me and asked if I had a business card. I said of course.

"'Melinda LeBlanc,'" she read. "'Best of Show, New England Growers Design Competition, 1990 and 1991.'" She handed it back and said archly, "Very impressive."

"Keep it. You might have an occasion."

Lou had wrapped her white fillets in butcher's paper, an enormous bundle, and announced it was $35.97, three pounds on the nose. I leaned toward her to see what her name was, and if it was a joint checking account. "Harriet Vogel or Eric Spindell" the check said, her name first, not even in alphabetical order.

Professor Vogel left without pleasantries for either me or Lou. It made me wonder what Eric Spindell was like; that is, what drew him to this rather unlovable Harriet Vogel? What made them marry? And where did she get all these friends, these six or eight people coming over tonight to sit at her table and consume three pounds of expensive gray sole?

Another goddamn mystery in the science of personal attraction.

With the coast clear, I bought four stuffed quahogs and told Lou I'd heat them up in the microwave at work. He asked me carefully how my mother was this morning. I said fine automatically; she'd probably be in later for some chowder fish.

"How *is* her chowder?" he asked.

"Watery. She won't use whole milk."

"She's a health nut," Lou said fondly.

"A few tablespoons of cream in her chowder wouldn't kill any of us."

I noticed Lou looked sad at the "us," a reminder of who else might be at the table consuming chowder made by her with Schiner chowder fish. I saw how personal it might be between them—his ingredients lovingly transformed by her hand into a healthy supper, that her purchase of his raw materials was a ritual that had substituted for adultery. I wanted to signal to him that I knew, and that I was on his side.

"She could thicken it with a little flour and still leave out the cream," he said.

"I think she knows that."

"No good either?" he asked with a smile.

"You know her rules."

"I'm beginning to," he said.

We pretended that my visit was routine, that this wasn't the first time I'd been there in the role of Rosalie's daughter, Rosalie's confidante. I wanted to ask how his wife was, code for "in this country we divorce crazy women who stay in bed all day and call it a terminal illness." Instead I asked, "You alternate Saturdays with your brother?"

"I take three out of four Saturdays. I don't mind, and Manny's kids are younger. In fact I like Saturdays. It's busy—people getting their special orders for parties and company."

"Not too busy now," I pointed out. Two guys draw a living from this, in other words? Two families?

"We do a big wholesale business. I can tell you which restaurants here in town where I'd let you eat sushi."

I asked where. He said stay away from MacWhinny's; Tinker's, yes, Kobe's Grille and Sushi Bar, yes. All their fish was his except the smoked items—they came directly from a smokehouse in Maine—and the gulf shrimp. Different distributor.

I said I had already discovered Kobe's on my own; hadn't tried Tinker's since it changed hands; would only order meat at MacWhinny's from now on.

Lou looked worried suddenly. "I'm not saying that their fish's no good. I'd stay away from their sushi appetizer, that's all. I don't like to bad-mouth another local business. Especially the restaurant business. It's so damn hard to make a go of it."

Nice guy, I thought; a little too chamber of commerce-ish for me. Maybe a little wishy-washy, but I supposed that helped explain things—a guy who didn't wrap his wife up, bedclothes and all, and drag her to a shrink, wasn't a guy who was going to trash another man's fish. Still, could I imagine him leading my mother from the front of the case around back to the locker for a passionate embrace? Hard to picture, in his apron and his black rubber boots, but obviously it did the job. I wondered if I could accomplish the same thing, lead a customer by the hand to the back room and kiss him good. He wouldn't have to know I got my inspiration from Schiner Bros. Seafood.

I went home to change for the wedding and to tell my mother my impressions of Lou. He had already called her and said he'd enjoyed his conversation with me; what a sparkling personality I had; what a lovely young lady I was; how much I reminded him of her.

"What's with the wife?" I asked.

"Nothing! He works, he does the food shopping, he goes home and cooks dinner. If he goes out, it's alone or with one of the daughters when they visit."

"How long has this been going on?"

"Since the change—about five years."

"But he won't do anything about it?"

"She won't admit anything's wrong with her mentally except for saying she has MS—"

"Which she doesn't for sure?"

"No doctor thinks she has it and she's been seen by an army of them. She's even had the test where they use magnetism and put you into a chamber and your body glows in different colors according to what you have. She won't take no for an answer. Lou worries that they might find something really wrong with her, and he'll have called her crazy for nothing."

"I get it: 'In sickness and in health'?"

"Which is nothing to make fun of."

"Look," I said, "this is classic. How fast do you think she'd be out of bed if Lou gave her an ultimatum?"

My mother didn't answer.

"Has he ever done that?"

"She knows he wouldn't go through with it."

"He's a nice man, isn't he?" I asked, watching her face closely. She nodded quickly.

"And what good would an ultimatum be if it worked, right? She might just get out of bed and be fine. Cured! Back to being a real person."

My mother said, "I've thought of that. So has Lou."

"So, in a way, it's better to maintain the status quo?"

"We don't talk about it," she said softly.

"This wife has to be a pretty great actress to have kept this up for five years."

"I never met her," said my mother.

"Do the daughters know about you?"

"There's nothing to know. Not really."

"They should know that their father has a chance for a real life with a functioning woman."

My mother laughed.

"It's true! They shouldn't be protected. They're old enough to think of him as a human being with his own needs."

"I wasn't laughing at that. I was laughing at 'functioning.' I thought you were going to say 'lovely' or 'nice' or something like that. Then 'functioning' came out. It just struck my ears funny."

"No offense. I meant as opposed to her, the wife."

"Barbara."

"And what does this Barbara want? More attention from her husband and her daughters?"

"He's very attentive. He waits on her hand and foot, and I get the sense that he did plenty around the house before she was sick."

"Do you think he's had other women?" I asked.

"I know he hasn't."

"Because he told you?"

She said, "That's right."

"And you think he's telling the truth?"

"I know he is."

I said that was fine; I certainly was not implying that he couldn't be believed. My question to her, however, was this: What was her goal here, a Martha-inspired question.

What did I mean, "goal"? she asked.

"Do you want to marry him? Do you want to have a sexual relationship with him, and that would be enough? Do you have to do it all right—divorces, waiting periods, daughters' consent? What exactly are you hoping for?"

"Oh," said my mother. "I need a minute." I waited patiently. She said, "I'd like us to be together."

"At what price, though? That's the crux of this, really. Do you care more about being together than you care about all the loose ends?"

She asked what kind of loose ends I meant.

"Divorces, for starters. People do, in fact, leave their spouses and live together without divorces."

"In Harrow? Not if you own a business and care what people think of you."

"People will talk anyway unless Barbara dies and Lou publicly mourns her. There's probably no respectable way to get together short of that so you might as well enjoy each other's company now rather than in twenty years."

"What are you saying—we should run off together and shack up?"

"People do it all the time," I said.

"Not people like us."

"What's your alternative?"

"This. We keep it on the up and up; we see each other several times a week and talk on the phone whenever the coast is clear. I had romances like this in high school. You can be in love with someone and not sleep with him. This idea that you have to sleep with someone as the only way to express your feelings is not everyone's cup of tea. Sometimes it's just not practical."

"C'mon," I said, "you don't think he's dying to sleep with you? Men want sex. He's your age, right? Hasn't slept with his wife to speak of? This guy is hornier than you care to think about."

"He's patient. He's had to make do for a lot of years."

"And do you know why you're telling me all this?"

"Why?"

"Because you're recruiting me to your side because you need my organizational skills. And I'm the only person whose approval you wanted, even though you might not have been *consciously* seeking it."

"You're awfully quick to send Gerry packing," she said after a short silence.

A nice enough stepfather and all, I said, but not around enough to develop an attachment to.

"He's very fond of you."

"I'm fond of him, too."

"He never asks me how I spend my household money, and he's happy when I buy myself a new dress and have my hair done. A lot of couples don't have joint checking accounts—"

"I think you love Lou Schiner, and you don't love Gerry and that's what we're down to."

"I knew you wouldn't be shocked about Lou," she said, "but I didn't think you'd take his side against Gerry's."

"I think you and Lou Schiner want to be together, you've behaved honorably, you haven't cheated on your spouses and you both deserve some happiness."

"Lou has a business to run, and a partner who's his brother, and three daughters who he loves very dearly."

I tsk'd loudly. "Would you stop buying fish from someone because he was living in sin?"

"*I* wouldn't—"

"You don't think people feel sorry for him, living with a crazy woman he doesn't love? You don't think his customers would be happy for him?"

"This isn't California," my mother said, invoking her favorite example of life-style anarchy.

"Maybe you two should move to California. No one there would give you a second thought."

My mother thought this over: freedom from judgment; the freedom to rent a little house and live there as Lou and Rosalie, refugees from small-mindedness. "We would have to go away," she said. "Not necessarily all the way to California, but someplace where people wouldn't know what we had come from."

"I'm for staying here and for you two being together despite the flak."

My mother said, "I'm not a rebel."

"Look—Gerry's hardly ever here. He would *not* freak out over a divorce. Yes, he'd lose his home base and he'd have to change his letterhead, but all in all, I think his life is on the road."

"Still . . ."

"What?"

"Twice-divorced," she said. "I hate the sound of that."

"Then don't say it."

She sighed, looked up at the clock on the microwave and asked what time my wedding was.

"I want to be at the house at three."

"Are you changing?" she asked.

"Definitely. I'm going to be a guest at this one."

She nodded, not paying close attention. A few weeks ago I would have taken her preoccupation to mean: Why not you, Melinda? Why not your wedding?

192

But today, she was thinking of herself and Lou, and that was good; perhaps she was thinking weddings weren't everything. You wished for them, and planned and dreamed, and then they didn't work out.

21

One of the More Eventful Weddings I've Done

As usual, I went to the bride's house first, a few steps ahead of the photographer. I wore my tailored gray flannel suit with a veiled black velvet hat that made me look like a wealthy European widowed young. Paulette's father let me in, told me for the hundredth time he was allergic to chrysanthemums. I reassured him that there was not a mum in sight, that he'd be wearing a sprig of lily of the valley—

"No chrysanthemums in my wife's corsage, either, right? 'Cause we'll be dancing."

"None. I swear. She and Paulette explained that very carefully."

He motioned I come inside, suddenly impatient. "Paulette's in the bedroom; they're all in there. Want me to bring that up?"

I held on to my carton and said, no indeed. The florist got to place the flowers in the proper hands; I'd pin his boutonniere on for the photos then take it back for the ride to the church and put it on again just before the ceremony.

Walking up the stairs I said over my shoulder, "You look very handsome."

He grinned and said, "Oh, yeah?"

I told him the tux looked great; it wasn't a rental was it? . . . It *was?* It fit so well, I thought it had to be his own.

"Nah. That formal shop on West Ridge Road. Shirt, shoes, everything."

"Amazing," I said.

He straightened his shoulders before turning away, momentarily not the father of a twenty-nine-year-old bride. Sometimes I amazed myself, how easily I said these things.

Of course I knew Libby had designed the wedding dress, but I hadn't expected to find her in the bride's bedroom with a needle and thread. Paulette, a chiropractor, was dressed and standing obediently with her hands by her sides, her spine the picture of alignment. The dress was two-piece, long-sleeved, high-necked; a lacy Victorian blouse and a long skirt of pleated silky fabric. She saw me in the mirror and cried, "I lost weight since the final fitting! The waist isn't doing what it's supposed to do."

Libby, in blue jeans rolled up two turns at the ankle and pink ruffled crew socks, was fussing over Paulette's middle. I said hi first and asked if it was serious. Libby said she was cheating, taking tucks where needed, moving the hooks; please remind her to do the final fitting not more than two days before the wedding from now on.

"It's absolutely beautiful," I said.

"The lace in the inset is from her First Communion veil," Libby said.

195

"Whose idea was that?"

Paulette laughed and said they had put their heads together to come up with some family heirloom lace. Her mother wouldn't sacrifice her wedding veil, still hoping that one of her other daughters would like it enough to use it as is; after that, they went down the list. Paulette's grandmother had made all four grand-daughters' First Communion dresses, so this was one piece of fabric she could cannibalize as her own.

"Well, it's gorgeous. Your grandmother had a great eye."

"That's what I said," added Libby. "Whoever would have thought to use Princess lace for a little girl's veil? I built the blouse around it." She cut off the thread with an expert snap. "That should do it."

Paulette swiveled from the waist up, elbows in the air, and pronounced the fit perfect.

"Don't be afraid to eat, either. It'll hold fine." Libby got to her feet with a groan. Paulette said she should have a cushion between the hard floor and her patella.

"Let's see it with the flowers," said Libby.

I took Paulette's bouquet from the carton—a loose-stemmed spray of delphinia, coquette roses, white lilacs and Queen Anne's lace—and placed it in her arms. She cradled it, and all three of us cooed.

"Not too big?" I asked, fishing for praise.

"Perfect!" said Libby. "The look is exactly right, very Victor-ian."

"Where's the photographer?" I asked.

"With my sisters. We sent him away for the alterations."

"I'll get him," I said.

He stuck his head in instantly, as if he'd been lurking outside. I knew this guy from a hundred other Harrow weddings, a *Sentinel* photographer who free-lanced on weekends. "Ready, girls?" he said cheerily. I also knew the shot: in the mirror, dressmaker pretends to fuss with dress; florist pretends to fuss with hair wreath. He began to set it up, but Paulette said, "Let's just get a shot of the three of us. We don't have to pose."

"Whatever you want," he sang.

Libby took a pinch of skirt fabric in one hand and held it out, claiming the dress; I took back the flowers and held them up as I would a trophy. Paulette smiled good-naturedly between us, and the photographer said, "hold it," and "again." He asked, "Want to sit down at a mirror and put on lipstick or anything?"

"No," said Paulette. "No stock shots if I can help it. We discussed that, right? The true meaning of 'candid'?"

"Sure," said the photographer. "Whatever you want. It's your day."

"Let's get everyone together downstairs," said Paulette.

I picked up my carton and slipped out the bedroom door first. Libby said she'd walk behind Paulette and play lady in waiting. The family, hardly a serene crew, was in the living room, pulling on gloves and checking the collective hundreds of small covered buttons going up the attendants' backs. I pinned on Mrs. Fontana's coquette roses, Mr. Fontana's lily of the valley, and passed around the identical bridesmaids' bouquets which were less grand versions of Paulette's. Easing away for the photographer, I joined Libby on the stairs and asked her if she was coming to the wedding.

She said she wasn't; her job was done. Not like mine, with all the setup I had to do.

I said the church was ready; I'd gone there first: a spray of baby's breath and Jack Frost roses at the end of every pew; two fantastic arrangements in antique iron urns at the altar, right out of a Victorian engraving, heavy on fronds and juniper branches and flowering herbs.

"I'm sure it's perfect," Libby murmured, her eyes on Paulette's waistband.

We watched the bridal party duck in and out of formation.

I made myself ask casually, "Did you have a nice time last night?"

"Last night?"

"With Dennis and Nick and Lyman?"

"You mean at dinner—"

"I saw all of you walk by. You looked as if you were on your way somewhere fun."

"Just to MacWhinny's."

She didn't get it; she didn't know that I was saying, *I saw all of you—without me—walk by and I was hurt and angry.* I said, "I would have come if you had asked me. Or I could have met you there later."

"It wasn't a big deal. We were discussing the softball team. You certainly didn't miss anything." She looked perplexed, as if she was having trouble imagining such a slight. Of course she couldn't: that was what enabled her to wear Dutch-boy haircuts and homemade party dresses for four years at Harrow High and then make a career of it: not worrying about what her friends thought.

"What softball team?" I asked.

"Brookhoppers. Dennis wants to sponsor a team."

"So?"

"In the coed league. He needs three women on the field at all times. He figured he could talk you and me into it, and maybe his sister. Or Francesca's nice daughter."

"Robin's a pretty good athlete. I bet she'd be interested."

Paulette called up to Libby, saying that the skirt felt great—not to worry.

"It should be fine, and if it's not, I'll run over."

"Aren't you coming?" I asked.

"I can't. I left the shop to run over here."

"Can't you close early and come afterward?"

She shrugged. "I'm not dressed."

"So? Whip something up!" I turned back to the bride. "Did you know Libby thinks she's not coming to the wedding?"

"Of course you are," she answered.

"And I could use your help. There's twenty-some-odd tables to decorate and I'm on my own today."

She opened her mouth to protest, but I had an argument ready: There's always extra food and extra seats: assorted no-shows, people on strange diets, people who drink too much over hors d'oeuvres and wander into the wrong function room. She could fill me in on the softball team and besides, I knew the caterer.

"Who is it?" Libby asked.

"Fabulous Fetes."

"Good?"

"The best, and gorgeous. They garnish with flowers."

Libby laughed. I felt better, enough to coax, "C'mon. What else do you have to do tonight?"

"What time do you think it would be over?"

"You could leave any time."

"You wouldn't consider me a crasher?" she asked Paulette.

"Be serious," she answered.

I said, "Saint Bridget's, until . . . probably four-thirty, then Moss Creek. A little champagne, a little music, a little dancin' with a handsome usher; a little romance, a little rum cake. . . ."

"Okay, I'll *go,* but I have to get back to the store first. My mother's the only one there."

"Go."

She waved to the Fontanas, who were at attention for some photographic purpose Paulette was protesting. Nice people, I thought. They stopped to thank Libby for her house call, to tell her how beautiful the dress was, to underscore her welcomeness at the wedding.

"Wear your dancing shoes," I called to her from my supervisory perch.

"Bring a date," called the bride.

She didn't make the ceremony. No surprise, I thought: one customer arriving a minute before five can keep you in the shop an extra half hour, even if you've got the keys in the door and an evening purse in your hand.

But she was at the reception, looking the way a designer could only hope her dresses would look in print ads; quintessentially Libby, full skirt, off-the-shoulder sleeves, scoop neck, black puckery cotton with gold threads woven in, flat shoes, blond hair fluffed and lipstick dabbed; dots of gold at her earlobes her only jewelry.

With Roger Stanley Bonak.

My cousin Roger, wearing his blue Sunday suit and textured maroon tie. They weren't quite holding hands but looking as if they'd just recently and reluctantly let each other's go.

I didn't exactly gasp when they walked into the foyer together; after all, there could be any number of reasons why a tall, doughy, prematurely balding florist would accompany Libby tonight outside the dictionary definition of "date": Escort. Pal. Chauffeur. Navigator.

I walked over to greet them. "Sorry we missed the ceremony," said Libby.

"How's it going?" Roger asked. "Your job pretty much done?"

I nodded. "Twenty-three tables and the ladies' room. I'm off duty."

"You weren't serious about needing an assistant, were you?" asked Libby.

I said I wasn't; it was just a way I dragged reluctant friends with nothing to do on a Saturday night to receptions.

"It took longer than I expected. I had this dress at the store, but Roger had to run home to change and shave." She said it unself-consciously, as if she routinely talked about Roger's ablutions and Roger's body in the act of undressing then dressing.

He smiled foolishly, but I could see he was proud of himself, proud that he was like the other guys now, the cool guys who cheat on their wives with beautiful babes and get away with it.

"Where's Robin?" I asked.

"You here with a date?" he asked cheerfully, ignoring my question.

"Not exactly." Conrad's band was playing; I had condoms in my purse.

"Everything looks real good," said Roger. He looked around, nodding. "I'm glad you talked Libby into coming."

Where was all *this* coming from—this Libby business? Of course, if I pressed them, they'd weasel out of a formal confirmation. I turned to Libby. "And in all that time I was twisting your arm about coming, you never mentioned you were hesitating because you already had plans."

"It wasn't anything concrete," said Libby.

"Just your usual Saturday night understanding?"

"Sort of."

"Which has been going on for how long?" I asked.

They looked at each other. Roger smiled first and raised his eyebrows as if saying, Go ahead, tell her.

"How long?" I asked. "Shock me."

"A while," said Libby.

"Months?" I asked.

"One," Libby answered. She must have thought I was feeling left out again because she said kindly, "I almost told you today at Paulette's house."

"I don't want to know about this! Why would you think I want to know?"

Libby opened her mouth in protest. She and Roger exchanged looks acknowledging they'd misread my code of sexual ethics.

"I can't believe you're saying this," said Libby.

"I can't believe you'd just show up here as if it was perfectly kosher."

"This is a Forget-Me-Not wedding," said Roger, "and Libby designed the bride's dress. Paulette personally invited her."

"I thought you were good at keeping secrets," said Libby.

"I'm good at keeping my own secrets," I said.

She opened her eyes wide for effect and said, "I don't see you running off to Candee Riley and telling her you slept with her husband a week before her wedding."

I groaned; that's what Libby took away from that episode: Melinda, a fornicator herself, could be trusted with this sort of thing.

I said, "What were you thinking—that this was your coming-out party. Or did you think I'm the only one here with eyes in my head?"

"We're here as guests, for God's sake. I designed the wedding dress and Roger owns the shop where all the flowers come from."

A white-gloved waiter, finally, came by with champagne glasses on a tray. We each took one and murmured our thanks. Libby and Roger had the nerve to raise their glasses—infinitesimally, but I caught it—in a nauseating salute to imagined love.

22

The Last Man on Earth

Roger as paramour—an unbelievable concept. Robin had hinted that he was enthusiastic in bed, but I had shrunk from hearing any more. Besides, I figured, consider the source: they met at the voke school, went steady for years, learned sex in each other's bed.

It just goes to show you that persistence from one party and loneliness from the other can put together a Roger and a Libby. How in the world could the same woman who loved Dennis find anything at all in my cousin Roger?

And what about Robin? It would be a disaster on all counts—Libby next door, me Libby's friend; Roger and Robin's partnership; the kids, the house, the perpetual calendar. What if it was Robin left to manage Forget-Me-Not, sniffling, leaning on me?

Later, several phases down the road, divorced, spunky again, treating me as if we were partners in man-hunting.

I tried to see Roger as a man, not as my younger cousin, not as Papa Jan's inferior assistant by the highway, not as my humorless boss. But Roger Stanley Bonak: receding lank blond hair, round-faced, round-shouldered, flat butt, no charm.

I had followed Libby into the ladies' room mid-salad (endive, watercress, roasted red peppers, local goat cheese) with the excuse that I needed her personal products and a touch of her lipstick.

"What would you like to tell me?" I asked her, after checking for eavesdroppers in the toilet stalls. "And don't say, 'About what?'"

"I assume you mean Roger." She reached under her skirt to smooth what turned out to be a sewn-in underskirt of black net.

"Of course Roger."

I waited for her answer, appraising my arrangement of Bridal Pink roses and baby's breath. A little too all-purpose, I thought; should have recreated the altar urns on a small scale; brought in the herbs, a nice touch for a bathroom. Part of the problem was a euphemism of a beribboned wicker basket next to my flowers holding Tampax—the management's thoughtful party favors.

"Pretty," she said.

"I was just thinking they're a little clichéd."

"Roses are everybody's favorite."

I said I know; not mine, though, unless they're an oddball strain. This was not the result I derived much pleasure from. Robin could have done this arrangement, I was sorry to say. . . . Anyway: How did it happen?

Libby spoke in a flat voice, the way you report your side of the story to the opposing attorney. Her first response, she told me, had been what I would have expected: go away, Roger; I'll pretend you never came in here.

Then? I asked. You actually felt something stirring inside you for Roger?

"Yes I did," Libby said, a challenge. She turned toward the vanity mirror and fluffed her bangs, a few hairs at a time pinched between two fingers. Finally she said, "I don't expect you to understand, and I certainly don't expect you to approve."

I spoke to her reflection in the mirror. "When you told me about Roger coming on to you a while back, coming into the store about coordinating your window displays, you hadn't wanted anything to do with him."

"I know I *said* that. . . ."

"But you changed your mind?"

"You think you know him—"

"I do! I work with him every day. I've known him his whole life."

"He thinks you still see him as Roger, the pain in the ass."

I pressed my lips together. There were no other possible interpretations of Roger. I knew him through and through and the man *was* a pain in the ass.

"What about Robin?"

"He's not in love with Robin anymore."

"How handy."

"I know it's hard for you to see this," said Libby.

"Is it the sex? Is he great in bed, and he's filling a void? Because you don't have to call that love, you know."

"Nobody's calling it love."

"Roger isn't in love with you?"

"What he's feeling is real, but it's also a symptom of things being wrong with Robin. If it hadn't been me, it would have been someone else."

Doubt it, I thought. How many other women would have been worn down by Roger? "I don't have a man, either—"

"But you have chances, even if they don't go anywhere. You meet men and if you felt like it you could have sex with anyone in town."

This was interesting: *sex with anyone in town.*

Oh, really? I said. Like who? I named the owner of Buddy's, a known bad boy famous for hitting on his waitresses; I named the registrar of the college; I named Miles Getchel and my stepfather; I named the chief of police, the collector of taxes, our state senator.

"I mean ordinary people," said Libby. "Guys who you run across at the shop or at weddings."

"Is that what you think? I meet guys through *work?*"

"A lot of your customers are men. Billy Riley was a customer."

"Please. That was hardly worth mentioning."

"No," said Libby, "I disagree. Men are at least half your customers, and the ones who come in, come in alone. Plus you go to the weddings and meet the eligible friends of the groom."

"Is it that you want Robin to find out? On some level, you're hoping to be caught?"

"No," said Libby. "If Robin found out, Roger would just deny the whole thing and we'd cool it. For a while, anyway."

"No offense, but are you physically attracted to him?"

Someone else might have answered with a dreamy smile, but not Libby. She said, "I find him quite compelling."

I laughed; I had to. *Roger compelling.* "This has everything to do with what else is going on in your life, you know."

"For example?"

"If Dennis had responded in some way, you never would have looked at Roger."

"You can go to hell," said Libby. "I'm just sorry I let you talk me into coming. In a way I wanted you to know because I thought it might make you feel . . . included."

"What are you going to do when people figure out you're here together?"

"They won't if you don't tell them."

"Nobody told *me!* I put two and two together without much help from either one of you. You don't think Robin will, too?"

"Roger doesn't want to break up his marriage, and I don't want to marry Roger—"

"And you think that's it? You can keep it in a neat little compartment called 'having an affair with my next-door neighbor'?"

"That's right," said Libby.

I walked a few yards away and flopped into the flowered chintz armchair outside the stalls. "In my wildest dreams . . ."

Libby raised her voice. "What? In your wildest dreams you can't imagine sleeping with someone you weren't madly in love with because it gives you something you don't have? Or in your wildest dreams you can't imagine anyone being attracted to Roger? Am I on the right track? You're the only Main Street merchant who's allowed to sleep with a married man?"

"Please."

"It's true."

"Billy Riley hardly counts."

"Why? Because he was only engaged at the time?"

"Because that was one time. It was *not* an affair—we didn't even lie down when we did it. It was a bad idea, a minor outlet."

"Well, so is this a minor outlet."

"For you, maybe."

"Is it on moral grounds that you're protesting this? Or family grounds, or commercial grounds, or what?"

A good question. I tried to analyze my distaste for the whole matter. Was it personal, professional, ethical? Was it my grudging but basic loyalty to Robin, who built her life around the Roger-Robin legend of two peas in a pod?

207

Libby prodded me: would I tell her to get out of a similar relationship if it were another married man on Main Street?

Of course not, I thought; wasn't I pushing my mother on Lou Schiner? I said, "Doubt it."

"Okay, then. It's not religious or moral. That leaves your own personal ties to Roger and Robin."

"It's a pretty big lie to carry around all day in the shop."

"Roger carries it around all day in the shop and then takes it home."

"Well, good for him. What a prince; what a talented guy!"

"You get used to keeping a secret," said Libby, "and after a while it doesn't seem so huge."

"You don't avoid her?"

"I never see her in the course of a week."

"I guess not. Makes it so much cleaner that way. . . ."

"Are you going to tell her?"

I pretended not to know that my answer was an unequivocal no.

"Roger doesn't want a divorce—"

"If he divorced Robin he'd be doing it so he could marry you, which I assume is not your romantic goal in life."

Libby peered at me as if trying to understand the foreign phrases I had just uttered. Finally, she said bitterly, "You think I have a romantic goal left—a romantic bone in my body? Do you? Are we still waiting for something like a happy ending and true love?"

I said, "I am."

"Not me."

"So why mess up Robin's life—and Roger's, too, if you're not in love with him? I guarantee he's madly in love with you and no matter what he spouts about this being a casual affair, he's full of it. Roger's not the type."

Libby said, "We've been in here too long. I'm sure they took our salads away by now."

Our tablemates were a selection of quasi-invited guests— musicians' girlfriends, an engaged couple who were taste-testing the caterer and were there at Fabulous Fetes' expense; Roger, Libby, and I. Our salads were gone.

I used the time to pitch my services to the engaged couple, named Pam and Pass. "What kind of a name is Pass?" I asked him.

"French. Short for Pascal."

"Neat," I said.

He rolled his eyes and I immediately liked him. Then Pam said wryly, "We're *not* having matchbooks printed up with 'Pam and Pass,' no matter what you say," and I liked her too.

The band was playing schmaltzy music. A few guests, the ones who danced to anything and had trophies at home, were darting about with their smart steps. The musicians' girlfriends pointed out their sweeties: the drummer and the bass player. I didn't tell them I belonged in their group, that I was the mystery woman Conrad serviced every few gigs.

"We don't usually get invited to eat," said the drummer's girlfriend, who wore pants and a bolero jacket of a space-suit material. I was dying to exchange looks with Libby over it, even with us in mid-crisis. I called across the table to her: "Libby! . . . have you ever worked in this material?"

Libby knew exactly what I was up to. She said, "I'm sorry to say I haven't."

"Where did you get it?" I asked the drummer's girlfriend.

"New York," she said apologetically.

"My clients tend to be conservative . . . a lot from the college," said Libby.

"Do you have a store?" asked the bass player's girlfriend.

Libby told her: Rags for Sale, on Main.

Here? they asked. Neither had been in, but then again, they weren't from Harrow.

"Libby apprenticed at a big design house in New York," I said.

"Albert Nipon," she added.

"Did you make that?" one of them asked.

Libby nodded. The girlfriends smiled politely, trying to look enthusiastic over something cotton and cap-sleeved.

"She made the wedding dress," Roger said.

"It's a knockout," said Pam, future bride.

"You design it or just make it?" asked the one in Mylar.

Libby said both; it was a period piece, though, rather than an entirely original—

"How much does something like that go for?" asked the other girlfriend.

Libby said, "More than you think."

Pam and Pass stood up and said they were going to dance until the entree came—try out the band, too.

"Do you know what they're serving?" I asked.

"Salmon en croute," said Pam.

The bass player's girlfriend returned to Libby as soon as Pam and Pass moved away. "You don't want to say?"

"I make it a policy never to quote the price of a wedding dress at the actual affair."

Libby and I smiled at each other briefly. There was no such policy; it was just rare to meet someone tacky enough to ask at the event.

"You married?" the same one asked.

"No," said Libby.

"Would you make your own dress? Your own wedding dress?"

Libby laughed and said, indeed: she'd been sketching it her entire life.

"I bet," said the bass player's girlfriend.

I broke in and asked, "Any of you serious with them?" pointing my chin toward the band.

They shrugged their yeses, neither with great conviction. I sensed a competition between them over whose boyfriend was closest and truest.

"Well," I said cheerfully, "keep me in mind for the flowers."

"We live in Connecticut, though," said the bass player's girlfriend, whose dress was a steely blue crêpe and whose hair was a peculiar shade of deep burgundy.

"How'd you meet these guys?" I asked.

"At her wedding," said the Mylar one, reaching for her friend's pack of cigarettes.

"I'm separated," the other one explained.

"How long were you married?"

"Too long," said her friend, blowing smoke toward the ceiling.

"My husband has psychological problems, which didn't come out until we were legally married."

I told her I was sorry, then repeated, You met this guy, the drummer—sorry I don't know his name—at your own wedding?

"Ronny. It's not like it sounds. I was in love with my husband at my wedding. I didn't even notice Ronny."

"They ran into each other after the crazy stuff had started, and he remembered the booking."

"Well," I said, "that was lucky."

"They're nice guys," said the one with the burgundy hair. "They're not into the kind of stuff you hear about with musicians —drugs and groupies. They're normal guys who happen to be musically talented."

I said I knew that; I knew Conrad. He and I had done several weddings together, and we had become friends.

"What's your name?" asked the bass player's girlfriend, squinting into her own cigarette smoke.

"Melinda."

211

They shrugged: Sorry. Guess we don't know you.

"We only see each other when our schedules overlap. Like this. I'll probably go out with him for a drink after he's finished."

"Maybe we'll all go out," said the one in blue, the separated bride. She put out her hand for me to shake and said, "I'm Terri. And this is Melody. Ronny is the drummer and Ron's the bass player."

"Don't say it!" said her friend.

"What?"

"That Melody is the perfect name for a musician's girlfriend. It's my real name. I didn't invent it."

Roger piped up suddenly, "Melinda used to be just Linda. She named herself that."

"That's funny," said Terri, "because Conrad made up his name, too."

"What was it?" I asked.

"I forget," said Terri. "Something like Conrad only plainer."

"It was, like, twenty years ago," I said. "I did it when I went into high school."

"How old are you?" asked Terri.

"Thirty."

She looked around. "Are all you guys around that age."

Roger and Libby nodded.

"Carl! His real name is Carl. It just came to me," said Terri.

Roger said with a tight smile, "Linda and Carl. Seem like fine names to me."

I ignored him and said, "They sound a little sluggish tonight."

"That's what I was thinking," said Terri.

"You can make requests, you know," Melody said. "They know something like five hundred oldies. You can just go up there, or you can pass them a note, or you can tell one of us."

Roger smiled at Libby, stood up, pushed his chair back in and

212

approached the band. If Libby hadn't been there I would have said, "This ought to be good."

I said, my eye on Conrad, "I haven't said hello yet."

"They've got a break coming up in another song or two, probably after this guy's request."

I leaned around Terri and Melody to ask Libby, as sweetly as I could, if she and Roger had a special song. She ignored my question, so I said to my new friends, "I guess not. They haven't been together all that long."

Up on the dais Conrad nodded to Roger and signaled, sure, you bet, end of this set.

"We'll soon find out," I said.

Roger returned, looking proud, and sat down. Libby refused to look at me.

All of us waited—us three girlfriends of the musicians. Conrad pulled his mike an inch closer to his mouth and said, "Our first request, ladies and gentlemen." He winked and said, "And of course since we know every song ever written . . ." The wedding guests laughed. A male voice yelled, "Far Above Cayuga's Waters." Conrad opened his mouth and clamped it shut, getting another laugh.

"They knew mine," Roger confided.

Conrad mouthed, "a one, a two, a one, two, three," then jerked his hands off the keyboard to sing the first line *a capella,* "When you're alone and life is making you lonely you can always go . . . downtown."

"Petula Clark," said Roger, swaying like a singing camper on a bus.

"Aren't you going to dance?" asked Melody. "That's usually what people want with a request."

Roger looked at Libby, who nodded but without enthusiasm. Roger followed her to the dance floor where he waved his arms and shuffled his feet in an unsuccessful imitation of Libby's wan flutters.

"What's their story?" Terri asked me.

"He's my cousin; he owns the shop where I work. He and his wife own it together."

Terri and Melody let this sink in until one of them asked, "This one's not the wife?"

"That's right."

We watched silently until Melody said, "How come you see great-looking girls with guys who are nothing special, but not the other way around?"

Terri laughed and said, "Don't kid yourself. He's doin' somethin' right."

"How long has it been goin' on?" Melody asked.

I told her not long, weeks maybe, but that I had just found out tonight. No preparation, no hints, just this—their arriving together as brazen as anything. Roger and Robin have two kids, two girls, Laurel and Heather, but I guess Libby is too much of a prize, the kind of woman he always saw as unattainable, to just exercise a little self-control and obey his marriage vows.

"What's his wife like?" Terri asked.

"Cute. Short and energetic; straight brown hair, chin-length, barrettes. Looks about sixteen."

"She doesn't know?" Melody asked.

"Robin? I doubt it."

"This won't last," said Terri shrewdly. "Screwing's one thing, in the privacy of your own room—maybe he's extra nice to her, takes his time, whatever it is she likes—but it's another thing to be seen in public, especially after a while when the sex becomes routine." She shook her head, cigarette and all. "No way . . ."

"Pretty arrogant, though," said Melody, "coming to something like this for the whole town to see."

"He wants to get caught," Terri explained. "He doesn't want trouble, but he can't stand not showing off his honey."

I told her that's what I thought—Roger who never even looked at another woman and vice versa can't help flaunting this particular prize; that his ego wouldn't let him keep it a secret, like a little boy. *Exactly* like a little boy.

Meanwhile, Conrad was up to something, mouthing directions to the two Rons and to the guitar player, grinning slyly as if to say, Let's give 'em what they want, boys.

We knew soon enough: a seamless segue to an *a capella* rendition of another first line: "I . . . know a place where the music is fine and the lights are always low. . . ."

"Do you believe the shit they know?" said Melody.

"You can't dance to this," said Terri.

Roger looked doubly delighted with what his request had spawned. Libby continued to dance coolly.

I said, "They think people will just assume they're here on wedding business, thrown together at the same table and that's it."

Terri disagreed. "He's into it. Look at him. He's dicking her and it's written all over his face."

Roger *was* looking obscenely pleased with himself. "He's such a jerk," I murmured.

"And no one looks jerkier on the dance floor than someone who's a jerk," said Terri.

I searched for Pass and Pam. They were looking anything but jerky, dancing close, talking, swinging out every so often in a modified jitterbug spiral. Nice. A few couples away, the bride fox-trotted by with her new father-in-law, smiling self-consciously as if to say, He doesn't know any other step. The groom played at dancing with a little girl in a long, plaid taffeta skirt, letting her feet touch the floor for pirouettes but raising her off the floor for tangolike strides.

And thrashing in their midst was Roger, grimacing with the music as if "I Know a Place" had meaning and mystery to a lover such as he; as if his clumsy pelvic rotations were, for all the world to see, sex on the record with the lovely and talented golden girl of Harrow, Libby Getchel.

Con came down to our table while we were on the salmon course. He kissed me on the lips and said, "You've met the girls, I see. He pointed to my fork, then at his mouth. I fed him a taste of the salmon en croute.

He made a face. "It is *not* possible to make this in large numbers and get the fish right. You overcook it to begin with, then really kill it in the reheating."

I winked at Pam and Pass. "Scrap the salmon."

"Have you done other weddings with this caterer?" Pam asked him.

"Who we talking about here?"

"Fabulous Fetes," I said. "Pam and Pass are scouting them for their own wedding."

"They're as good as you're gonna get," Con said. He sat down on the empty chair between me and Roger. "And they make the stuff look great, if you're into that. Big on the esthetic."

"We noticed," said Pam.

"Their poached salmon's terrific; it's not that they can't do fish. It's just this pastry thing people ask for. . . . What are you looking at, a summer wedding?"

"October," said Pass.

"You could still do a cold poached salmon in October. Particularly if you had a hot entree. Prime rib or rack of lamb."

"We haven't thought about it," said Pam. "We're not sure yet even whether it's going to be sit-down or buffet."

"Definitely, buffet," said Con. "It's much looser—more dancing, more table-hopping. People who come stag get to meet other people. . . ." He reached over and took a baby carrot off my plate. He held it up by its green nub and said, "See, like this. Even their vegetables are pretty." He wiped his hand on my napkin and reached into his inside jacket pocket with two long fingers. "Just in case you don't have the music locked in, either."

Pass took the silver business card and said thanks.

"Got the date yet?"

"October ninth."

"We might still have it open," said Con. He smiled. "You listen and see if we're your sound. We do everything from black-tie-Gershwin-Michael-Feinstein to our own sound which is kind of Gary Burton, and everything in between."

Roger said, "You know a lot of oldies, huh?"

Con smiled a star's smile and said coolly, "You hit us lucky, pal. We can't always reach back."

"This is my cousin, Roger Bonak. Roger—Conrad Zimmerman," I said.

"Heard a lot about you," Con told Roger.

Libby leaned around Roger and said, "I'm Libby Getchel," in the determinedly polite voice of someone miffed at not being introduced.

"Libby made the wedding dress," said Terri.

"No kidding?" Con asked.

"No kidding," said Libby.

"She's here with Roger," said Melody.

Libby touched her mouth with the maroon linen napkin. "Actually," she said, "I'm not. We're working. Roger is Melinda's boss and I'm here to see that the lower half of the bride's dress doesn't fall down around her ankles."

"At least not yet," I said.

"It's a fantastic dress," he said, "and I say that as someone who's seen a lot of brides."

"Any of them yours?" Libby asked.

"Me?" he asked, and looked in my direction as if only someone who had subscribed to his sexual service could fully appreciate the irony of *that* question.

"Conrad is a bachelor," I said.

"What about you?" he asked Libby.

"You mean am I married?" She shook her head.

"This is the singles' table," I said, "except for Roger who's stag tonight. . . . Pam and Pass, who are single in name only—"

"More like the service table," said Libby. She went around in order, pointing, "Florist, florist, band, band, caterer, caterer, seamstress."

"Bandleader slash emcee," said Con, pointing to his own ruffled shirt, "who has to get back at the mike before the father of the bride comes looking for him."

"We were sayin' to Melinda that maybe we could all go out for a drink or something later," said Terri.

"Love to," said Con, already on his feet and sliding away.

"If you asked me to dance," I said to Roger while Libby was up at the dessert table, "at least you'd give the *appearance* of being here with no one in particular. The more women you dance with, the better."

"I'm a big boy," he answered.

"You wish. You love the idea of this, don't you—having a mistress. You, Roger Bonak, just like a guy in the movies." I checked Libby's progress. Good; a long line at the make-your-own chocolate fantasy. "You know what this reminds me of, don't you?"

Roger pursed his lips in protest.

"My father! He runs off with the first babe who licks her lips in his direction."

"That's really low," said Roger. "Your father was completely irresponsible."

"How is this different?" I demanded.

"It's *different*, because I'm living with this. I'm not running off, abandoning my family, and I'm not bringing it home to Robin."

"You think you're being *discreet*? You think people won't see what's going on after this? They'll be looking for signs that this wasn't just their imagination. You've planted the seeds good here tonight."

Roger wrapped his hand around his coffee cup and stared at it. "I'm not giving up Libby," he said quietly. "You only get one life."

"She doesn't love you," I said, checking the dessert line again.

"I know that."

"So what's in it for you—besides the obvious?"

Roger smiled ruefully, still staring at his cup. "The obvious is a lot."

I asked what their routine was—her house? Her store? The van?

"Her place," he said. "I park at least two blocks away."

I waited a few beats before asking, "Are you going there tonight?"

"I assume so."

"And then what? You go home and slip into bed, or do you take a shower first?"

Roger turned away, refusing to answer such a rude question.

"Do you think Robin suspects anything?"

"She doesn't. I act real normal around her."

"Where is she tonight?"

"Home."

"Where does she think you are?"

"She knows I'm here."

"I still can't believe it," I said.

"That's because you can't imagine a woman finding me attractive, other than Robin. That's what you can't believe."

"No. The unbelievable part is that you'd cheat on your wife.

It's like, if Roger Bonak can screw around, if Roger and Robin's marriage can break up, then nothing is sacred. No couple is safe. What do you think it does to my outlook as an unmarried woman who can't imagine a second date with the same man, let alone something permanent? I'm cynical enough about this stuff without you demonstrating that nothing ever works out."

"That's not my job, is it? Being a model husband so you can have the right outlook. You're acting like I was cheating on you."

Libby was walking toward us with a plate of out-of-season fruit. She sat down next to Roger, arranging her wide skirt evenly around her as if posing for an aerial shot. Her composure depressed me: Here I try to improve myself—as an artist, a daughter, an employee, a friend, an object of desire where appropriate—and nothing changes for the better. Meanwhile, Libby, without improving her character or even getting up from the sewing machine, finds something that resembles happiness.

It was suddenly too much—everywhere bodies dividing, the halves dancing, whispering, proposing, mating. I rose quickly, excusing myself with the embarrassed wave that fends off help and denies that anything is wrong.

23

Another Date with Conrad

I waited politely to one side of the dais as Conrad finished, "I Love You Just the Way You Are." He'd untied his bow tie, left it dangling from his unbuttoned collar so he'd look more like a jaded crooner in a smoky club.

"Hi, babe," he said right into the mike.

I nodded curtly: leave me out of the song, thank you.

"You all know Melinda LeBlanc, the genius behind the flowers here tonight? Can we put our hands together in a tribute to her talents?" A polite smattering of applause. "I'm going to take five, but that leaves Ron and Ronny and Skip up here, so don't sit down. And you guys still sitting down, get up off those tushes and find a lady." He swatted the mike away and stepped down next to me.

"Want to get together later?" I asked.

He took my chin in his hand and said, "She's seriously asking if he wants to see her later?"

"She's not taking anything for granted. Which I believe is the deal."

Now he took my face between both of his hands. "When you and I book the same affair, you don't have to check my date book for conflicts." He kissed me on the lips and I thought, even his quick pecks employed his tongue.

"Melody and Terri asked if we could all go out for a drink afterward."

"*After?*" he said coyly.

"After you're done here?"

"After I'm done here," said Con, his lips on my hair, "I'm going to be sticking my throbbing wogga into the pussy of my dreams."

"And how would you say that in table conversation?"

"Tell them that," said Con. "They'll understand. Or tell them it's late and you have to get up for church tomorrow."

"I'll just say I'll take a rain check. They were probably being polite."

"You look sinful in that suit," he said, nuzzling again. "I love the statement you're making—gray flannel, all business. I love that I'm the only guy here who knows there's a lace teddy underneath. . . . What color is tonight's?"

"Pink."

He bit his knuckles theatrically. "I'm supposed to get through the rest of the night knowing that?"

"You'll make it."

"What material?" Con asked.

"Silk."

He groaned.

"What do you do when I'm not around?" I asked.

"Ooh. A serious question. . . . You mean sexually?"

"Yeah. What does the horniest guy in America do between the occasional weddings in Harrow where I happen to be involved?"

"Ouch!"

"It's a reasonable question—do you get like this when the clock is ticking and it's almost time to get out of your pants, or are you like this regardless?"

"You answer that: What was I like when we first met, I mean before we started dating? I carried on a normal conversation, even *with* the sparks flying."

"I guess so. . . ."

"I'm like an old work horse, doll. Basically I want to be in the pasture, doing what I like to do best. Take me out on the road, I'm slow. Turn me in the direction of home, and I gallop."

I pushed him away and said, "You don't have to sweet-talk me. We have a date. I won't change my mind."

"Just don't worry about the girls. They'll be doing their own nasty thing anyway."

"I'm not worrying."

He pressed my hand, said he had to get back; and then I had his door key. "This way you can leave whenever you're tired instead of waiting around here until the last dog is hung," he said.

I took it and said, "I'll probably be asleep when you get there."

"Daddy'll wake you up," he said.

I'll tell you: there's something about having sex with a performing artist, especially one who has just got off work, that seems less than sincere. Conrad had a way of watching himself, I thought; admiring every move, as if he's congratulating himself throughout on his technique. That he carried on a good deal about how great it was, how awesome, but part of his mind was scoring himself on a men's magazine quiz, "You Loved It, But Did She?"

Not the kind of thing you'd bring up over coffee, or ever: "Too good?" he would say. "I don't get it. How'm I supposed to make myself a lousy lay? That's what you're looking for?"

"I'm not sure myself," I would say.

"We're not talking about love here by any chance?" he might say. " 'Cause we know what we are to each other, right? I mean, don't think I don't feel love for you; in fact I'm a little hurt you think I could get this much into it without that feeling. That wasn't what you were saying, was it?"

I didn't know what I was thinking. Con slept, sprawled naked across his bed. I could have gotten back into my gray wool suit and slept at home, except that Con had read somewhere that the women you fuck should spend the night—that sincere lovers are hospitable hosts, too. So I made a spot for myself, tugging gingerly until I had enough navy blue sheet to tuck under my chin.

I reviewed the wedding—how I could have varied the arrangements subtly from table to table, and I should have brought the altar urns to the reception to frame the head table.

What else? With no one to talk to—Con was dead to the world as only a twice postcoital man can be—provoked by Libby and Roger, I reviewed the forms of love in Harrow as observed or experienced by Melinda LeBlanc in the last twelve months of her life: pointless and sexual. Adulterous. Dishonest. Convenient. Unacknowledged. Never going to happen.

24

All Things Considered

I called Dennis at home Monday night and got a busy signal for more than an hour. When I finally got through, I learned that one of his local commentaries had made it onto "All Things Considered." Old friends were phoning their congratulations.

"What was it about?" I asked.

"About a friend of mine, a black guy, who was fishing on the Battenkill and this other trout fisherman kept smiling and waving, and finally came over to shake my friend's hand and ask for advice."

"So?"

"He thought it was me. A case of mistaken identity, even though Matt is six-three and doesn't look anything like me. Like the Celtics rookie who got rolled by the police in Wellesley as a bank robbery suspect because he was black? I thought it was kind of funny—this white guy thinking, what's a black guy doing fly fishing? Oh, it must be that one who puts out the catalogue."

I asked if his friend straightened the guy out.

"Yeah. He said he looked real innocent, and said, 'Gee. I wonder why you'd take me for Dennis Vaughan?'"

"And what'd the guy say?"

"The usual—no apology. Just walked away, thinking he made an honest mistake."

"Did your friend get mad?"

Dennis said, "He moved to another spot upriver and figured he caught the guy's fish."

"Did you put that in?" I asked.

"I hinted at it; the trick is to sound wise and thoughtful but not self-important. I added some related things about when I worked in TV in Boston and people either took me for any number of athletes and black anchormen or felt for their wallets. Stuff like that. I think it was pretty good."

"I'm sorry I missed it."

"It was funny, too. I usually don't do that."

"I know. Maybe you should."

"It's not my strong point, but they like that ironic twist on life."

I asked who he'd heard from.

"A cousin in Indianapolis . . . a guy I worked with in TV . . . another guy who lived on my corridor freshman year . . . a woman I knew in Boston. You."

I told him I was calling about something else.

Dennis waited: what is it this time—gossip, pressure, constructive criticism?

"I heard you were putting together a softball team. Libby told me."

"I am. Are you interested?"

"Very much interested."

"Can you play?"

"Is that a prerequisite?"

"It helps."

"I can actually stop a ball in the infield one way or the other."

"Good; that's good. Can you hit?"

"I run fast," I said. "I've been used as a pinch runner."

"When did you do all this?"

"Growing up. I played with the boys in my neighborhood— serious, organized daily games. I had my own glove."

"How old were you?"

"Ten, eleven."

"Hitting?" he tried again.

"I have a tendency to swing late."

"But you know the game. That's better than Libby."

"I'm not bad with ground balls, as long as they're not coming too fast."

Dennis groaned good-naturedly. "Shake a tree and a hundred gloves fall out. What this team needs is some *wood*."

"You probably have some wood and you're being modest."

"Can't have too much wood."

"Who else have you recruited?"

"Nick and Lyman, Libby, my brother-in-law, Chris; one of my suppliers who played freshman ball at UMass; and that's it so far, plus a pitcher. We have time. My original idea was to have it made up of people who work on Main Street, which I interpret liberally. The coed league rules say you need at least three out of nine on the field to be women at any given time."

"What about Robin?" I asked.

"You think she'd be interested?"

"She's always interested in civic organizations. Can't you see her as the first-base coach?" I waited a beat then asked if he would have asked me to join the team if I hadn't asked first . . . con-

227

fessed I had felt a little sorry for myself being left out of the initial planning session; that I'd seen everybody walk by on their way to dinner at MacWhinny's.

"I knew you were working," he said. "Libby said you were working late to get everything ready for a Saturday wedding."

"I was. I wouldn't have been able to come."

He laughed and said, "Well, that makes perfect sense."

"It wasn't anything rational. Just my life."

"I'll tell you what," said Dennis. "As a vote of confidence, what if I make you the assistant manager, now that I know you're committed?"

"What does an assistant manager do?"

"Helps me make the decisions."

"What kind?"

"You wouldn't have to make coaching decisions—I'm going to be the player-coach; you'd help me with the other stuff."

"Like what?"

"Whatever you wanted to. Organizing stuff, setting up a practice schedule . . . the T-shirts."

"Am I the first one you asked?"

"That's right."

"It didn't come up the other night at your organizational dinner?"

"No it didn't," said Dennis.

I said, "I guess I'd enjoy it. At least you couldn't kick me off the team if I'm the assistant manager."

"I wouldn't kick you off the team," said Dennis.

"Libby didn't want to do it?" I asked.

"I didn't ask her."

"Just curious," I said.

"I didn't choose to ask her, as much as you refuse to believe anything I say about Libby."

"I believe you."

"We need women. She's on the team because she's on our block. It would be rude not to ask her, just like we'll ask Roger and Robin."

"I doubt if both of them will play," I said. "Among other things, they'd have to get a babysitter."

"Maybe they could trade off," said Dennis.

"Don't beg them too hard. If they're reluctant to join the team, just say thanks, maybe next year, or something like that, okay?"

Dennis laughed. "Good thing Nick and Lyman don't feel that way."

He thought I meant I get enough of Roger and Robin during the day; please don't make me play softball with them at night.

"That's entirely different. Nick and Lyman love you," I said.

Dennis didn't respond head-on to my statement. He answered by asking if I'd heard the name they had come up with.

Let me guess, I said; a fishing motif: the Mariners? The Whalers?

"Pathetic," said Dennis, "although you're in the ballpark."

I pictured the blackboard at Schiner Bros. Seafood: The Swordfish. The Mackerel. The Jumbo Shrimp. The Farm-Raised Catfish.

"The Lunkers," said Dennis proudly.

"The Lunkers?" I repeated.

"It means a fish that's big for its breed."

"The Lunkers," I said again.

"We thought it sounded funny, too; like we don't need all that much talent for a name like that. And if by any chance we turn out to be decent, the name'll be ironic."

I had heard this delight in his voice before, the times I'd seen him talking on the phone to a customer who had caught something wonderful or fished somewhere beautiful. He would pace with the receiver cradled between his ear and shoulder, straining the cord, too excited to steer clear of whoever was in his way.

"What about uniforms?" I asked, looking for ways to stretch the lunker talk, to preserve the joy in his voice, and the warmth.

"T-shirts. Otherwise you look as if you're taking it too seriously. The team from the Artisans' Loft has these uniforms that look like cyclists' outfits. They're too into it—they drink Gatorade on the bench and give each other high fives. We're just cool. We're gonna be the *fun* team. Shirts and visors, that's it. I figured we'd use my logo on the back, enlarged, with the trout speckled in green, brown and hot pink. And on the front: The Lunkers. White shirts, neon-pink lettering."

"What's their team called?"

"The A.L. Champs—A.L. for Artisans' Loft; A.L. for American League? Get it?"

"I hate them already," I said.

"Thatta girl," said Dennis.

"When do we start?"

"June."

Months before my advice and consent were needed. "Guess we have plenty of time," I said.

"First," said Dennis, "we need players. Ask around; any tall, rangy guys come in looking for flowers—"

I told him to forget that; where would I find any men at work?

"You don't get any male customers?"

"Robin waits on the walk-ins."

"I've seen you wait on customers."

"When I'm alone."

After a pause he said, "You could always ask your boyfriend."

I asked where he had heard I had a boyfriend.

"It's a small town."

"What did you hear?"

"A guy in a band. I don't know his name."

I certainly was not going to expound on the fine points of my purely tactile and easily misunderstood relationship with Conrad. I said, "If I'm not mistaken, you've renounced your stake in any of this."

He thought about that for a while. "I don't like my friends getting involved with the wrong people."

"I think we shouldn't discuss each other's social life. I don't particularly want to hear who you're dating."

"I'm not dating anyone."

"And that's fine with you?"

"I'm making progress," he said.

"How so?" I asked.

"For one thing . . ." He stopped. When I prompted he said, "My ex-wife is going to pitch."

"Iris," I said pleasantly.

"She's good. Played for a women's team that made it to the playoffs when she was in high school. She actually has an earned-run average."

I said I was surprised: him wanting Iris on his team. Considering.

"That's life, though, isn't it? You always end up playing on the same team as people you have a history with. Friends, enemies, ex-wives . . ."

"Miscellaneous paramours."

"Miscellaneous paramours."

I thought of saying "one-night stands," but hesitated. It was a little bald, even for me.

"Were you going to elaborate on that?" he asked.

"On what?"

"I don't know—after paramours. I thought you were going to say something else."

"Were *you?* I cut you off."

"No, no, you didn't. Not at all."

231

I laughed. "Aren't we the souls of politeness?"

"Above all else," he said—a little grimly.

"It might have been Iris. I was going to ask if having her around would ruin your fun."

"I thought about it. I decided having no pitcher would get me down worse than having my ex-wife on my team."

"It's not like you hate each other," I offered.

Dennis said dryly, "I wouldn't go that far."

"It's just that you've made peace with your divorce?"

"Something like that."

"Is this new?"

"She's being a little more civil when we run across each other. A lot of my stomach-churning had to do with her attitude."

"Do you hate her guts? Just between us managers?"

"Nothing I can't handle."

I said that was good, I was glad I had called him. . . . And in the future could he check with me first when he heard my name linked romantically with unsubstantiated males? I'd return the favor, naturally.

"Sounds reasonable."

I said, "I should hang up so more people can call with their congratulations. I'm sure I'll talk to you tomorrow."

"Sure," said Dennis. "Bring your coffee over."

"I'd like that."

His pause was eloquent: *What have I done? Doesn't "I'd like that" sound like the acceptance of a date? Could it signal that she views tomorrow's visit as more meaningful than today's?*

"Someone's always around," he said.

I see: A woman can't imply she's looking forward to anything in a man's presence—a poke in the eye, a cup of cold coffee—without him worrying if her expectations are too high. Well, fuck you, Dennis; fuck all men.

232

"About my being assistant manager," I said. "Maybe you should take that under consideration before committing yourself."

"Did I say something wrong?" he asked. "You sound mad again."

Truth? You think I should have spoken the truth? Blurted out some declaration at this late date?

Well, I didn't. I said good night and sorry, whatever, for sounding cranky. Congratulations on "All Things Considered."

It was professional advice. Martha says women stink at confrontation—her dissertation; soon to be a chapter in a college textbook. Men hate the truth. It's only on television with scripts to follow that they hear you out with wet, grateful eyes.

In real life you tell them how you feel, they tell you they're flattered. Then they cross the street when they see you for the rest of your unmarried days.

25

House Call

My mother called me from the supermarket where she had a two-day job passing out low-fat microwave french fries and coupons therefor. "I'd like to talk things out with you," she said.

"What things?" I asked.

"You know," she murmured.

"You can't talk there?"

"Exactly," she said with the firm brightness of someone being overheard.

"The Gerry question?"

"Partly."

"The Lou question?"

"Yes," she said briskly. "I hope you'll be home for dinner."

"Sure. Something happen?"

234

"I'm leaving in fifteen minutes. I'll pick up some fish on the way home."

"You do that," I said.

"Anything you want from here?"

I told her ice cream, but not the healthy kind. A pint of Dastardly Mash or Chunky Monkey. It wouldn't kill me.

She cooked in the white lab coat she wore at the supermarkets to look like a nutritionist with a degree. I asked if this job was over.

"One more day, then I'm at Shop Rite for two days."

"Did you bring any home?" I asked.

My mother was standing guard by the broiler, both hands in large quilted mitts. She frowned at me over her shoulder and said, "Frozen french fries?"

"I like french fries."

She ignored my challenge, turning back to the sole.

"Julia Child likes french fries. I read in *Boston* magazine once where they polled gourmet chefs about their favorite junk food, and Julia Child said, 'The shoestring potatoes at McDonald's.'"

My mother turned two oven dials to Off with a click. "Julia Child got cancer."

I was setting the table—my mother liked plastic place mats protecting the embroidered kitchen tablecloth. I waited a few moments so I wouldn't snap at her, then asked, reasonableness itself, if she worried more than most people did about the food she ate.

"I know you think I do."

"Only because it seems like a full-time job. And you can be preachy about it."

My mother slid a portion of sole from her stainless steel spatula to my plate. "Lou gives me a full pound no matter how much I ask for," she said.

235

"Maybe it's sublimation."

She asked who and what I was talking about.

"You're always worrying about what you eat."

My mother took a bite of her unseasoned sole and said, "I cooked it just right."

"It could use a little sauce or something."

She passed me a saucer which held two quarters of fresh lemon. "Not if you really love the taste of the sole; if you appreciate its own flavor." That was her condiments argument, which had become a moral one: if you were good enough—smart enough, really—to appreciate what was pure and natural, you didn't need to hide it under tartar sauce.

I went over to the refrigerator and got my jar of salsa from the outlaw shelf. "In normal families," I said, "I would spoon this on top of my fish without apologizing for it."

My mother squeezed a few drops of lemon on her fish to show that she, too, could be an adventurous eater.

I said, "You never cheat."

"What's sublimation?" she answered.

"Doing something that's socially acceptable in place of something not so socially acceptable. Sex, usually. You never cheat on your diet because it gives you control of at least one area of your life."

My mother passed me the bowl of shredded steamed cabbage. I shook my head no. "Is this something you've been accusing me of for a long time?" she asked.

I said, no; just this minute, actually. But talking to Martha on a regular basis had sharpened my psychological insight. " 'Accuse,' by the way, was the wrong word," I said.

"Martha," she repeated as if it were a solution to a puzzle.

"Schiff-Shulman."

"I know who Martha is."

"My shrink."

My mother had been slipping the spatula under a second portion of sole, but left it on the platter. "Officially?"

"For fun," I said. "Someone with the right degrees to bounce my life off."

My mother went back for her piece of sole and wordlessly offered me seconds, too. I said sure, it was delicious fish. Pass the salt and pepper. "What kinds of things do you discuss with her?"

"You know," I said.

She pressed her lips together then said, "Men?"

"Bingo."

"And what does she say?"

I laughed. "It's a wide open subject. She says different things about different men. Depending on the guy and the circumstances."

"Can you give me a for-instance?"

"Well . . . Nick."

She squinted. Nick hadn't registered.

"Nick, from Brookhoppers? Dennis's associate?"

"Nick and Lyman," she said.

"There was a little . . . thing. I was told that Nick was interested in me."

"Who told you?"

"Lyman. And Dennis, sort of. So I looked into it, and Nick was too shy or too weirded out to respond. I described the whole thing to Martha after the fact and she had some opinions."

"Could I hear them?"

"I can't remember her exact words, but the gist was that Nick is young and under Dennis's thumb. Something like that."

My mother frowned, suggesting that it was just as well I wasn't paying an hourly fee for such nonadvice. "I don't understand," she said.

"Nick works for Dennis. I'm Dennis's friend." I smiled as if that certainly settled that.

237

"Dennis would be jealous?" she asked tentatively.

"Ma. No. Forget it."

"I'm not following—"

"Look: Martha has a talent for seeing things clearly, even if I'm not explaining it well. Nick is beside the point." I reached for her plate, and she nodded her permission for me to clear. From the sink, I heard her say to my back, "Do you think Martha would listen to me and give me some advice?"

I shut off the water and sat down quickly. "About Lou?"

She nodded.

"Tea?" I asked.

"Please."

I said carefully, "I could call Martha right now before you change your mind."

"I'm thinking it's a good idea," she said after a few moments.

I dialed Martha's number. I'd have to speak in code, because Martha knew everything I knew about my mother's lust for Lou. Stephen answered. I asked if I was interrupting their dinner and he said no, he had a seminar on Thursday night so they ate obscenely early. I greeted Martha's hello with, "Could you come over and have tea with me and Rosalie?"

"What's up?" asked Martha.

"My mother would like to talk to you. I told her what a good confidante you are."

"Whose idea was this?"

"Rosalie's." I smiled at my mother.

"Is this on the level?" Martha asked.

"Absolutely. I'm thrilled she wants to talk."

"Does she know I know?"

"Absolutely not," I said, trying to make it sound like an answer to a wholly different question.

"When?"

"A.S.A.P. Water's on for tea."

"Are you forcing me on her?"

I held the phone up to my mother and said loudly, "Ma, am I forcing Martha on you?"

"No you are not."

"Hear that?" I said into the receiver.

"Okay. I need ten minutes here. Tell Rosalie I'm flattered."

After I'd hung up, my mother took a third plastic daisy from the drawer and set Martha's place with a careful precision I knew meant she was about to say something quarrelsome.

"She said she'd be right over," I called from the sink.

"I bet she knows the whole story."

"Which whole story?"

"Mine."

"Unh-uh."

"You never said a word to her about me and Lou?"

"Ask Martha. Psychotherapists don't lie."

"She's your friend. She's not going to break any of your confidences just because I ask her what's what."

I sprinkled scouring powder on the appropriate sponge—we assigned three for different duties—and wiped the sink. After a minute I heard her say, "You don't have to lie to me, you know."

"I don't," I said automatically.

"I know you think you have to protect me from the real world, but I can take care of myself. I can roll with the punches every bit as good as you can."

I said I knew that, really. I'd been shown that very fact by the Lou Schiner caper. And of course, her surviving my no-good father's running off with the Linda tramp.

She was sitting now, teacup and saucer centered mathematically on her place mat. Her face changed when she heard that name, and I realized that until now she had shielded me from this hatred.

"Thirty-one years," I said. "That's a long time to get the kind of look I saw on your face when I said her name."

My mother didn't answer.

"You know what it makes me think? It makes me think the wound never healed if you hate her that much."

She told me to rinse the green sponge well, and to hand her the yellow one; she'd do the table. "You can get over something enough to live your life and do what you have to do," she said.

"But you never really get over it?"

"She didn't want him! She left town and went back where she came from, and to this day never sent me any kind of word to show she was sorry for stealing my husband."

"Ma—you couldn't really expect you'd ever hear from her. Who would do that, call the abandoned, pregnant wife of the guy you seduced? Only a masochist would do that, and if anything she sounds like a spoiled brat."

"She is! A fifty-two-year-old spoiled brat."

I narrowed my eyes accusingly.

"Maybe I called her," she said.

"Recently?"

She said, taking a sip of tea first, swallowing fastidiously, "July twenty-eighth."

My birthday. I raised my eyebrows. "Just a coincidence?"

"I always call her on your birthday. I called her when you were born and it's become a tradition."

"You hot shit," I said.

She looked surprised, as if I were the first to suggest an act could be both criminal and defensible.

"What do you say?"

"I say, 'This is Rosalie LeBlanc. Today is my daughter's birthday'—or 'yesterday was' or 'tomorrow will be'—I vary it so she won't expect the call on any particular date; then I say my piece and hang up."

"What do you say exactly?"

My mother traced the petals of her place mat before saying, "Different things."

"You can get arrested for telephone harassment."

"I'm careful. And I only call once a year."

"How'd you find her?"

"MacMillan's alumni affairs office. They fall over themselves trying to be nice if they think it'll bring a donation." We heard the crunch of tires on gravel—Martha's Jeep.

"What does she say when you call?"

"Nothing! She hangs up, but in a different way each year. When we were still young she'd say, 'Go to hell' before hanging up. Then, when she got that out of her system, she'd just bang the receiver down. When we hit our forties, she'd hesitate before slamming the phone down, which gave me the idea that she was thinking of saying something to me. . . . A couple of years ago, around the time we turned fifty, there was this moment of silence so I said, 'Did you ever get anyone to marry you?' Not, 'Did you ever get married?' but *Did you ever get anyone to marry you?*"

The doorbell rang. I said, edging backward to the door, "I'll die if you don't let me tell Martha this."

"You know what her answer was? 'You're a very bitter woman, Rosalie.'"

I opened the door to Martha's hug. "Hi, Rosalie," she said over my shoulder.

"Doesn't she look all grown up and professorial?" I asked.

"We see each other all the time," said my mother.

"At the supermarket," Martha supplied.

"Did you have dinner?" my mother asked.

"Absolutely. But you go ahead."

"We ate—fish from Schiner Brothers," I said.

"Lemon sole. Very nice," said my mother.

"Always," said Martha.

"Are you a customer?" my mother asked.

Martha checked with me first. "They don't know me. Stephen's the one who shops for fish. I guess that makes me not a customer."

"Good," said my mother. "For this conversation, I mean."

Martha sat down, her coat still on. "Is it important to this conversation that I not be a customer of Schiner Brothers?"

My mother winced a ladylike yes, but said nothing.

"Do you want to tell me why it's important?"

My mother looked at me.

"Do you want me to start?" I asked.

She looked at Martha, a look that said *not just yet*.

I laughed and said, "You want me to leave, don't you?"

Martha opened her eyes with bland innocence, her I'm-only-the-shrink look.

"Ma?"

"I wouldn't mind speaking to Martha privately."

"But it was my idea."

After a diplomatic silence Martha said, "You know, in couples' therapy we interview the partners separately and then, depending on the nature of the problems, we bring them together for subsequent sessions."

"Except this isn't marriage counseling between her and me. I'm her sponsor. She wants to talk to you about her husband and her . . . life. I'm the facilitator." I smiled proudly at pulling out such an inspired title.

"Look," said Martha, less painstakingly, "go upstairs and watch the news and we'll call you down when we're ready."

I left, not exactly sulking, but thinking, this is what it would feel like to have a sister, and to be banished while she conspired with our mother.

* * *

I watched the rest of the network news, switching to "Jeopardy!" at 7:30. Then it was eight o'clock and I hadn't been summoned to the kitchen. I went down to the top of the stairs on the second floor and yelled, "I'm ready whenever you are."

Their voices were just a murmur, with no discernible response. I called again, "I'm coming. Ready or not. Time's up." As I entered the kitchen, they continued to talk with the intensity of two women trapped in a double date who like each other but hate the guys. Martha had moved one seat closer to my mother and was leaning forward, her chin in her hand, listening to what appeared to be the most fascinating story ever told.

"Mind if I join you?"

"Rosalie?" said Martha.

"We have no secrets," said my mother.

I sat down, sliding my cup of cold tea to my new seat assignment. "Any insights?"

"Plenty of insights," said Martha. "The question is, any decisions?"

"She agrees with you about one thing," said my mother, "and that's the idea that my not wanting to be married to Gerry has to be considered separately from my wanting to be with Lou." She turned to Martha for affirmation. Martha nodded her along. "And I'm blurring the issues when I talk about not wanting to stay married to Gerry."

"I knew that."

"Martha says I don't do any kind of meaningful talking with Gerry. Maybe I have to rediscover what I found there in the first place—"

"To reconcile her unconscious choices in a husband—maybe security or family expectations—with her romantic ones. . . ."

"She doesn't love Gerry," I said impatiently.

Martha waited for my mother to answer.

"She's in love with Lou," I said.

"Maybe," said Martha.

"Aren't you?"

My mother, the good catechism student, echoed *maybe*.

"Have your feelings changed?"

She checked with Martha, a look that said *stop me if I misspeak*. "My feelings for Lou haven't been tested in any way. We're still experiencing the first blush of love, like teenagers who have a crush on each other from afar but have never had a real date. That's not what you base a divorce on."

"They see each other practically every day," I said. "They've known each other since they were fifteen. And they've kissed in the cooler."

Martha laughed.

"What's so funny?" I asked.

"You're such a romantic. It's very sweet."

"Sometimes these situations call for romance. Rosalie's in love with her fish man and he's in love with her. And I don't think she'd be falling in love any differently if she were single. She'd go in there and they'd make eyes at each other and after a while they'd kiss, then have a few dates, then he'd propose. Her so-called marriage—"

"And his," said Martha. "Don't forget that thorny little fact."

"Okay, *their* so-called marriages come into this only because they complicate things legally. But it shouldn't be used to keep them apart."

"Of course it should," said Martha. "People take marriage vows, which their friends and relatives and counselors are supposed to uphold."

"Is this a code or something—you have to say this obligatory speech about marriage vows so you can hold your head up in counseling circles; like you took an oath in graduate school, but now we can get down to business and get Rosalie laid?"

"How crude," said Martha, finally peeling her coat off, "yet how astute."

I insisted that my mother leave the room—my turn. "She never talks about my father—" I began.

"Ever?"

"Not to me."

"Can you imagine? Something like that festering for your entire adult life?"

"Married to someone you don't love," I prompted.

"What about you?"

Me?

"He's your stepfather, the only father you ever knew. You don't have some ambivalence about her ending that marriage?"

"I want her to be happy."

"You didn't answer my question."

"I was eleven when they got married, and the only reason I went along with it was because my mother could give up her full-time job, and I'd get to be maid of honor."

"Are you sure? There's no bond between you?"

I shrugged. "He's pleasant enough."

"That's it? After twenty years? Seems pretty cold-blooded."

"He's never around. In real time I've probably known him three or four years."

"Must've been hard to share your mother after having her to yourself for your whole childhood."

I said, "Is that from the *Journal of Step-Parenting Psychology?*"

"It must have been particularly hard at eleven," she repeated, undeterred.

"It was."

Martha waited for a few moments, then said, "Because?"

"Because I didn't know him that well, and suddenly he was

245

living with us, in my mother's room. They hadn't gone out on that many dates; at least it didn't seem like she had known him long enough to marry him."

"Or to disappear into her bedroom with him."

"Men's cologne and deodorant in the medicine cabinet all of a sudden. Soap on a rope. I knew every time they had sex because he'd shave before going to bed and I'd hear his electric razor droning from the bathroom." I put my fist to my cheek and demonstrated with sound effects.

"You never got to feel comfortable around him?" she asked. "Even when you were older and presumably less horrified by your mother having sex?"

I said I knew what she was thinking: I was stunted. I had the emotional maturity of an eleven-year-old whose idea of marriage came from television where perfect parents slept in twin beds and sensible pajamas.

"No," said Martha.

"Can't I just dislike the guy's personality? Can't it be incredibly annoying to live with a champion salesman?"

Martha leaned back and asked carefully if I was—just possibly —urging my mother to do something romantic and impetuous and, well, heartbreaking, as a way of experiencing a vicarious thrill, since my life might arguably be called . . . socially unfruitful at this juncture?

"Am I pushing her toward Lou as a substitute for having anyone to push myself onto?"

"More or less."

"As in: 'Get a life, Melinda'?"

Martha shrugged apologetically.

"I've thought of that." I put more water on to boil, and sat down again. Martha asked softly, tapping my arm once, then leaving her hand there, "What *is* new with you, kiddo?"

"Nothing."

"What are you working on?"

"Nothing great. Another wedding Saturday; a big banquet at the Harrow Inn Sunday."

"How was Randy and Paulette's wedding?" she asked.

I said it was okay.

"Didn't you say Conrad's band was playing."

"That's right."

"And?"

I said in a monotone, "I went back to his apartment and fucked him. It was very nice, doctor."

"Was he a *mensch*?" she asked, her favorite character test.

"No more than usual."

"Are you going to see him again?"

"Probably."

"Next gig, you mean?"

"That's right, Martha. He's using me for sex. We have no relationship outside our incidental one. He's a loser. I'm a jerk. You're right again."

Martha smiled and said, "I guess that puts me in my place."

"You deserve it."

"For asking how a wedding went, a wedding of two locals with a large guest list culled from the immediate population, yet there's nothing else to report?"

"Do you know something?"

"I know you. I know you'd have called me to report on the banalities of such an affair, so the fact I haven't heard a word means there's something knocking around in your head."

I looked at the wall clock instead of her and said, "Several things, thank you very much."

Martha inched her chair closer to mine and said, "Great. Like what?"

"Confidentially?"

"Of course!"

247

I looked directly at her this time, waited a beat and said, "Cousin. Roger. And. Libby."

Martha's eyes widened first, then her lips parted to mouth a drawn-out *no*.

"It's true. I got it from the horses' mouths. They came to the wedding together."

Martha whistled.

I said I knew; a biggie. Ramifications up the wazoo.

She tilted her head in the direction of the stairs.

"I haven't told her."

"Robin?"

"Nothing."

"They came as a *couple?*"

"Pretty much. Of course they thought nobody would put two and two together."

"And now you're in the middle. How considerate of them."

"Exactly!"

"Libby and Roger," Martha murmured. "Talk about unlikely couples."

"I'm not talking to her," I said.

"Because . . . ?"

"Because I'm being unreasonable," I said.

"You mean you haven't gone out of your way to talk to her, or you refuse to talk to her when you meet face to face?"

"Both," I said with the conviction of someone who hasn't had to test either scenario.

"What do you think's going to happen?"

"I know what's going to happen! Libby's going to get sick of Roger and tell him to get lost, and Robin will already have figured it out because he's mooning around so much. So everyone will be miserable."

"And you'll be blamed," said Martha.

"Me?"

"Sure. You're Libby's friend, and you'll be perceived by Robin as part of the conspiracy."

"No I won't."

"I'm not saying it's logical, but that's what happens. You won't be perceived as a neutral party. Believe me, I've seen it happen—the friend who knows about the neighbor's affair tells the injured party; the affair ends, the couple stay together, and both stop talking to the friend who did the informing."

I thought this over and said, "You're not always right, either."

"Keep out of it," she said.

I looked at the wall clock again. "What about Gerry and my mother? She's upstairs thinking we're solving her life."

Martha checked her watch and made a face. "We haven't even scratched the surface with you."

"We can pick up next time where we left off. She's going to want a plan."

"What else is knocking around in your head, besides Libby?"

"Can you have lunch tomorrow?"

"What's tomorrow? Friday. Yes. Give me the key words so I can *hak* you if you forget."

Key words? Okay, I said: Softball; Dennis Vaughan.

Martha smiled and said, "I like that."

Now, about Gerry, I said. Poor guy; we can't even focus on him long enough to get him divorced.

"Do you think he'll be devastated?" asked Martha.

"Surprised; inconvenienced because this phone number is on his letterhead. But will he lose any sleep? Doubt it."

"Do you think he cheats on your mother?"

"All the time."

"Do you know this for a fact?"

"I don't need to. I saw *Death of a Salesman*."

"With Dustin Hoffman?" asked Martha. "Or the movie with Lee J. Cobb?"

I laughed and said, "You don't give a shit about Gerry, either."

Martha persisted. "Does he love her?"

"Nah."

"Are you sure? He might not be demonstrative, but—"

"Look, she won't fool around, even though they're the perfect candidates for it—absentee husband, invalid wife—so I think she should clear the field. That's my position. If Gerry's in love with her, here's his golden opportunity to say so. Maybe he will, but I suspect he won't. That's it; I rest my case."

"You're tough."

"She wanted my help, and I think this is what she counted on me to say."

"Look. You don't divorce a guy in one night. We'll call her down, we'll say Rosalie, here's what we want you to think about: blah blah blah, Gerry; blah, blah, blah, Lou; blah, blah Lou's wife the crackpot; how you'd feel if such and such didn't happen; would you still want the divorce. Blah, blah, blah. What is your goal, let's talk in a week."

"Fine."

We nodded solemnly, a pact. I called to my mother. She said she'd be right down.

Martha whispered, "You, however—tomorrow, lunch. Faculty Club, one o'clock. Softball. Dennis Vaughan."

26

Iris Signs On

I love eating at the Faculty Club, even with its unremarkable food (turkey pot pie, shrimp salad on croissants, Waldorf salad); in spite of its unfriendly stares from untenured professors wondering if you're interviewing for their jobs. It's a nice space, as we retail merchants say, white and gallerylike, with faculty art well lit against exposed granite walls. I like it more than Martha does—it's not egalitarian enough for her because staff is excluded —but she indulges me once or twice a semester.

We met on Monday, because Robin said my wanting to take a lunch hour on a Friday was quite unbelievable, frankly. Of all days, as if I hadn't been doing this for enough years to consider Friday out of the question.

Okay, I said. *Okay.* Excuse me for living. I needed to talk to

251

Martha over some critical issues affecting my life, but I'd postpone until Monday, as long as that was a dead enough day for her to grant me a lunch hour. And since when was she starting to sound like Roger?

"Roger is not always unreasonable," said Robin.

"All right, I'm sorry. I shouldn't have asked."

"If Martha's your friend, why can't she meet you after work some night?"

"She came over last night. I'd talk to her this weekend, but, as you know, I'm working Saturday and Sunday."

"Oh, which reminds me," said Robin.

"What?"

"Roger's going to do the setup for those affairs. He thinks it's time he did more on that end."

"Really?"

"He says with you doing the big jobs and him doing the walk-in stuff, he's not growing."

I said, "Roger's not so great on the big jobs—on seeing the big picture, like in a wedding. His taste is a little . . . corny."

"He wants to learn," said Robin.

I couldn't help myself. I said, "He must have enjoyed Randy and Paulette's wedding."

"He did. Although I think he was embarrassed that Forget-Me-Not had two florists showing up for the reception and the meal. I'm knocking twenty-five dollars off the bill for that reason."

"Paulette expected me to stay after I'd spent a couple hours setting up."

"I'm not saying you weren't welcome."

"Yes you are. You're implying that I crashed the wedding and embarrassed my employer."

Robin shook her head with her eyes closed until I stopped

talking. "Roger is going to try to be more creative—that's all I'm saying. And you won't have to work every wedding and every affair. He plans on being more artistic. He's had a very good teacher, after all," she said.

"Why all of a sudden?"

"Taking on more, you mean?"

I nodded. Robin said, "Boredom, maybe."

"Mid-life crisis?"

"At twenty-nine?"

"Figuratively," I said.

Robin ignored me with a bright smile as the harness bells announced the arrival of a customer. I disappeared into the workroom before I could be consulted.

I ordered a Reuben and Martha had the salad plate, which was an ice-cream scoop each of tuna salad, potato salad and cottage cheese. She said she'd been ordering it for twenty years since coming here with her father as a little girl.

"What are you working on today?" she asked.

I told her a funeral with all bulbs.

"Who died?"

"Mrs. Horne."

"The newspaper Hornes?"

"The mother. Ninety years old. White tulips, narcissus. They spent a fortune. The employees sent an arrangement of Casablanca lilies that practically took up the whole van. Everyone chipped in. And a beautiful message that the editor of the living pages composed."

Martha said, "I shouldn't laugh, but I used to read her restaurant reviews aloud to Stephen—Adele B. Horne, right?—and howl. She'd always try the most pedestrian thing on the menu, then say, 'I ordered the onion soup, the veal parmigiana with a side

253

order of spaghetti and Jell-O for dessert . . . So did my companion.' "

As she chatted I saw Iris Lambrix enter and give her faculty I.D. number to the woman seated by the door. Martha turned around to see what was distracting me. She said quietly, "I forgot to tell you—her contract's not being renewed."

"Iris? You know this for a fact?"

"Her department voted in her favor, but not by a big enough margin, so now she'll get a hearing, where every student who ever hated her gets a chance to testify."

I asked if people ever pull it out.

"Sure. The ones who are really popular with students. Then they pack the meeting and have placards about 'Those who can, teach; those who can't, write papers.' You pretty much don't have a prayer if you're an Iris Lambrix with no constituency."

"They don't have enough black professors as it is," I said.

"They need her more than she needs them," said Martha. "She should be the CEO of some big corporation. She'll make ten times her salary here—a black woman with a Ph.D. in management?"

"When's the hearing?"

"Not for a month. They have to give everyone lots of notice so they'll have time to come to her defense."

"She must be ready to kill."

"Or ready to sue," said Martha. "I would."

"Maybe she *is* a terrible teacher."

"It's a popularity contest! The male professors can be pompous douche bags and still have graduate students fighting over them for teaching assistantships. But women have to be *nurturing*"—her voice curled around the word contemptuously—"which is what Iris is up against."

Iris sat down at a table near the door, facing away from us and apparently unaware of our presence.

I told Martha about her bitchy posted hours in Stedman House; about Dennis's impression that the students were afraid of her.

"And he married her after that?"

"They were two of the few black professionals in town. He mistook that for their belonging together."

"It was their choice to live in Harrow. It couldn't have been a major priority to associate only with black women."

"He chose Harrow because it made good business sense, not—"

"Does he date white women?"

"Date?" I repeated.

"Date? Go out on dates. As in 'girlfriend'? And don't say the word 'Libby.' You're a broken record on that score."

I said neutrally, "He's attracted to white women. I don't think that's a problem."

Martha stared for a few moments, maybe even less, and said, "You've slept with him, haven't you?"

"I have not."

"You know you can tell me."

I asked why she jumped to that ridiculous conclusion.

"It makes sense," said Martha. "You're always pressing the black-and-blue spot named Libby, even while Dennis swears up and down he's not interested."

"I've abandoned that campaign. He's not carrying a secret torch for Libby."

Martha said, "I still don't get it."

"What's that?"

"Your pushing them together. Unless it's guilt, that somewhere along the line you fell in love with him yourself and had to push him into Libby's arms because she called it first."

I said, "I'm not that good a friend."

"I hate to disabuse you," said Martha, "but yes you are. You're also in love with Dennis."

I said, Look: I am not. There was something there, all right? Once. One night. Okay? It happens. That's what you're picking up, a little history and that's all. Both of us have managed not to let it affect our friendship, which was lucky, considering the way men handle these things. Billy Riley? Remember that jerk? He can't even buy a fucking bouquet-of-the-day from our pail on the sidewalk without blushing. Dennis is much much more mature; no comparison."

I could see a new thought invade Martha's brain. "Do black people blush?" she asked.

"Probably."

"I think they don't. I read a piece in the science section of the *Times* that said blushing may not be involuntary after all. They think people do it because it reflects favorably on your character —makes you look as if you're modest. It's actually a kind of coyness, and you've conditioned yourself to have this response because people react favorably to it."

At least in her academic mode she'd stopped talking about Dennis. That was one of the tedious but often useful things about being friends with a professor: every damn thing reminds them of a piece they read in the *Times*.

I said soon I was going to march over to her table to express my sympathy or whatever was appropriate, and say I was looking forward to being Lunkers together.

"Lunkers?" Martha repeated.

"The Lunkers, our softball team. Dennis and I are managing it, and Iris is going to be our starting pitcher. Obviously, we're in bad shape if she gets the ax and leaves town."

"I get it: 'softball and Dennis Vaughan.' That's what you

wanted to talk to me about." Martha flattened her scoop of cottage cheese with her fork before taking small, unhappy bites.

"Maybe I'll just welcome her to the team, and not say anything about the vote in case she thought we were gossiping."

"Since when are you interested in softball?"

"Dennis is sponsoring a coed team and needs a few women. I said I'd play, and I'd be his assistant manager. Iris is going to pitch."

Martha said with a cool smile, "What a forgiving man to ask his lesbian ex-wife to join his happy little social club."

"It's not just a courtesy; she pitched for real on a team in New York."

"And when push comes to shove, winning is more important than one's own personal hatred of one's ex-wife. That's a male thing: you put up with less-than-perfect teammates because you know that it takes five or nine or eleven to play. I read a book about it once. Women aren't raised playing pickup games of football, so they expect excellence from everyone on the team."

I said, "Very interesting. Now I'm going to ask my pitcher if she'd like to join us."

"Fine," said Martha.

"Don't let them take my sandwich away."

I walked to Iris's table. She was writing in a notebook, scowling with concentration. I spoke her name softly. She looked up, narrowed her eyes slightly as if dredging up my name and my connection to this spot. "Melinda," I said.

"I know who you are," a reprimand meant as a compliment.

"How are you?"

"Have you heard?"

"About the vote?" I nodded.

"I expected it," said Iris.

"How could you have?"

"I'm not a popular teacher and I'm not one of the boys. Far from it."

"Look, I'm having lunch with Martha Schiff-Shulman, and she's not one of the boys, either. Would you like to join us?"

"I've already ordered."

"They can bring it to our table."

"I find people being nice to me all of a sudden," said Iris.

I laughed.

"I'm not kidding. I'm the object of everyone's solidarity and pity. The crossroads of sexism, racism and homophobia. A one-woman bias festival."

Iris hadn't discussed her sexual orientation with me, so this was new ground. I said, "Are you going to fight it?"

"Sure. If the president's stupid enough to let it go through."

"Martha's on your side. You can talk in front of her," I said.

"What department?"

"Psychology, but she agitates all over."

"How do you know her?"

"She went to high school with me."

"Is she friends with Miss Libby, too?" asked Iris.

"No."

Iris transferred her napkin from lap to tabletop, accepting my invitation. Martha was waiting, looking hospitable. She stood and extended her right hand to Iris as I led her to our table. "Boy, do you have a good case," said Martha in greeting.

"What'd I tell you?" I murmured to Iris.

"Sit," said Martha. She pantomimed to the waitress that Iris was here now, and her order should be rerouted accordingly. Returning to Iris she said, "Are you angry yet or are you still groggy from the one-two punch?"

Iris said smartly, "Interviewing lawyers today and tomorrow."

"Have you two formally met?" I asked.

"I'm sure, somewhere along the way," said Martha.

"Heard you were a faculty kid," said Iris.

"My dad was political philosophy and my mother was a secretary in Theatre."

"Retired?"

"To Chapel Hill," said Martha. "An enclave of Yankee professors emeriti." Using Iris's exact tone, she added, "Heard you had a mean right arm."

"Left," said Iris. "Southpaw."

Martha turned her palm up with a flourish. "Your coach."

"Assistant manager," I said modestly.

"Go on."

"Honest," I said. "They need women."

"Another good reason why you can't leave town," said Martha.

"I'll be around. I'm not running away so fast. And I've got ties in the community."

Without blinking Martha asked, "Your lover's here?"

Iris nodded.

"Does she do something transferable?"

"She's an artist, so theoretically, yes."

The waitress, a studentlike woman with a single blond braid and round wire-rim glasses, brought Iris's soup and sandwich combination. Martha and I said we'd like coffee . . . if it wouldn't be too long in the coming. When she left, Iris said, "I think she took one of my classes. That pout looks familiar."

"They shouldn't use students as waitresses here. You can't slander them over lunch without worrying about spies."

"I do it anyway," said Iris.

Martha laughed and Iris joined in—in pretty sprightly fashion for someone with lawsuits to file.

"I knew you two would hit it off," I said. I retrieved my shoulder bag from the back of my chair and said I had to run, coffee or no; wanted to be in the shop when the clock struck one.

Martha's expression changed instantly. "But we hardly got to talk at all," she cried. "That was the whole purpose of lunch."

"But we ran into Iris, so it's nice all around. . . ."

"I'm sorry," said Martha. "I really wanted to . . . get down to certain things."

"That's right," said Iris. "How's it going since our last lunch?"

I squeezed Martha's shoulder, said I'd take a rain check. Meanwhile, there was nothing to report.

I left them, their antennae vibrating—two nosy social scientists with time on their hands and much in common.

27

California's Nice

My not speaking to Libby for a whole week went unnoticed, apparently. I visited her at the shop Saturday afternoon and said, "This makes me very uncomfortable."

Libby looked up from her hand sewing and said, "What does?"

"Our not speaking."

"I just thought you were busy and our paths hadn't crossed," she said.

"No busier than usual."

"Are we still not speaking?" she asked.

"I haven't decided."

She smiled slyly without looking up. "You must be considering it if you came in today."

I said there was only one thing I was considering and that was not taking sides and not getting caught in the crossfire between Roger and Robin or Robin and her.

"But you are taking sides," Libby said. She checked her work on the bridal-looking material and appraised her invisible stitching. "You're taking the side against Roger, which I'd call taking Robin's side."

I repeated Martha's theory without attribution: I'm the link between Forget-Me-Not and Rags for Sale, which, when the shit hits the fan, will make me the architect of this particular sin.

"Are you saying that Robin will be madder at you than she'd be at me. Or at Roger?"

I said, on reflection, that maybe I *was* inflating my role a tad. Maybe Robin would turn to me for comfort, particularly when I renounced the whole unfortunate mess.

"She'll probably never find out," said Libby.

"I hope you're right."

"Between the business and the girls, she's really not tuned in to much else."

"Is that what Roger thinks?"

"Roger says she's amazingly . . . consistent. She has her routine, and she doesn't depart from it. It's as if—" Libby slapped the back of one hand into the palm of her other—"this is my life, my marriage, nothing's ever going to change, including my husband, so I never have to look up from what I'm doing to check it."

" 'My wife doesn't understand me'?"

"It happens to be true in this case."

"Look," I said, "I work with Robin. I don't need any outside consultant telling me how difficult it is to live with her, or how easy it would be to get sick of her. But they're *married*. The whole town sees that as the right side to take; not some Roger's-unfulfilled argument."

Libby picked up her sewing again with a shrug that testified to my unworldliness.

I continued, "You might think this is all very manageable, but it's not."

"It's manageable as long as you don't tell Robin."

"You think I'm the only potential informant on Main Street? You don't think Roger's capable of blurting it out in the middle of an argument, on the theory that once it's out of the bag she'll throw him out and you two can live happily ever after?"

"That's not what I want," said Libby. She snipped another length of white thread from a giant spool, and, threading her needle on the first try, said she had more pressing problems. Rags for Sale was not making it. High rent was the reason, along with slow-moving dresses at prices too steep for MacMillan students. They were wearing short black skirts with chartreuse accessories in all seasons, and Libby's dresses were too whimsical for the hard, dark look they were cultivating as they left their teens.

Libby told me she had never made a profit, not even in prom season when it seemed to me that dresses were flying out of the store. "I can't do this," she said. "I have to face facts: if I'd been able to turn this around it would have happened by now."

She said she was thinking of closing before she killed herself in the prom and wedding rush, which turned out to be for naught anyway. Sell everything off at a going-out-of-business sale, pay some of the bills, borrow some more from her parents, do what she had to do to get out from under this huge responsibility.

"Then what will you do?" I asked.

"Take a few weeks off, then get a job."

"What kind of job?"

"Sales? Maybe at a gallery. . . . Maybe something at the college."

"You'd work for the *college?*"

"If the right job came up."

"Like what?"

"In the art gallery, or in public relations. Maybe Admissions."

"I thought you hated the college."

"What would you have me do? Wait on tables at Francesca's?"

"No! You're a designer. You should design dresses."

Libby pushed back her blond hair then restored her bangs. "I tried that, didn't I?"

"For a while. Maybe not long enough."

"I thought by this time I'd have a staff, and I'd be designing the whole time, with other people sewing them up and other people on the floor. I can't do it all. Even if I could, physically, it wouldn't be paying off. I am not good at the business part of it."

"Couldn't you get a partner? A business person who'd free you up for the creative stuff?"

"Who'd buy into a bankrupt dress shop? No one with any great financial insights."

"It's worth a try. People always put businesses up for sale."

"I'm no good at this. I can design and sew and sell but I can't do all three. I don't want the responsibility."

"Bad attitude," I said.

"Why?"

"You know: the woman stuff. What the Martha Schiff-Shulmans of the world would say."

"Martha's doing all right for herself on their two salaries. She could have afforded my dresses. Ever notice her shoes? She spends plenty for her hippy outfits."

Martha hated Libby's party dresses. She said they reminded her of Mamie Eisenhower. I skipped over Martha and said, "You could work from your house."

"Maybe."

"Sure you could! You have a following. And you could

specialize! Wedding gowns, maybe. Or just gowns for all occasions. Advertise in *Bride's* magazine. Do mail order."

"Mail order's expensive. All that stuff is."

"I just think you'd be sorry if you gave it all up."

"Or maybe I'd be relieved. I'm sick of sewing. I'm sick of Main Street. I shouldn't have come back."

"Would you say that if things had worked out with Dennis?"

Libby said slowly, staring as if this was for the record and the last time she'd repeat herself, "Dennis is a lost cause. Over." She turned back to her handwork and said easily, aimlessly, "You can have him."

"Why would you say something like that?"

"You don't find him appealing?"

"Of course he is, but I say that as his buddy, the same way I'd hope—"

"I should warn you," Libby continued confidently, "he's not very accessible. I don't think that's going to change so fast."

"You mean, what a ludicrous idea—Dennis turning to Melinda if he passed on Libby Getchel?"

"He could find you attractive," said Libby. "I know a lot of men do."

"That's right."

"I wasn't implying anything. I meant, 'Lots of luck. Go for it. I've given up.'"

"Because now you have Roger?"

"Roger's in no position to help me out with the store."

"I meant romantically."

"It's an affair," she said, her voice flat.

"No future, no commitment?"

"Isn't that what you're campaigning for?" She opened a small box and picked about its contents with a tweezer. They proved to be seed pearls, and from the frown on Libby's face, inferior ones.

"No good?" I asked.

She didn't answer immediately, then said, "The white's a little off." She plucked several from the box and laid them on the white fabric. I said they looked fine to me.

"Too gray," said Libby. She picked and prodded among her finalists until she had a small pile. I returned to her earlier hopeful note. "Are you less and less thrilled with your affair, or is that putting words in your mouth?"

"Roger, you mean?"

"Who else are you having an affair *with*?"

Head bent, Libby said, "I think it'll run its course."

"And then?"

She looked up. "We'll stop seeing each other."

"And then what? Back to business as usual?"

"Except that I won't be here."

"Might not be the worst thing in the world," I said. "Maybe you'll find you're better suited to work for someone else, now that I think about it. Or some*place* else."

"I'm not moving yet," she said.

"California's nice. And don't forget warm—you'd have a much bigger call for summer dresses there."

"I thought you disapproved of California."

"For *me*. Not for everybody. Millions of people love it. You could probably work in the movies doing wardrobe. They get screen credit for that."

Libby shook her head primly. "I don't think so."

"Because of your parents?"

"My parents?"

"They were so ecstatic when you moved back."

Libby shrugged. "I like Harrow," she said. "I wouldn't know a soul in California. All my friends are here."

"Roger?"

"I expect Roger and I will stay friends," she said.

"And me?"

"I hope so."

I assumed there was an apology in that phrase, that she meant, "I hope we salvage a friendship even after the damage I've done, the distress I've caused you by sleeping with your cousin. Despite the lack of interest I've demonstrated in your social and emotional life; despite my complete self-absorption."

I said—and note how I gave her the benefit of the doubt just like every other time she applied for it—"Maybe business will correct itself and Rags will survive. Maybe you won't have to leave Main Street. And you know what else? You know how these things work?" I continued—such a good friend—"I bet as soon as you give up Roger, you'll meet someone, Lib, and he'll be the one."

28

Permission

The most astounding sight at my own dining room table: my mother, my stepfather and Lou Schiner having coffee after what appeared to be a fish dinner.

Gerry sprang up to kiss me hello, something he didn't do when there was no company. His shoes shined, his smile wide, his hair arranged to disguise his baldness, he could have been calling on customers.

"You know Lou from the fish store," Gerry said.

"Sure I do. Hi, Mr. Schiner."

My mother said nothing. She was dressed in my black wool jersey Libby Getchel; she'd personalized it with a silk kerchief tied around her neck, pep squad style. I said, "You look terrific."

"I tried to call you for permission," she said.

"You look about eighteen."

Lou turned red in the face and scalp. Gerry boomed, "She always looks eighteen."

My mother asked if I'd like some halibut—Lou's treat. See, he'd delivered her order, and they had started talking about their daughters—Lou has three—and they'd lost track of the time; then Gerry had driven up and there was enough fish for a party, so Gerry had convinced Lou to stay when he heard Barbara was sick and not cooking. And why was I so late for dinner? She'd been expecting me around five-thirty. . . .

I apologized as gracefully as I could, considering she hadn't been expecting me at all. I asked Gerry how long he was staying this time.

"I've got to be at Yale–New Haven first thing tomorrow, then I'm going south—New York, out to the island, back up through Westchester."

"Sounds like a long trip," said Lou.

"A week; about average for me."

Lou asked if he minded being on the road.

"*Mind,*" said Gerry. "You do what you have to do. They give me a car and I get all my expenses, and nobody tells me where I'm supposed to be on any given day. I've been with Cardiotech for fourteen years; some of the guys I used to sell to in purchasing are heads of whole hospitals now. I get invited to cardiologists' Christmas parties. I worked out a nice program where we donated televisions to CCU waiting rooms in a couple of big teaching hospitals in Philadelphia."

"That's nice for the families," said Lou.

"Sure it is," said Gerry. "It's good for us, too. We're respect-ed in the field. I've got my accounts established, so it's pretty much maintaining them rather than knocking on a lot of new doors."

"So, Lou," I broke in. "Fabulous Fetes does *not* do justice to your salmon when it's en croute."

He brightened at my comment, even with its negative catering report. "Overcooked, I bet."

"And reheated."

"Ten minutes per inch," he said. "That's all they need to know."

"What's Melinda referring to?" asked Gerry.

"Lou's fish," said my mother. "He supplies a lot of the local caterers."

Gerry said to me, "You know that these two know each other from high school?"

"I heard that."

"We didn't know each other well," my mother murmured.

"I'm from the Boston area," said Gerry. "Ever hear of Malden?"

"Sure," said Lou.

"Ever get out that way to do your buying?" my stepfather asked, settling into another pitch.

He was good at only that. He hadn't seen that her dress was not meant for him; hadn't noted that there was abandon in her chocolate cake ingredients—almonds, sugar, butter-cream frosting. Hadn't questioned Lou's presence, Lou's suit and silk tie. Didn't care that his wife's fishmonger called her Rosy.

Lou left soon, declining leftovers for Barbara, thanking Gerry for inviting him to join their table; the one grave nod between hostess and guest.

Moved by the same public impulse that made him kiss me hello, Gerry followed my mother out to the porch where he put his arm around her in happily married fashion, and waved good-bye to the newest account in his Friend file.

29

Of All the Revolting Developments

I asked Martha if she would define the term "sociopath" so that, in light of what I was about to tell her, I could determine whether Libby, Roger, Robin or I fit the diagnosis.

"Uh-oh," said Martha.

"Do you have five minutes?"

"What happened?" she asked.

This: I was cleaning the morning's shipment of mums and carnations, worrying because my work sink was clogged, when I received the following telephone order, the caller having asked for me by name: One dozen long-stem red roses, to Miss Libby Getchel, Rags for Sale, 333 Main Street.

271

"Message on the card?" I asked the slightly familiar voice.

"You don't recognize your confrere?" he said, emphasis on the "con."

"Conrad?"

"Of course."

I didn't say anything out of equal parts shock and confusion: could he really be ordering romantically symbolic flowers for another woman—one I had introduced him to; and, further, if he had the gall to do that, why call me when any employable florist could box a dozen roses with almost equal competence?

"Can you get those out this afternoon?" he asked.

I said stiffly, "I would hope so. We're right next door."

"That's why I called: I figured even if I missed the delivery deadline, someone could run them over to her."

"Like me?" I said.

"Whoever," said Con.

I found my voice, finally, and said, "I think it would make a nice statement: here's flowers from Conrad Zimmerman, the most recent man I slept with, passing the baton to you. Hope you enjoy getting screwed as little as I did."

"You're mad!" said Conrad.

"You don't see any reason why I'd be mad?"

"Can you tell me?"

"You don't call a woman you're sleeping with to send flowers to another woman. Especially when they work next door to each other and the girlfriend of record introduced you."

"I am stunned," he said after a few moments.

"Not as stunned as I am."

"Because," he prodded, "because . . . ?"

"You don't do this kind of thing, all right? I've been working with flowers for a long time, and no one's ever been insensitive enough to pull something like this with me."

" 'Pull something like this,' " he repeated, with a note of victory in his voice, "am I pulling something or am I being completely, utterly honest and aboveboard with you about what's going on in my head right now? Sending flowers to a woman I feel very attracted to. Not sneaking around calling FTD, but ordering them through the only florist I know personally."

I said flatly, "You are great. You are quite a guy. I should have thought of that instead of thinking you're a total asshole. I wasn't thinking clearly."

"Look," said Conrad. "I'm not insensitive. I knew this might give you some pain. But I'm not into playing games. This is where I'm at right now, and I thought this was a way of presenting that truth."

"Well, thank you so much," I said.

"Maybe I was wrong," he said.

"Like, maybe there was some middle ground between slipping me your door key and having me deliver flowers to your next victim."

"Melinda," he said sorrowfully. "Melinda."

"Do you want baby's breath?" I asked.

"If you recommend it."

"Boxed?"

"As opposed to what?"

"Arranged. Boxed is forty-two. Arranged is fifty-nine."

"Boxed," said Conrad.

"Message?" I asked.

"Just 'Con,' don't you think?"

"I don't think anything."

"Just 'Con.' "

"You got it," I said, in the quiet, demure voice with which one punishes such transgressions.

*   *   *

I decided it would be worth the trouble. Frank lent me his cap and I walked next door, carrying my version of what best spoke for Conrad's intentions: a dish garden with an unsightly eight-inch, prickly protuberance, two small fuzzy cacti at its base, and my own carefully crafted message: "For you, babe, when I can't be with you. Con."

"Delivery for Miss Elizabeth Getchel," I announced as I came through the front door.

There were two customers in the shop, apparently a mother and daughter, fingering swatches of material. I waited, knowing Libby would see something deranged in my face and grow increasingly uncomfortable.

"We were thinking, a different pastel for each bridesmaid, maybe in the pink ranges."

"Or in every range, like a rainbow," said the daughter.

"Like Necco Wafers," Libby added helpfully.

I moved a few steps closer. "Rainbow weddings are so tacky," I said. "If you had any taste you'd stick to something simple and elegant."

All three faces registered the bewildered amusement of women unaccustomed to deliberate offense. Their heads swiveled to consult Libby and to find meaning in this curious display. "Melinda," she said evenly. "I don't think they realize you were kidding."

"I'm a floral artist," I said. "I know what I'm talking about. And when they're through here, I don't want them next store asking me to spray-paint their bouquets."

Libby stood up and said, "Please excuse us." She murmured something else to the customers which I guessed identified me as a furloughed mental patient who insulted customers up and down Main Street but was basically harmless.

I sidestepped Libby, and strode to the back corner, placing the obscene dish garden on the glass top of her accessories case. *"Pour vous,"* I said, and left, tipping my hat to the nervous mother of the bride and her foolish daughter, who looked much too young and satisfied to be getting married in the first place.

It was a mistake to charge his account for the price of a dozen long-stem red roses, boxed, or to charge Conrad anything at all for my own personal floral statement. In the real world, acts like these don't go unpunished.

Conrad was the least outraged. After all, I was the lover scorned and he was too hip to register chagrin over the career florist's equivalent of climbing to the top of a tower and spraying the campus with bullets. Libby found out about the undelivered roses when she called Conrad with her thanks for the lewd yet oddly romantic gift and to report, incidentally, that Melinda had become a madwoman in the process.

He swore later that he called Forget-Me-Not only for an adjustment on his MasterCard, certainly not to complain about such a rude switch in flora—hey, she was only acting human and he could dig that.

And it didn't help when the mother-and-daughter wedding shoppers marched into Forget-Me-Not to say that a woman from the state hospital was impersonating their delivery man.

Accordingly, I was fired.

Roger said the actual words with Robin standing a few feet behind him looking oddly satisfied, as if she had ghostwritten his diatribe. I stood there, my voice lost to some automatic, stupid sorrow.

Roger said, "We looked the other way for a long time because you were family."

"You had warnings," said Robin. "I talked to you any number of times about your job performance."

I needed to insult them deeply, to say, "You are ordinary people, without talent. You are the ones who should be grateful to me."

Instead, straining not to cry, I said something truer and crueler: "Papa Jan would have turned over in his grave if he knew I was working for you."

A satisfied look passed between them: *how perfect, how Melinda-like to remain disrespectful to the end.*

"Who do you think is going to do the Frankel wedding?" I asked.

"Roger. And I'll help," said Robin.

"She'll cancel before she lets that happen."

Roger's mouth twitched. "Maybe you should've thought of your customers before you shot yourself in the foot."

"We even talked about letting you buy into the business one day if you straightened out," said Robin. "You could've been a partner if you'd been a different kind of employee."

I strode between them to the cooler, the madwoman unleashed, and grabbed a bucket of red roses, a branch of baby's breath, an unlikely stem of huckleberry, and shoved them into Roger's hands. "Here. A dozen long stems, past due. Deliver them yourself to Miss Libby Getchel so there's no mistaking what an honest and honorable man you are."

Roger didn't move; he looked through me with the steadfastness of a secret service agent in an angry crowd.

It was Robin who took the bucket out of my hands and told me to leave, but in such a weary, wise-mother fashion, that I knew she knew.

30

Adrift

Michael, the assistant to the president of MacMillan, woke me with his phone call, asking me if I could meet with Frederika, his boss, that afternoon.

"I don't think you want me," I said, not even trying to sound awake.

"We heard. I called you at the shop and Robin said, 'Melinda is no longer in our employ.' I asked if she knew where I could find you, and she said, 'Are you one of our clients?' I said, 'That depends what happened to Melinda.'"

"You really said that?"

"I did, dear," said Michael. He was one of those witty and effeminate twenty-five-year-olds, smart and sarcastic beyond his years.

"Because you suspected foul play?"

"I could tell by her tone—prissy and curious at the same time, you know? I wanted to slap her smug little face through the telephone."

"You're a pal," I said.

"Who do they think they are? Do they expect to hold on to their esthetically demanding customers if you're not the designer?"

"Evidently."

"Well, I say fuck them. They're not getting my business."

"You don't have any business, Michael."

"The college's! I'm the power behind the throne. Frederika doesn't have any loyalties to the shop if you're not in it, so we follow you."

"Except that I don't have a job."

"You don't need a job. You just need some flowers and some scissors. Frederika has seventy-five coming for cocktails Thursday night and we don't want a bowl of mangy daisies for a centerpiece."

"I'm gone," I told him. "It's over. I haven't even gotten out of bed today."

"Ooh, how tragic," he said. "Did you call a hot line?"

When I laughed, he plunged ahead confidently. "You're just experiencing shame, which happens no matter how much you hated the job or how much you know, intellectually, it's for the best. In our culture, we fall apart when we get fired. Protestant ethic, and all that."

"Did you ever get fired?"

"Get serious," said Michael. "I could have filed some great civil suits if I had a litigious personality. You think everyone likes having me around? Frederika's the only boss I ever had who appreciates me."

"I wasn't appreciated. They think Roger can do what I was doing."

"Who wants *Roger* hanging around their chi-chi functions? Not the president of MacMillan College. Could I even trust him to send a plant to an open house?"

"Probably. And I could tell you what to ask for in a center-piece—"

"*You're* doing it," said Michael.

"How?"

"I don't know how. You're the artist. Go buy some flowers somewhere—wherever your cousin gets them—and stick them in a vase, which I can get you from her vast collection—and make us something that goes with shrimp and crudités, for God's sake. Buy some oasis and a good pair of scissors and get to work at your kitchen table. Cocktails are at six."

"Which day?"

"Thursday. All the time in the world."

"What's today?" I asked.

"Are you asking that for effect like you just came out of a coma?"

"You woke me up."

"It's an emergency."

I still hadn't agreed to produce his order. I said, "If you're dead set against Forget-Me-Not, I could tell you who else could do a decent job, and what to order. You can't go too far off in that situation."

"Oh, she's a consultant now," said Michael.

"It's going to cost you if I do it myself."

"As if it's *my* money."

"What if I say two pieces minimum, one for the library table in the foyer and one for the buffet table?"

"I'd say deal."

"What's she wearing?" I asked.

"That's why I love you," said Michael. "You think your cousin

279

Roger would ask what Freddie's wearing to a cocktail party? Hold on. I'll buzz her."

He came back on the line after a long pause. "Navy blue if I can make it to the cleaner's; red if I don't," he said.

"Definitely get to the dry cleaner's. I'll use pinks and purples. Maybe I can get some poppies in the right shade." I asked who the guests would be.

"Locals," said Michael. "Town and gown relations; the mayor, the town council, administrators from both sides. The annual unspoken apology for being nonprofit and paying no property taxes."

"What time again?"

"Six. The working masses like their suppers early."

"There isn't any chance Robin and Roger are invited, is there?"

"As what?"

"I don't know—shopowners. Main Street merchants?"

"And if they were? You live in this town, too, and you're the florist of record at this affair. You're going to have to learn to bid them a cool hello and move on to the next guest or else you'll be putting too much energy into avoiding them. Which brings me to what happened. I assume it was artistic differences?"

I groaned and said it was a long story, perhaps best saved for a two-hanky lunch.

"C'mon. Just the highlights."

I said in a monotone from the depths of my pillow, "A man I was seeing ordered roses for Libby Getchel. I brought her a phallic dish garden instead."

"A sight gag! I love it!"

"There's more to it," I said, warming up to my new, discretion-free, ex-employee's point of view. "Roger is sleeping with Libby from next door."

"Don't toy with me," said Michael.

"He was. I know for a fact—"

"Is it still going on?"

"I don't know. Libby has a new admirer."

"Your sweetie?"

"Someone I'd been seeing."

"Seeing or *shtupping?*"

"Mostly the latter."

"Ugly!" Michael yelled. "This is an ugly little town."

I heard his other line ring; I asked if he had to answer it.

"Don't you dare hang up," he said.

There was a long wait. He got back to me and asked, all business, if I could hold longer or could he call me back. "I'll wait," I said.

"Speak of the devil," his voice announced a minute later.

"Libby?"

"Roger, worried. Doing a little inept customer relations."

"What did you tell him?"

"I said we had nothing coming up for them in the foreseeable future, but would keep them in mind for any straightforward, prosaic pieces which didn't require artistic expression."

"Did you tell him I was doing a cocktail party for you?"

"Should I have?"

"Not yet. If I pull it off from the kitchen and you ask me to do more, then you can tell them anything you'd like."

"Of course I'll ask you to do more. At these prices, I'll look like the genius."

I sat up straighter in bed and said, "I haven't set any prices."

"No overhead, remember. And I know you'll be happy to pass the savings along to your customers."

"It's not coming out of your pocket."

"That's true, but I know Freddie. She likes these little line-item savings. It'll make her favorably disposed toward placing orders for functions that don't necessarily cry out for flowers. I'll remind her that you're cheaper than Forget-Me-Not, and that'll be that."

I said, "I'm getting out of bed so I can find some start-up capital."

He exclaimed in good soap-opera falsetto, "You mean I've given you the will to live?"

"Sure," I said. "Free-lance florist. I wasn't one ten minutes ago."

"I'd have some stunning cards printed up *tout de suite*," said Michael.

My mother said, "I'd ask Dennis Vaughan. From what I understand, he does all right."

She was washing dishes at the sink, wearing yellow rubber gloves because she thought passing out coupons to housewives required silky hands. Maybe, I thought, I'd get something going from the house and I'd build it up enough to support a secretary. My mother could do the Robin stuff.

I was eating one of her Jane Brody omelettes, two egg whites but only one yolk. My mother announced that Michael's call was a tribute to my talent and to the depth of customer loyalty—a variation on the theme she'd stated a half-dozen times since I'd told her—and that Dennis, as a good businessman, would most likely be delighted to back me.

I said, "I can't ask Dennis."

"I'm talking about a loan with interest—"

"Which is a terrible position to put a friend in."

"Because you don't think you'll be able to pay him back?"

"Neither a borrower nor a lender be," I said halfheartedly.

"You'll pay interest," she repeated.

"I can't ask him."

"You're going to ask the wholesaler, though, who's practically a stranger."

"That's different. That's credit from a supplier who wants my business in the future. There won't be any interest charges unless I screw up."

"I don't see what the big deal is," she offered. "You go in there, you ask to speak privately with Dennis, you tell him you lost your job without notice or severance pay, and that you're starting up your own business. Also tell him you have one important client and hope to build on that." She gestured, yellow glove palm up, as if to say, that's it, that's your speech. Done and done. She turned back to the sink.

I need gloves like that, I thought dully—rubber gloves, a routine, a religion. Maybe they help a woman who's failed at everything important come down to breakfast; a woman who has nothing in her wallet, no money, no truthful business cards, no snapshots of men or babies. A routine could help, if my mother was any test: wash in the soapy water; dip and rinse in the clear water; stack for maximal sheeting action, just in case the manufacturer of her dish-washing liquid dropped in to film a commercial. "I'd give you the money myself if I had it to give," I heard her say.

"I know that."

"But I don't, and I'm sorry."

"You shouldn't be sorry. I'm the one who's worked at a dead-end job, knowing I wouldn't last and not putting any money away for something like this."

"Whoever thought you'd be fired! You worked for family. Family doesn't fire their own."

"I committed fraud," I said, repeating Roger's official finding.

"It was a practical *joke*."

"Right. And I happen to work for the two unfunniest people in America."

My mother turned her face toward me and allowed a faint smile. "They are, aren't they? Ever since Roger was a little boy he's acted like an old man. I don't know if he could ever take a joke."

I refilled my coffee mug from the glass percolator on the stove, and decided to tell her, my secretary, my housekeeper, my banker, that Roger's goody-goodiness did not preclude cheating on his wife. I chose the words for maximum dramatic effect. "Here's the real reason I'm not working there anymore: your nephew was sleeping with Libby, and Robin found out."

My mother didn't cry out in busybody ecstasy, nor did she recoil in moral indignation. She said quietly, "What does that have to do with you?"

"I'm not sure, but it's some psychological phenomenon Martha predicted."

"I think I can picture why."

"You can?"

"They probably want their privacy to yell at each other or punish each other or whatever they need to do to stick it out. Where else are they going to let it out? Not at home in front of the girls. So they don't want to have to walk on eggshells at the shop, and they don't want to see the looks on each other's faces when you come back from having coffee with Libby."

"Which, I might add, is ancient history. I had already stopped doing that before I brought the cactus over because of her taking up with Roger."

"You know," said my mother, "I never liked that girl. I felt there was something very selfish about her; takes over her parents' house and lets them go live in elderly housing. *Then,* she turns around and becomes Roger's mistress."

I laughed at that, "mistress"; at Roger having a mistress, and said nowadays when we slept with people it was referred to as having lovers rather than mistresses unless we were nobility or congressmen.

"How come she doesn't have a regular boyfriend, an attractive girl with her own business?" my mother asked.

"She does now. That's who the dish garden came from."

My mother squinted at me. The fine points of cacti versus long-stemmed red roses had been lost in the bigger picture of me getting fired by her brother's son, the clearly inferior Roger.

I said, "Conrad, this guy I'd been seeing, ordered roses for Libby—through me, from him, to Libby. Which made me slightly crazed and also made me put together cacti that looked like erect genitalia in place of the roses."

She turned all the way around, her back to the sink. The corners of her mouth tilted up into the slightest smile. "I like that," she said. "I'd like to think I would've thought of that if I was a florist."

"Our dark side," I said.

"How come I never met Conrad if you were seeing him?"

"I only saw him at weddings. He's a musician."

My mother made a face: *what do you expect from a musician?*

"You're right," I said. "He was a jerk."

"Did you date?"

I repeated *date* as if it were another outdated phrase.

"Did you sleep with him?" she tried again.

I carried my plate to the sink and handed it to her. I asked if she really wanted to discuss it.

She pondered the question, then asked, "How much of a jerk?"

"More than most."

"He's in love with Libby now?"

"As much as he does that kind of thing. He's very big on living for the moment, doing what feels right, I'm okay, you're okay."

She was trying to put a face and a name on this new kind of romance in which a man slept with a woman, but never met her mother and never called the house. She said seriously, "Men and women should like to do other things together besides sex."

"So I've heard."

"I think they shouldn't start off with sex, but it should be something they lead up to gradually."

"Sometimes, though," I explained, "there's this huge thing, a huge attraction, right from the beginning which gets in the way. You have to get beyond that so you're not just mistaking the lust for long-term interest. That's one argument for not putting the sex off for too long."

My mother said sadly, "You sound so expert."

"It was my point about you and Lou. You're probably torturing each other unnecessarily. Just go do it and see if you're still pining for him after you've had sex. Maybe you both just need a good release."

She wiped her hands with a dish towel, gloves and all, then pulled them off carefully by the fingertips. I followed her upstairs into her beige and brown bedroom. It was budget-hotel, masculine decor, selected for Gerry's conjugal visits lest he feel he was an outsider in a feminine world. I had once asked her how she would decorate the master bedroom if it were entirely up to her. She had answered so enthusiastically about Laura Ashley wallpaper and dotted swiss; about ceramic light switches and bureau scarves, that I had known she'd asked herself the question, allowed this one proper fantasy among the sinful ones: what would her life look like without Gerry?

I helped her make the double bed her way, briskly straight-armed, each of us on one side. I asked if Gerry's surprise visit changed anything. Was she closer to telling him the truth?

She did the least Rosalie-like thing I'd ever seen her do: she dropped on the just-made bed, face up, and bent one arm across her face. "I don't know," she said. "I don't know anything."

I sat down next to her. "You know you love Lou Schiner."

She stared at the ceiling without blinking or answering.

"You *something* Lou Schiner, right? From afar. Enough so that you're considering a divorce so you and Lou can . . . I don't know—be together?"

"I'm so stupid," I heard her say.

"No you're not."

"You don't know what I'm talking about, so don't argue with me."

I lay down next to her and looked at the same ceiling. "Do you want to tell me why you're stupid?"

She shook her head no.

"It's about Lou, though? Am I right about that?"

She nodded, but just barely, and I could see tears forming in her unblinking eyes.

"Did his feelings change?"

She shook her head.

"Did yours?"

Tears ran over her lower eyelashes and onto her cheeks.

"It was easier before, when it wasn't acknowledged?" I asked gently.

"Why did I tell you?" she wailed. "I had a crush on my fish man and he kissed me, and I started this whole big thing, and then we brought Martha into it."

I reached across her to the box of tissues on her night table. "Here." She blew her nose, but didn't wipe the tears off her cheeks.

"Are you crying because you told me, or because you don't feel the same any more and you're afraid you'll hurt his feelings?"

She shook her head under her crossed arms. I asked if she could tell me or if I had to guess. "I don't know why I'm crying," she said.

"Is it because you have a big decision to make?"

"I don't *know*," she said. "If I knew I'd tell you."

I told her I had a sense of what was wrong; why this conversation, today, affected her more than others.

"Why?"

"Because we're talking about men who jumped into their love affairs with both feet—even someone as pathetic as Roger. . . and you're listening and thinking about Lou, who hasn't been moving this relationship forward. Not asking you to run away with him or even to jump into bed with him—"

"Not in so many words . . ."

"He's not the type to leave a sick wife. That was my impression—that he's strictly law-abiding."

"Which makes it sadder, his having the kind of love affair of the spirit that he can manage. I don't think he's going to find that again so easy if I push him."

I sat up partway, leaning on my elbows. "Maybe it's going to remain a love affair of the spirit. Maybe that's just your speed."

She nodded solemnly. "It is my speed."

"Maybe you could even do without Gerry's conjugal visits and get by strictly on whatever you want to call it with Lou."

"You can call it love."

After a silence, watching her watch the plaster ceiling swirls, I said, "Don't you think you should tell Gerry that you want a divorce?"

She said, "Lou wouldn't divorce Barbara just because I was free."

"We already know that," I said.

"It's so much easier to let things . . . to not go through that." She sighed. "Poor Gerry."

"No offense, Ma, but Gerry's life is selling pacemakers. I've never really noticed him buying into this marriage, except as a professional accomplishment: I've got an expense account, a company car, a wife in Massachusetts. . . ."

"In other words, bite the bullet, tell the truth. Otherwise I'm lying to myself all the time when Gerry comes home?"

"Comes home and gets into bed."

"Even though it's easier not to rock the boat?"

"Yes."

She said triumphantly, "Just like you?"

"Me? I'm not married. I'm not divorcing anyone, either, except for Roger and Robin."

"I told you I've changed," said my mother. "I see things now. I know the way you feel by the questions you ask me."

"So?"

"I'm talking about Dennis Vaughan."

"What about Dennis Vaughan?"

"What I'm saying is, if I have to be honest with myself and do something that's hard, then why shouldn't you?"

I asked if she meant asking Dennis for a loan.

"No I do not."

After a few moments, I lay down again and crooked my arm over my eyes. "It's much too late," I said.

She pulled herself up and patted my knee, smoothing the material of my pajama leg. "I'm calling Gerry, which isn't going to be so easy."

"You mean, 'I will if you will'?"

"Tell him," she said.

31

That Night

It seemed to me that Dennis's face showed both concern and relief when he looked up from pink invoices and saw me.

"How did you hear?" I asked.

"Francesca."

"How'd she hear?"

"Libby."

"My best friend Libby. Did she pass along the reason?"

He straightened the pile of invoices and reached for a stapler. I intercepted it and repeated my question.

Dennis said, "I don't believe everything I hear."

"What did she say was the reason?"

Dennis said lightly, "Fraud."

"That's right," I said. "Fraud. Armed robbery. Murder. Sodomy."

"I didn't believe it," he repeated.

"When did you find out?"

"I just heard this morning—"

"And you've been extremely busy?"

He looked at me and said pointedly, "I called you, if that's what you mean."

"When?"

"About a half hour ago. Your mother said you were at the bank."

I said that was true.

"It sounded important."

"I filled out an application."

"For what?"

"It's confidential," I said. "Family stuff."

"A loan?"

I said so what? Hadn't he applied for a loan when he started his business?

As I spoke, Dennis moved slowly along the case to the cash register. When he reached it, he opened it softly and apologetically with a bounce of his fist.

"What are you doing?" I asked.

"Please let me do this."

"Forget it. I'm not taking money from you, Dennis."

"What's it for?"

"Nothing."

"I'm only asking so I know how much to give you. I don't care what it's for."

"Just flowers," I said.

He lifted the coin compartment to expose the cache of bigger bills. He took whatever was there, fifties, a hundred, replaced the drawer, then counted out all the twenties from their compartment. He reached for my limp hand and curled my fingers around the bills.

291

After a minute, I put five twenties in my wallet, but gave back the rest. I said, my voice unsteady, "You'd better put a note in there to remind yourself why you're short."

"I won't forget."

"I'll pay you back Friday."

"Are you crying about the job?"

I said I wasn't crying. I was just a mess.

"Why won't you take my money?" he asked quietly.

"I did take your money."

"Not what you need."

I said I couldn't explain it, all right? Just old things between us which I'd rather not go into at this particular point in time.

"I want to know," said Dennis.

"I don't want money from you," I said, staring at gadgets in the display case below us.

"Because . . . ?"

"I don't want to say."

"Because?" he repeated.

"Because of our history. Because I know you feel guilty," I said rotely. "Because I know a couple of hundred dollars would be an easy way to settle an old debt."

I didn't look at him. I heard the drawer shut, and his voice push out the words as if they were the saddest ones he knew: "I danced with you and danced with you and I took you home with me."

"What about it?" I asked, bracing myself for the other half; the part where he explained how he was black and I was white and how sexual gratification was a very small piece of the cruel American pie.

Nick appeared suddenly from the back room. He stayed in the rear of the shop near the waders, his arms folded, not disguising his interest. When I turned toward him, he didn't look away. I thought I saw an encouraging nod pass from Nick to Dennis, but

292

so slight it might have been imagined. Dennis said, his eyes on my face, "I have a hard time saying what needs to be said."

I leaned over the counter and said slowly, "You're a goddamn radio commentator. You find things to say about a fucking *trout*."

Dennis almost smiled. "Is that right? You're the one who won't talk to me."

"You're nuts. You set the terms—"

"But what about since then? You kept pushing me away even though I tried—"

I shook my head: you absolutely did not try.

"Diana's *wedding*. It's like that night got surgically removed from your brain."

I pushed my hair away from my face, straight back from my forehead and held it there for clearer visibility. I said I wished that was true, that I could forget, but it was so much the opposite that for ten months, it's made things very difficult for me, that one night together.

"Look," said Dennis, "when I went into Forget-Me-Not to talk to you, I said things by the book because I was nervous, but it wasn't what I wanted to say—"

"Yes it was! You weren't the least bit torn."

"Maybe not at first—"

"But what? You changed your mind but you forgot to tell me?"

"You kept saying, 'You're right, Dennis. I agree with you. Let's be friends.' Every time we talked . . . *every* damn time we talked."

"Because I know about men! It's easy for them to get carried away at night, all dressed up on a dance floor. Well, we did. You enjoyed yourself, but by daylight I was this easy mark, leftover popular girl of the wrong race."

Dennis closed his eyes.

"It's true! You were sorry in the morning—the oldest cliché in the book."

He stepped closer. "For a leftover popular girl, you have very low self-esteem."

"Yes I do. Too bad yours is worse." I was still holding a hank of my own hair. I let go of it, and Dennis reached over, barely touching it back into place. He said quietly to Nick, "I'd like a few minutes in private with Melinda."

Nick shook his head. "You think I'm leaving you two incompetents to settle this thing on your own?"

"We don't need you to monitor our conversation."

"Since when? Please answer her question."

I said, "I think Nick knows more than I do."

"Which has made for a charming winter," said Nick.

I said to Dennis, a stage whisper, "I've never known your employees to be this rude."

"*I've* never starred in a goddamn soap opera where two people won't tell each other what's going on," said Nick.

Dennis said softly, "What was your question? Maybe I can answer it now."

"She *asked* if you were like other men *or* whether sex meant something to you and whether you're ready to bring her home and take a stand," Nick supplied.

I said I hadn't actually asked those things in so many words, but they were excellent questions.

Dennis turned so Nick couldn't eavesdrop as easily. "It meant a great deal to me, more than I could handle. And now I can't imagine why I never told you that."

If I had had any hope left at all, I would have cried with relief at the regret in his face.

"Dennis isn't done," said Nick.

After a hostile glance over his shoulder, Dennis continued. "The champagne and the music might have helped"—he smiled —"and that dress. But it wasn't accidental. I had wanted to . . . I had known for a long time, but I'd been scared because

294

of my marriage, and because of work we'd be practically an office romance with all of those problems. So I'd convinced myself that your behavior toward me wasn't anything special—"

"That's it, you know, my problem in a nutshell—the flirting. It worked in high school for getting dates but it doesn't translate well into mature relationships."

"It worked fine," said Nick impatiently. "He came back from his sister's wedding totally besotted."

"He was?"

"And then he started intellectualizing it, *politicizing* it; completely ignoring the forest for the trees. You wanna talk to *me* about ten long months?"

Without looking directly at either of them, I said I had been the same way after Diana's wedding. Exactly.

Nick said tersely, "Can you be more specific? Anyone?"

"You know," I said. "In love."

From his station against the wall, Nick emitted a televangelist's, "*Thank* you, Melinda! Thank you, Jesus!"

I laughed and Dennis rolled his eyes. Nick said maybe now he could run out for a late lunch, a little of this nice spring air. Walking by, he squeezed my arm.

"You can come out from behind the counter now," I said to Dennis.

When he took my face in his hands, it all came back: that night; a spotlit singer crooning across ten months, and the best man, my lost hope, asking for the dance.

32

Everything Must Go

He has never taken another woman fly fishing, not even Iris when they were married; not his mother, not his sister. He stands behind me in the river, his right arm covering the length of mine, his gloved hand on my wrist. "Picture the face of a clock," he says, "and trace the arc between ten and two." I stand on my toes, barefoot inside his spare waders, and let the big water of the Starkfield wash me back.

"Again," says Dennis. "Closer to twelve than to two."

My line, leader and fly splash in the water a few yards away—a terrible cast. He takes the rod and demonstrates. "Not too far back, then one, two, three, and four." His Grey Ghost drops from the sky and lands gently twenty feet away from where we stand. "You want a soft landing," he says, "or you'll scare the fish away."

He can stand in the river for hours, reading the water, narrating as he goes along—"the current's too strong here, too fast for a fish, so let's try behind this rock where he might be able to hold. I'm using a woolly worm, not a purist's fly, but it does the job." Hours later he hooks a gorgeous rainbow, hurrying to a calm enough spot to land the fish, only to release him, murmuring compliments and good wishes.

I finally tell him the truth: I hate the actual fly fishing. I like fishing off a dock with bait, even night crawlers, and I like taking the fish home and—excuse me for living—eating it. Was this a test and have I failed?

"You seem to like being here," he says, after considering my confession.

"I like being alone with you," I say. "I like the picnic aspect of it. I love your fly-fishing lessons. I like standing in the river and feeling like I'm walking on the moon."

He grins. "Well, that's something."

"And I love you," I say.

"I love you, too," he answers, calmly and quietly like the fine fisherman he is.

I couldn't help myself: I went to Libby's going-out-of-business sale. Martha went on and on in her MacMillan way about it being a metaphor for Libby's moral bankruptcy, but I said no; she made too many dresses that no one wanted to buy until a sign went up announcing, "Everything Must Go!"

Martha said, "How about if we go in together, and we pretend you're shopping for a wedding dress?"

I told her we weren't in high school anymore. Besides, would I ever in a million years let Libby Getchel think I'd get married in one of her rags when and if such an event took place?

"I've built a career on my insight," said Martha, "so don't give me any crap about *when* and *if*." We were outside Rags for Sale, chatting happily if not self-consciously, the way women act when they think their sworn enemies are watching through plate glass.

"Her fabrics are good," I said. "It's the nineteen-fifties party dresses that did her in."

"Did you ever tell her?" asked Martha. "Did you ever say, 'Libby, I think you're very talented, but have you read *Vogue* lately?'"

I said no. I had liked her dresses when we were friends—

"Shades of *The Emperor's New Clothes* . . . and, excuse me, but when was Libby Getchel ever your friend?"

"I think you won't be coming in with me," I told her. "I'll meet you at the store."

There was a crowd of customers inside, but the wrong population for Libby's dresses, older sale mongers looking displeased with the still-high prices. She was talking to a frowning customer, but looked up when I walked in.

I went straight to the peach silk and chiffon flapper dress with black beading, the very one I had harassed Iris about, now reduced by half.

"May I try this on?" I asked overpolitely, the first words we'd spoken in a month.

It didn't look quite right when I got it on; it needed Iris's height to maintain its lines, but I wanted it anyway—it was the freest and softest of her dresses; what might have been if she'd paid any attention to what makes people comfortable.

I hinted at something like that when I paid her. "I can't believe this never sold. Do you ever analyze that kind of thing?"

She studied her creation, holding it by the shoulder seams for a long good-bye; her expert hands barely skimmed the sheer fabric as she folded it and swathed it in tissue. "The bead work alone . . . ," was all she said.

I wrote out a check from my new account, which announced my new address and venture.

Libby studied it and read, "'The Perfect Arrangement.' Catchy."

"I'm on my own now," I said.

She smiled coolly. "That's not what I hear."

When I didn't answer she said, "You and Dennis. The talk of the town."

"We expect that," I said. "We don't let it bother us."

She eased my dress into a pink and aqua Rags for Sale shopping bag, soon to be a collector's item. "I guess I'm not going to get any credit for the way things turned out," she murmured.

I asked what she meant.

"Wasn't I the one who suggested you consider Dennis romantically?"

"Elizabeth," I said, "first of all . . . ," but I stopped. She had her own version, her own reality.

After reading my check again, she said she'd try to remember "The Perfect Arrangement" when brides asked her to recommend a florist.

I said thanks, I'd appreciate any referrals.

"Likewise. I'll be designing out of a studio when I close up here."

"Where will that be?"

"My house. Same phone number."

"Same basic designs?"

"Whatever people ask for, within reason."

I smiled. "No Mylar, though."

"Mylar?"

"The musicians' girlfriends? At Paulette's wedding?"

She shook her head, sorry. Then: "I'm very happy. You know how it is—the professional side of your life becomes less important when the emotional side is successful."

"Or just the opposite: it lets you get back to work."

"Whatever," said Libby. "I may try something else. I may get a real estate license."

"Well," I said, helping myself to the bag. "I always loved this dress. I think it was meant to be, when you consider how many people passed on it."

"I'd do pale hose and a black shoe with a small heel and a strap across the instep."

"I remember. And a white glamellia in my hair."

"Final sale," she said. "No exceptions."

It was a small town. We'd work the same weddings.

I wished her well and left.

33

The Postseason

The biggest surprise in our lineup was Martha Schiff-Shulman, who had form at the plate and speed on the base paths. She'd been added to the roster at the last minute after showing up to lend moral support, then clamoring to pinch hit. In her first at-bat, she whacked a single to deep center and stretched it into a double.

We needed her, womanwise, since our team's coededness had shrunk. Neither Libby nor Robin had been informed of our practices or games, or polled for their T-shirt size in the wake of our personal differences. I avoided Robin and Roger, who plugged along at Forget-Me-Not, letting their dyed daisies and chrysanthemums speak for themselves.

Libby slipped away, taking Conrad with her, to her house on Adams Street. Her hand-carved Rags for Sale sign remained above the door, waiting for a new tenant; a hot-pink leaflet taped to the window announced that designer Libby Getchel had reduced her practice to the creation of one-of-a-kind formal and semiformal dresses, by appointment at her home. The downtown grapevine reported variously that her landlord was negotiating with a goldsmith, a futon maker, a chocolatier.

One early game, a five-hitter by Iris and a near-win, gave us false hope for the season. In fact, we never won a game and we never got better. Iris, who was flying around the country on job interviews, got worse. But if she was a disappointment as a pitcher, she was a champion chatterer and heckler from her New York softball days, who taught us "no battah, no battah, no battah," and a host of other insults, which did not come easily to a team of Main Street merchants. Iris and Martha got awfully thick over the summer, united by MacMillan politics, outdoing each other in overpraising Dennis and my comanagement talents.

Dennis would roll his eyes and tell them that subtlety was not their strong suit; that they could relax and we'd be fine.

"You weren't fine," said Iris. "You were very unfine for years, and this was way overdue."

Martha would join in, beaming like a real estate agent at an open house. "Humor us," she'd coax. "We waited a long time for this. Can't you just sit back and enjoy being the team mascots?"

And you can imagine how they felt about Nick. He accepted the credit, bragging in his newly assertive way, that he deserved a Nobel Peace Prize; that it was akin to Jimmy Carter getting Menachim Begin and Anwar Sadat to embrace on national television.

"You guys," I would begin, shaking my head as if words failed me over their silliness and not, as was actually the case, over being the object of so much, well, love.

* * *

In true Lunker fashion, we scheduled our postseason banquet early, before our final two games, because Iris was moving to Cincinnati at the end of August for a high-powered job with Procter and Gamble. The banquet was at Martha and Stephen's house, a sit-down dinner despite our offers of potluck contributions.

As with everything else, she did it beautifully and made it look easy. No Chinette plates, no screw-together plastic wineglasses; but French Champagne and Mexican beer, flowers by me (insisting I charge her full price or she wouldn't accept delivery). A welcome excuse to dust off the good stuff, she said, when we exclaimed over place settings of china and crystal and napkin rings. "All presents! We didn't buy a single thing. And I'm offended you think I'm this bourgeois."

She produced chicken *mole,* and spinach enchiladas for the vegetarians. Dennis's mother sent a jelly roll, my mother a buckwheat rotini salad, and Schiner Bros. Seafood, who sponsored a winning rival team, a bag of cleaned, deveined shrimp.

Only Dennis and I knew there was to be a presentation. Over coffee, he rose, slipped on his Lunkers visor, and said dryly it was time for their managers' remarks. I was sitting to his left with two trophies in a brown bag at my feet, happy to stare at my lap while he talked.

"It is not in the spirit of the Lunkers," he began, "to recognize one player over his or her brothers and sisters for special honors. First of all, we all gave equally, and, secondly, we pretty much stank across the board." (Applause and hoots.)

"But my assistant manager and I wanted to establish an MVP award because every team needs one. And besides, a 'trophy' has a special meaning in fly fishing: it is a great fish, a thrilling fish, a champion fish caught because you used the right fly for the right stream, on the right bank, on the right day, and you've been rewarded."

That was my cue. I reached down and took out the first of the identical trophies, a gilded man swinging a bat, his body twisted into its follow-through, his face upturned like Babe Ruth watching his last home run. Dennis took it from me with a businesslike nod.

"First, for her offensive talents, for always hustling, for being the only one who overran first base, no matter how many *times* I begged you people to overrun the friggin' base; for her cooking, her hospitality, her general good humor, and, especially, her seven runs batted in, a Lunkers record, we hereby present this to Martha Schiff-Schulman, spelled wrong, but hey."

Martha jumped to her feet, sashayed once around the table, blowing kisses with both hands, meeting high fives, pantomiming her swing and finally, brandishing her trophy over her head.

"And so quiet and ladylike," Dennis added. He smiled fondly, and reached for the second trophy. "Next we honor a man," he began and stopped, his voice catching unexpectedly.

"A player who," he tried again.

"A player without whom . . . "

I looked around the table, bracing myself for the usual wisecracks, but saw instead faces straining to prompt words he couldn't say.

"As for Nick," he managed, but only that.

I touched his hand before I stood and said, "The managers' next trophy honors our golden glove, our human vacuum cleaner at short, who never made more than one error per inning and sometimes fewer, the only one who knew our signals or who ever used them. For these achievements, and for others"—and here I almost stopped—"we hereby present this trophy to a fine friend, Nicholas McGowan, as most valuable defensive player on the Lunkers in their only season."

Nick stood up and faced us. He touched his right hand to his heart, the best speech of all, before accepting his trophy in a dignified, almost Nobel fashion.

When everyone settled down, Stephen refilled our coffee cups. My slightly intoxicated teammates began clanking their demitasse spoons against their porcelain cups.

"So what about next year?" Lyman yelled above the din.

It was a question for us as manager and assistant manager: What *about* next year?

Martha told me later that she observed some skin-tone changes in both Dennis and me as if the question had some personal context. And then that lovely moment when he slipped his arm across my shoulders and we smiled; smiles of such abiding affection—her phrase—that one could only imagine what he was whispering into my hair.

And the ovation? What was I *analyzing:* joy among the lip readers over the future of our team.

My Thanks to:

Herb Childs and Bob Belmer of Childs Flower Shop in Florence,
Mass.
—fine florists and good sports;
Victor Lipman, compleat angler and dear cousin;
Beverly Daniel Tatum and her book, *Assimilation Blues;*
everyone at Pocket Books, especially my editor, Jane Rosenman,
and Bill Grose, editorial director;
Deborah Slobodnik, my sister and own personal Martha
Schiff-Shulman;
my birth editor, Stacy Schiff, and my agent, Lizzie Grossman;
Julia Lipman and Blanche Cooney
(whose eating habits are no one's business but their own),
and most of all to my husband, Bob Austin.